Durso is a native New Yorker, who once owned a literary bookstore in Los Angeles, ran English language programs in New York and Istanbul, worked retail, wrote for a newspaper, wrote advertising copy, was a professional Boy Scout, and has lived in Turkey, the world's largest museum, since 2008.

Dedication

To the many dedicated teachers in Turkey, but especially to a few I was privileged to work with and know: Rukiye Uçar, Altynai Bakenova Polat, Nayat Bağ, Erdem Demirci, and Nejla Karabulut.

Also to Ali Rıza Esmen for making the suggestion to come here in the first place.

Leonard Durso

ISTANBUL DAYS, ISTANBUL NIGHTS

AUSTIN MACAULEY PUBLISHERS™

LONDON • CAMBRIDGE • NEW YORK • SHARJAH

A CIP catalogue record for this title is available from the British Library.

ISBN 978-1-78693-787-1 (Paperback)
ISBN 978-1-78693-788-9 (Hardback)
ISBN 978-1-78693-789-6 (E-Book)
www.austinmacauley.com

First Published (2017)
Austin Macauley Publishers Ltd.
25 Canada Square
Canary Wharf
London
E14 5LQ

"I am listening to Istanbul, intent, my eyes closed.
A bird flutters round your skirt;
On your brow, is there sweat? I know.
Are your lips wet? Or not? I know.
A silver moon rises beyond the pine trees:
I can sense it all in your heart's throbbing.
I am listening to Istanbul, intent, my eyes closed."

Orhan Veli Kanık

Cast of Characters
In order of appearance

Hasan Çentitaş: 30's rising young star in film circles in Istanbul, went to US to get a PhD in Media, met & married Katja, returned to Istanbul to work for Bekir in the new university but who died tragically from a heart attack one morning after leaving his wife asleep to go play basketball with some high school friends.

Katja: a dance instructor/choreographer, in her 30's, from Sarajevo, Bosnia originally, she met her husband Hasan in NYC when both were at Columbia University, she was getting her MFA in Dance and he was finishing his PhD in Media, and returned with him to Istanbul to work at the college. Her personal history is marred by tragedy—her father, mother, brothers, and older sister were killed in the civil war that ripped Yugoslavia apart and her husband died in June on a school yard basketball court early one Sunday while playing with his friends. Though in shock for a month afterwards, and in a foreign country, she slowly is emerging into life with the help of her late husband's mentor Bekir. A great cook, a lover of jazz and opera, she has terrific legs and the sexiest walk in Istanbul.

Bekir: the visionary who creates colleges, 50s, tall, moves with the grace of a former dancer which is what he was during his youthful college days; also was a member of the Communist Party and spent some time in prison during the 80s coup and was tortured. Still liberal in his political leanings and a great believer in the power of education. Family was originally from the Black Sea and he is very proud of that and also being able to speak Laz.

Michael: he's been chair of the Theatre Department for four years, ever since the university was founded. Before that, he was chair of a theatre department in California where he also occasionally acted in shows. As he approached 60, he longed for an adventure and responded to an ad for his present job in Turkey. Before that he had dreams of retirement on a beach somewhere with his cat, a glass of red wine in his hand, and the time to read all the books lining his walls. Instead he ended up in Istanbul and has not regretted it since.

Özge: Mustafa's wife of 25 years.

Murat: 40's, married with three children, two girls of three and seven and an infant son, holds a PhD in American Studies and a masters in Musical Theory and Composition, has composed some short choral pieces that played at a few festivals and is currently working on an operetta he hopes to conduct himself.

Philip: British, 50's, from a working class family, graduated Oxford on an academic scholarship, teaches playwriting and screenwriting, intellectual, has written stories, plays, screenplays, even independently produced his own work, is fascinated with building structures around a single word, rereads Proust every year, and though very social, can withdraw for long periods of time to submerge himself in his work, loves taking long walks wandering around the city and has a fondness for collecting old photographs and postcards.

Meric: early 30s, an acting teacher/director, restless, always seeking something just out of reach, has an MFA in Acting and studied at The Stella Adler Studio in NYC, passionate about theatre, acting, drink, and women, not necessarily in that order.

Gamze: late 20s, costume designer in the theatre department who is leaving to get married to her boyfriend in Adana in August.

Simon: early 40s, department head of the English Preparatory Program who is returning to his college in Michigan in August.

Jennifer: late 20s, blond, blue-eyed, exceedingly attractive young Prep teacher from Ohio who came to Turkey right after graduating from grad school in search of adventure and found it and romance at the college, is madly in love with Meric and will do whatever is necessary to keep him madly in love with her.

Meral: an English Prep instructor, married, no kids, 30s.

Elif: an English Prep instructor starting her fifth year of teaching, late 20s, unmarried, loves poetry and the theatre.

İşmigül: an English Prep instructor with one year of experience, lives at home, a shopaholic, 20s.

Fersat: a student in the film department whose shyness has, at times, made him appear backward but who has always been alert to whatever was happening around him and found, after being given a camera for his birthday one year, a way to record what he saw in ways no one who knew him would have ever imagined. It was more than his eyes; it was his voice, too.

Berat: a student in the theatre department and one of the lead male dancers. He has since he was a child been graceful on his feet and though he at first wanted to be a footballer, he found that majoring in dance not only suited his artistic temperament but also allowed him to be surrounded by beautiful, shapely young women who enjoyed being held in his arms.

Elena: a student in the theatre department and the lead female dancer. Is a foreign student from the Ukraine: long legged, blonde, blue eyes, every Turkish man's dream of a goddess from the North who not only dances like the wind but is as free.

İrem: Michael's assistant in the Theatre Department, 32, wants to be a director, has a degree in Cultural Studies from Sabancı University and an MFA in Theatre from the University of Michigan, worked for a few years after college and though she loves her job, often thinks of returning to the US for a PhD. Cooks dinner for Michael every Saturday night, watches old movies with him, and considers him her best friend.

Deniz: mid 30s, slender as a model, is a costume designer who studied in London for three years, paints at home in her top floor apartment with a skylight that she's converted into a studio because of the light, loves to paint barefoot in a short, silk dress holding her brush like a knife while playing music, mostly Turkish pop or lately The Rolling Stones. She is filled with energy and loves change so much she is constantly rearranging the furniture in her apartment and adding clothes and shoes to her wardrobe.

Dave: a visiting professor from a US college that has a faculty/student exchange agreement with the college. He will run the English Prep Program for one year before returning to America. Is originally from Indiana but left the state for his current college in New York after a painful divorce. Eventually became the Director of the English Language Institute (ELI) as well as editor of the college's literary magazine. Was quite a ladies' man in his younger days but has, for the last few years, found himself without female companionship and has not been able to adjust to that very well.

Brenda: early 30s, from Britain, recently divorced from a husband more interested in writing love poems than the actual performance, a recent graduate of a PhD program in Media Studies, presented a paper at a conference that Bekir attended in London and, having finally been granted a divorce, jumped at the chance to teach in another country.

Sönmez: Murat's wife, late 30s, pays more attention to the children than him.

Mert: 50s, Chairman of the Board of Trustees, owner of the college, has known Bekir from their student days when they were young communists and briefly imprisoned together in the early 80s coup.

Meltem: a student in the theatre department, a born actress, has as long as anyone in her family can remember acted out all the parts in every movie or TV show that she has watched, donning costumes, applying make-up, changing her vocal register, even appearing either taller or shorter as was required, to everyone's delight.

Onur: Murat's best friend, 40s, teaches finance at another university.

Mark: Brenda's ex-husband, 30s, poet, more interested in writing about love than demonstrating it.

Pelin: a young student in the Theatre Program with a minor in Music who wants to study eventually in America. Besides wanting to be an actress, she sings with a trio of musicians from the Music Department at the university in local clubs and bars. Is heavily influenced by the torch singers she listens to, emulating vocal styles and mannerisms, exuding a world-weariness from life's experiences she sorely lacks but would desperately love to acquire.

Naım: a waiter at The Hamsi Pub.

Mermati: a waiter at the Hamsi Pub.

Osman: barman at the Belfast, a popular bar in Moda, in his early 20's, a former language student taking some time off from college to work.

İrem's mom: widow, early 50s, lives to see her daughter married with children of her own.

Brenda's mom: late 50s, concerned for her daughter's well being and marriage.

Cast Map

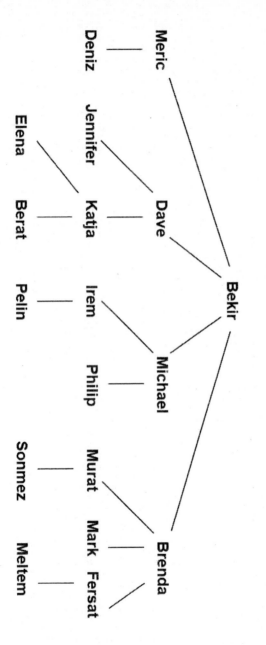

Overture

It begins at a funeral, never an easy place to begin in any country, in any culture, though there are some who use it to commemorate a life well lived, with photographs of those important events in all our lives: birth, school days, graduations, weddings, children, if we are lucky, vacations, family picnics, friends and relatives gathered around on holidays, changing hair styles and hairlines, fashions come and gone, smiling faces around dinner tables, in backyards, on trips to warmer climates with beaches and sand. But here, today, we have no such photographs for here, today, we bury a young man, only 36, a man who was still in the process of acquiring those moments yet to be captured on camera and stored away in our collective memory.

We stand at the mosque as the Imam reads from the Qur'an and there is murmuring of voices following along, hands raised palms up, female heads covered, moist eyes, and some sobbing, a solemn group of friends and colleagues surrounding the young widow, a woman named Katja who endures the burial of her husband. She stands mute, numb, one supposes, from the shock, and her knees buckle as she throws first a white rose onto his body covered in a burial shroud lying there in his grave, then a shovelful of dirt onto his body, that body she had clung to not so long ago as they slept in the bed that will now offer no comfort to her again. But Bekir, the university director, holds her firmly on one side and Michael, the theatre department chair, on the other and they both help her move off to the side while other friends and colleagues from the university, some former students of his, and some of the university staff all pass by, dropping a shovelful of dirt onto his cold, still form.

Afterwards the cars and minibuses bring everyone back to the school where tables are set-up with food and beverages because Bekir knows Katja is in no condition to host this herself, nor is her apartment large enough to accommodate everyone. So he turns the school and its staff over for this occasion and his wife Özge is in charge of organizing it while they all attend the service.

Katja sits in a chair at what could be considered the head table if this were that kind of occasion, a wedding, say, or a graduation party, but being a funeral, no one thinks of it that way. But people do file past offering condolences that she more or less acknowledges with a nod of her head or a faint smile or sometimes both. First, of course, there is Murat who though he never worked alongside her late husband in the film department since he is the head of the music department, he still, like Michael who stands at her left side, worked with him on committees. And though Murat feels awkward since he always felt somewhat threatened by Hasan because of his close relationship with Bekir, who stands at Katja's right side, and being the head of the school is thus supervisor to them all, he still can't help but be moved by her loss.

Next comes some film department faculty including Philip who teaches script and playwriting for both departments and who awkwardly bends over to kiss her cheeks which she is too distracted to notice. Then there are the theatre faculty, among them Meric, the acting teacher for the Turkish track students and the other director of showcase productions besides Michael, and Gamze, the costume designer who is leaving in another month to marry her fiancé and live in Adana, and then the English Prep teachers, led by Simon, a visiting instructor from America who is returning

22

to his college in Michigan at the end of July, and the other teachers including Jennifer, Meral, Elif, and İşmigül, and students, of course, from his film classes, like Fersat and Meltem, as well as from the theatre and dance program, especially her favorite dancers Berat and Elena, and Michael's assistant and protégé İrem. So many others, all filing past, with moist eyes and mumbled words of condolences, all looking sorrowfully at Katja who sits dazed in her chair, and making meaningful eye contact with Bekir and then Michael, this sad parade of colleagues and students showing their respect for a fallen teacher lost so early in life on a basketball court on a Sunday morning.

And afterwards, they mill about the exhibition hall of the college, nibbling on food, sipping soda or water, speaking in hushed tones of the departed, and casting furtive looks at the young widow lost in mourning with Bekir and Michael still at her side.

And finally the ordeal ends for her. Bekir drives her home and Özge helps her get settled before they both leave her to lie in a semi-catatonic position on the bed, still in her black dress, her eyes closed, wishing herself asleep.

As for the others, well, they drift off back to their lives and we will let them go, except for a few who we will follow till the end of this day.

First there is Philip sitting in a bar watching the world go by. He is thinking about mortality, his own in particular, and wondering just where the time goes. He had liked Hasan, a polar opposite version of himself in some ways: a PhD in hand, a credible academic resume, papers presented at the right conferences, articles on up and coming Turkish directors who live in other countries like Germany and Italy, a book in progress about the artist as an alien in a foreign culture, a promising career ahead of him in academic circles,

23

a beautiful, foreign wife, a man destined for success. And now, a generation still behind Philip's own, dead. Ah yes, Philip sighs. The good really do die young.

He sips his beer and watches a young couple walk past him to another table in the back. He can't help noticing the way their jeans hug their hips, the young man's hand sliding down to rest somewhat possessively on the small of the back of the young woman, the smiles they each have as they lean forward over their table whispering in the semi-darkness.

Youth, Philip thinks. Where did it go and how come one can't get it back? Surely, with modern science making such gains, there can't be a pill one could take which would allow one at least a fleeting moment of youth recaptured. A night, say, once a month, a weekend in the country, a candlelight dinner, an hour under the sheets.

Of course Philip never really thought he would ever be anything but young since he did not imagine he would live long enough to grow old. He himself had never really expected to make it into his fifties, much less beyond that, but here he is firmly implanted in that decade and though he smokes three packs of cigarettes a day, he still can't quite get himself to think beyond the month. It is a flaw in his character, he thinks, but he does not know how to plan ahead beyond 30 days. It is possibly the reason his last lover gave up on him as a losing proposition, since no matter how often he was lectured on being fiscally conservative, Philip never seemed to listen. Actually, though, he did listen but he just never earned enough to do anything but live hand to mouth in London, and would still be doing the same thing if he were there. Here, at least, with a full-time job, health insurance, and a flat he can realistically afford, if he has no money left at the end of the month, he still does not have any debt, either. And since he has no dependents to be concerned

24

about, living this way suits him for the present. Perhaps if he ever worried about the future, he might rethink his strategy, but he has no belief in any time beyond the end of the month and so is quite content to continue this way until he stops breathing.

Then he thinks of Katja, alone in her bed, mourning a future she had envisioned but now is so cruelly denied, and he feels immense sorrow as he once again realizes how random happiness is.

Meric meanwhile is rolling over on his side in bed watching Jennifer's naked back and quite lovely ass disappear on its way to the bathroom. He rubs his hand across his abdomen and thinks he is a lucky man to be alive, in bed with a beautiful woman, working at a school he loves. Funerals always depress him but now, afterwards, he only has reason to rejoice. Poor Hasan, he thinks. Gone so young and by surprise. Meric did not know him very well since he was in the film department but he knows Katja well since they are both in the theatre department and all of his acting students must take her dance classes. He thinks he wouldn't mind dancing with her himself, then feels slightly guilty for thinking that. Hasan isn't even cold yet, and right away he is thinking of his widow.

He turns over on his back and stares at the ceiling. Jennifer will be back out soon and with luck she will stay the entire night. These American girls, he thinks, are so much easier than Turkish women. They are just the way he likes them.

His eyes begin to close, languid thoughts drift through his semi-awake mind, and then there is a weight on the bed, Jennifer's hands on his chest, combing his hair back from his forehead, licking his ear. "Miss me?" she breathes.

25

"Always," he says, and takes her in his arms, his fingers working their magic, and any thoughts of death far removed from either of their minds.

And then to Michael who sits on his couch, his cat purring in his lap, while Miles Davis plays on his stereo in the living room and İrem is busy cooking something, which he knows will be delicious, in his kitchen. He thinks he really should get up and go help, or at least watch, but the cat keeps him anchored on the couch and Miles' trumpet kisses the air around his ears and he can't seem to rise to the occasion.

İrem appears wearing the apron she keeps at his place and carrying a glass of wine for each of them. "I've finished with the mezes," she says, "but the fish needs to bake a little longer in the oven." She smiles as she sits opposite him and hands him the wine. "But knowing you," she says, "I knew this would be welcomed."

"You know me too well," Michael says and touches his glass to hers. "To life," he says.

"Yes," she says, her smile turning slightly melancholic.

They are quiet as they sip their wine, each listening to the trumpet, lost in their own thoughts, a world apart and yet closely bound together. Then Michael clears his throat, takes the remote in hand, and skips to the next CD in the player, a Frank Sinatra disc, and says, "Care to dance?"

"You want to dance now?" she asks, only slightly surprised since nothing he ever does surprises her for long.

"Yes," he says. "I do. Don't you?"

She smiles, stands, and, after carefully untying her apron, says, "Not with this on."

"Ah," he goes, "but it is so charming on you."

"You say that because I cook for you," she says, "and you'd like me to continue doing that."

"Well," he admits, shrugging, "there is a bit of self-interest here."

She holds out her hand so he can lead her to the center of the room and then they embrace, he holding her ever so lightly, she floating on air, and slowly they begin to dance to Sinatra singing *I've Got You Under My Skin* and death, remorse, all the cares of the world seem to fade away as the cat watches serenely from his position on the couch and the night slips by.

Murat stands in his living room staring out to the courtyard below. His wife is asleep in the back bedroom, their three children also asleep in the bed with her, even the oldest at seven still preferring to lie with her mother than in her own bed. Only Murat sleeps alone, out here on the couch usually, or in the kids' room on the single bed that should be his oldest daughter's but is, more often than not, his now. He holds a glass of raki in his hand, the milky liquid offering some comfort on this night, though not enough to quell any thoughts of death and mortality for long. He wonders how his life turned out this way, alone in his own home, and alone especially tonight after just burying a colleague, an almost friend. Poor Hasan, he thinks. So much to live for and all gone because his heart was weaker than he knew.

Murat moves from the window and sits on the couch. He wishes he could sleep but his mind is too active, too many unnecessary images floating through, many involving women and none are his wife. Where did the passion go, he wonders, and stifles a cry.

He pours more raki into his glass, drops in some ice cubes from the ice bucket on the coffee table, and mixes in some cold water, but he knows it will take several more of these before his eyes finally close. And his eyes move restlessly over to the shelves of DVDs and CDs lining the wall next to his home entertainment unit. He picks a CD of Kazım Koyuncu and puts it into the CD player, slips the headphones on, and turns up the volume. And as the Black Sea music blots out all else, he leans back on the couch, closes his eyes, and sips his raki. It isn't the evening he would like to have after burying someone he had liked, but it will do. It has to. It is all he has left.

And finally, we end with Katja. She lies in bed, curled up in a fetal position, wishing she were anyplace other than where she is, in bed, the bed she shared with Hasan up to not so very long ago, the bed where she would lie in his arms, being held by him, inhaling his smell, feeling his arms around her, his breath on her neck, the warmth of his skin. She cannot believe she will never feel that again, and yet she knows it is over, over never to return, and yet how does she live knowing that, how does she go on?

So Katja lies in bed and cannot even cry. She can do nothing. Only lie there. In bed. And wait for the end of the world.

Part One
Fall

Scene 1
September

The early morning call to prayer from the local mosque wakes him, his now familiar alarm clock. The cat, too, stirs and stretches, looks over at Michael who keeps his eyes closed in a futile attempt to fool him, but the cat is wise to his tricks and pulls itself up, and slinks over to stare into Michael's face until he opens his eyes to acknowledge him. "Okay," Michael sighs wearily. The cat them plops down in the crock of his right arm, puts one paw ever so gently on his exposed forearm, and rests his head, closes his eyes, and falls back asleep. Michael, used to this routine, joins him. And they both drift off for another half hour of rest.

Katja wakes up in a cold bed in the morning, missing her husband's arms, his breath on her neck, the long, slow penetration she had grown accustomed to. This is a morning, a world, a life, she doesn't want to be in. A world without any relief from the loneliness that has been her life until she met Hasan. Her heart, her body, aches for him, turns in her bed, her legs open, yearning for him. Hasan, she thinks. My Hasan.

And this is not the first morning she wakes to a longing in her very depths that she knows she may never fill.

Deniz's dream: she is walking in a forest towards a man she does not recognize but knows intimately. As she approaches, there is a rustling of leaves in the upper branches of the trees and she turns toward the sound, startled to see a flock of sparrows, their eyes intently watching her every move. And she smiles in turn because that seems to be what one does to sparrows in trees, and yet it does no good, for the birds begin to fly and then soar forward, circling above her head, their beaks open, a chattering sound filling her ears, and yet it is not unpleasant and she awakes smiling, and thinks of her mother and fortune tellers back in Fatih and omens about money, good fortune and birds in dreams.

Dave wakes not knowing where he is, the bed, the room, the air he breathes unfamiliar. He gropes his way up to a sitting position and surveys his surroundings, his eyes adjusting to the room as the morning light filters in through the open window. And as he hears the morning call to prayer, he realizes he isn't back home on Long Island but in Istanbul, his new temporary home for a year. His heart slows down, his breathing normal, and he lies back to try to catch some more sleep before the alarm rings and he begins his new adventure.

Bekir's wife Özge prepares breakfast while he shaves, showers, gets dressed. It is a typical Turkish breakfast: olives, three types of cheese, some meat, a sliced hard-boiled egg, honey, jam, bread, a sliced tomato and cucumber. He eats without talking, just listens as Özge relays the latest news of their children, both at college now, from emails received during the night. He half listens, not because he isn't interested, but because his mind is on the school, this first week of the fourth year, the faculty, the staff. the months of preparation during the summer he endured to get to this point, the first gathering this year of everyone connected with this, the fourth college he has willed into being. And his mind cannot stay focused on anything other than reviewing all the last minute details, the registration process for new students for the next two weeks, the introductory remarks he must make in less than three hours. Most of these people are returning faculty from the last three years but there are some new people hired to replace those who have left and others to teach for the increased enrollment, so the mix is different,

33

is challenging, is just the way he likes it. Always a fresh challenge, always something slightly different, in this a university dedicated to the performing arts. And this year, his all-important year, must turn a profit, or else be on the verge of turning a profit for his contract to be renewed. For the Board of Directors are growing a bit impatient with his results so far, and he knows if he doesn't do something this year to guarantee a marked increase in enrollment and exposure for the college's programs, his tenure as director will be over. And with this on his mind, he sits down to eat.

Bekir smiles as he eats and Özge thinks it is because of their son's amusing stories that she is relaying, but it is because of what awaits him outside the door: another leg of a new journey on which to test himself once again.

Brenda's journey begins at the elevator and continues down the five flights to the ground floor where we watch her step out of the apartment house door and take in the rich aroma of freshly baked bread from the bakery across the street. Then it's the beginning of what will come to be her morning routine: her "merhaba" to the baker as she buys her morning simit and then the brisk five minute walk along Bağdat Street past all the shop owners starting to open up for the day until she catches a mini-bus for the rapid darting through traffic to the ferry at Kadiköy for Eminönü. She waits with the other passengers, Michael among them, though at this point she does not know him and so there is no look of recognition on either of their faces, while the ferry disembarks its passengers at Kadiköy before the gates open and both Brenda and Michael are swept up in the surge forward with everyone else onto the ferry to look for a window seat: Brenda on the first floor, Michael on the second floor deck.

Brenda's head is lowered as she immerses herself in a book, reading Evelyn Waugh's *A Handful of Dust* while the ferry pulls away from the dock and moves off toward the European side. She is oblivious to the other passenger's, lost in the world of the novel, a marriage unraveling, much like her own back in London, but this one being much more humorous, as fiction often is in regards to life.

Michael, meanwhile, on the second floor deck always feels relief settling in as he gazes out the window watching the coastline recede, the wide expanse of the Bosporus with freighters and smaller fishing skiffs scattered about, and then the landing at Eminönü drawing closer as they pull up next to the dock. The lines are thrown out and slipped over the moors, the gateways are slid across, and the crowd scrambles off, either over the gateways or taking giant steps from the boat to the dock.

Michael makes his way to the buses and boards one headed for Balat and stands for the short ride up the coast of Haliç, or as he likes to refer to its former name The Golden Horn, and sees the signs of early life as mothers push strollers along the waterway, enjoying the early morning hours of autumn. Some wear scarves, some without, but all stroll leisurely along. There are a few older women on benches watching grandchildren and one ambitious grandmother in head scarf, long sleeves, and baggy black pants is astride the exercise stirrups working her legs in concentrated motion to her own beat. Michael admires her concentration and wonders if maybe he shouldn't start exercising again.

Brenda, though, we see getting into a taxi and handing the driver the business card for the school and asks, "Okay?" He studies the card, looks back at her, her thin, pale face, her long, blonde hair, her long, slender neck, and nods, says,

"Okay" in reply and starts the engine, and they are off while Brenda makes note of the meter reading and gazes out the window at the same scenery Michael sees but with cooler, more remote eyes.

Murat sits at the kitchen table and watches his wife Sönmez breast-feed their infant son. She seems so blissful, so very much absorbed by his sucking that she is unaware of anything else in the room, especially Murat's own presence at the table. And this depresses him. Their three year old daughter is intently staring at the cereal in her bowl as if she expects it to somehow magically transport itself into her mouth and he wonders how he ended up like this: married, with children, and a wife who grows more distant with each passing day. He remembers how they used to touch each other all the time, as if they couldn't bear to be separated for a minute, a second, but now they never touch at all, except when she hands him the baby to hold while she prepares the bath, or at night when she accidently brushes against him in the hallway in the long cotton nightgown she now wears to insulate herself even further from his touch. And he wonders how they grew so far apart and if he'll ever again prefer to stay here rather than board a bus to go to work.

Dave has the easiest commute of all since he is in an apartment supplied by the school for visiting faculty from America or England, but he is, this semester, the only visiting professor and thus the sole occupant of this apartment. He stands at the window looking down at the waterway known as Haliç and thinks what a way to start the day. He is drinking a cup of tea and nibbling on some hazelnuts and wondering who is cutting his grass back at his home on Long Island, then dismisses that thought as he watches a small fishing skiff sail by. Life, he thinks, in a new city. Another adventure. Another new day.

Deniz meanwhile steps off the bus coming from Sultanahmet and crosses over to the school. Dave actually sees her while scanning the street looking at people stepping off the buses but he, of course, does not know Deniz so there is no look of recognition when he sees her. She is just another pretty woman crossing a street to him but we know different. We know she is on the alert looking for sparrows. And her heart beats a little faster as she steps through the school's front door expecting one to swoop down. She is almost disappointed when no bird appears.

Brenda appears, though, emerging from a taxi just outside the front door and Dave, looking at his watch, thinks he should get down there and meet some of the English instructors he'll be supervising this year in the English Preparatory Program. But first another player goes walking in just before Dave, the music department chair Murat who is still thinking about his wife nursing their infant son and wondering when he will once again have the attention of those breasts himself. And he, like the rest, finds his name tag on the table set up just outside the auditorium door and fastens it on his sport coat lapel while taking a seat two rows behind Deniz who sits toward the front, crossing her legs and studying the agenda for the day. And they are very shapely legs, which does not escape Dave's eye, for he sits in the row opposite hers across the aisle.

Michael comes into the auditorium then and though he is on the lookout for İrem, he sees Philip off to the side and settles in next to him. "Ready for an hour's worth of speeches in Turkish?" he asks.

"I wake up mornings thrilled by the thought," Philip says. "But won't İrem be here to translate?"

"That's the plan," Michael says. "But you know that quote about mice and men, right?"

"By heart." And he perks up a bit when he spies İrem entering the auditorium as she pins her nametag above her left breast, "It appears, though, that İrem is neither."

She takes a seat between the two of them and says rather casually, "Miss me?"

"All the time," Michael says, "but I try to repress it."

"Hmmmm," she goes. "Repression isn't healthy, you know." Then she turns to Philip and says, "Isn't that so?"

"Absolutely," he says. "This I can attest to."

"See?" she says to Michael.

"Are you suggesting I'm repressed?" he asks.

"If the shoe is the right size," she says and leaves it at that since there is movement at the front and the speeches begin. İrem does her best to deliver truncated versions of each and every one for both Michael's and Philip's benefit. Michael, for his part, uses all his former actor's skills to appear interested while Philip just tries to stay awake.

Other non-Turks like Dave and Brenda are completely lost since this is their first year here and are totally unprepared for this. Jennifer has Meric to translate and Katja knows enough Turkish from her almost five years of living with Hasan to get the gist of it all.

Mert, the chairman of the Board of Directors, speaks first and though his speech lasts approximately 20 minutes, İrem's translation of it is about a minute long and is that they, as staff and faculty of this school, are like a family and their role in the family is as parents and guardians of the students who will be like their collective children.

Both Philip and Michael look at each other but neither knows quite what to make of the look so their attention goes back to the closing remarks from Mert who speaks of the need of a school like this to contribute to the artistic life in the city and praises Bekir for his vision and his ability to assemble such a talented, experienced staff and faculty together.

This speech, of course, goes over well with everyone present because they are all here because of Bekir, the engine behind this endeavor. And everyone applauds as Bekir takes the stand.

Bekir's speech is short and to the point: this is a school devoted to the performing arts. He expresses confidence in all the staff and instructors whom he has personally selected for this venture. The next three weeks will be devoted to some orientation meetings, departmental meetings to plan curriculum and teaching schedules, and the final two weeks of student registration. There's a lot to do, he concludes, but he knows the people gathered here are more than capable of fulfilling their duties and proving, by year's end, that this will be the premier performing arts college in the city. Then he asks everyone to stand one by one and briefly introduce themselves to the assembly.

There are over 60 people who stand but we do not need to note them all now since most of those who will be our principals have been introduced already and the rest we will meet as this day continues. And later, during the reception that follows, it is only natural for our players to meet.

Dave is especially in his glory flirting with the Prep instructors who will be working for him, almost all female except for one lone male, especially zeroing in on Jennifer who is a native American like himself. "You've been teaching here long?" he asks her.

"This will be my fourth year," she says. "I've grown with the school."

He thinks she has grown rather well but keeps that to himself and rambles on about how this is a one year exchange for him. "I'm here this year and one or two of you will go to my school in New York next year," he says. "There's also a plan to send about 30 of your graduates this year to my college for their MFA degrees."

"Yes, I know," she says.

And though he tries to keep the conversation moving along, he notices it is flagging on her end, she being continually distracted by what is happening on the other side of the room. He glances over and notices the theatre group but cannot, for the life of him, figure out why she is so distracted by that group.

But we can guess, since Meric is obviously flirting with Deniz and Jennifer can't help but size up her new competition.

"Do you ever miss the States?" Dave asks.

"Sometimes," she says, looking back at him. "But this city grows on you."

And though Dave is thinking about growth in other directions, our gaze, along with Jennifer's, returns to the theatre group where Meric stands between Deniz and Katja facing Michael, İrem, and Philip.

"I love working with the Turkish track students," Meric says, "but hope one day you'll let me work with some of the English track students as well."

"Well I am contemplating a year end project that will involve both groups," he says.

"Really?" and Meric's eyes light up while both Philip and İrem look over quizzically at their boss.

"It's just an idea," Michael says, "and I have to get Bekir's okay first, but it'll be a full production done at the end of the spring semester. A play with music and dance incorporated into the text in both English and Turkish."

"Will we still do the end of semester showcases from both track students?" İrem asks, but in her mind she's also

40

wondering why he hasn't mentioned this idea of his to her yet, and can't help but feel a little hurt by this omission.

"Yes," Michael nods. "This other thing will be in addition to the two showcases at the end of each semester."

"That sounds like an ambitious expansion of the department," Meric says.

Michael nods some more. "It is," he says. "And it will involve all of you cooperating not only with each other but using student crews to help."

"I think this all sounds very exciting," Deniz says, her eyes sparkling with enthusiasm which Meric finds most appealing. "I feel so at home here already."

"That's great," Meric says, his wheels already spinning in regards to making her feel even more at home.

And İrem looks at Michael who realizes, of course, what her unspoken question is and says, "I haven't mentioned this before because I want to make sure Bekir will approve it first."

"And you think he might not?" she asks.

"Well this is the first year we graduate students who have completed the entire program and he might not want to make any changes in our operation."

And changes in the current operation are exactly what is on the mind of Murat as he looks into Brenda's eyes at this, their first official meeting, and his first conversation with the woman hired to replace Hasan.

Brenda, too, finds herself attracted to Murat's deep, sensuous eyes as he talks about the impact of Western composers, especially those of twentieth century masters like Ralph Vaughan Williams and Aaron Copland had on his life. She can't help but notice the wedding band on his finger, though, or his attempt to hide it as he speaks.

41

And Murat finds he has a hard time keeping his eyes from traveling to her opened blouse and the cleavage she so brazenly offers for view. "You'll like our students," he tells her. "Of course I've been teaching the language of music in both language track programs but those students who have passed the English Prep Program and have entered the English language track program in film will be your responsibility."

"I'm looking forward to it," Brenda says.

Then he studies her face for a second before asking, "May I enquire as to why you chose to come to Turkey to teach?"

"For the challenge," Brenda says, though if she is to be totally honest she would also add and to escape a messy divorce, but she doesn't know him well enough yet to be totally honest. Besides, she thinks she is often not totally honest with herself for she could no longer keep living in London knowing that any moment, in a pub, at the theatre, turning a corner on a street, she could run into Mark and then how would she ever be free of her marriage? No, the only way to flee from it, from him, from the mutual friends who kept looking at her as if she were making the biggest mistake of her life, from her mother's accusing eyes, was to leave London and thus she jumped at the first offer to go as far away from all things familiar as she could go: Istanbul. It is here in Istanbul that she will hopefully find herself and be free. So she smiles as she adds, "I've always been fascinated by Turkish history and culture."

"Well," he smiles, "we do have plenty of that to hold your attention." But he is thinking that if he weren't married, he would be more interested in holding her attention himself. That thought, though, is almost as unsettling as any action would be.

42

She, for her part, finds herself admiring his height, his broad shoulders, his dark eyes. She begins to wonder about what goes on in his mind behind those dark eyes. "I don't think I'll have trouble finding things to interest me here."

Dave, meanwhile, wanders over to the theatre crowd where he spies some very attractive women, thinking if he is going to look for someone to be involved with, it's always best to look outside one's own department. Besides, he thinks he might as well introduce himself to Michael, the only other American besides Jennifer at the college.

"So," Dave says, "how long have you been in Turkey?"

"This will be my fifth year," Michael says.

"You must like it then."

"There's much to fall in love with here," Michael says, and though he doesn't look İrem's way, he knows she is watching him.

Dave, meanwhile, begins a conversation with her about the theatre program and in the middle of her description, says, "Your English is very good. Did you study overseas?"

"In America," she says. "I have an MFA from the University of Michigan in Theatre."

"Ah," Dave says. "Great school. And so you teach here?"

"I teach but I'm also Michael's assistant."

"Ah," Dave goes again and thinks lucky Michael. And though he looks over to see if he's paying attention, Michael seems to have wandered off in his mind because he has the look of someone not consciously in the room.

Which is not exactly true, for he is once again thinking of his project, a play with music and dance but not a musical per se but a retelling of Shakespeare's ***Romeo and Juliet***, in English and Turkish, with subtitles flashing above the theatre like at City Center in NYC, with colorful costumes and

43

characters of all ages, with two different languages causing misunderstandings, and those two star-crossed lovers torn between their two families that are at war with each other, and a love that can never be in a world where a happy ending is unrealistic and tragedy looms over all. A play about life, about love, about gaining some sort of wisdom. A play that will be the culmination of everything he has thought or felt these last decades. His opus. Here in Turkey, before he has his own heart broken and he must leave.

Meanwhile Philip moves over to Katja and says, "And are you ready for the new year?"

She is almost startled, not expecting anyone to try to engage her in conversation, her mind off somewhere else, thinking of the past, perhaps, and seeing Hasan standing over by the film people and smiling her way. But Philip's voice brings her to the here and now and she smiles tentatively and says, "More or less."

"Me, too," he sighs. "Though I do so enjoy the teaching, I think I would rather, if I could afford it, not be bothered and have more time to write."

"You're lucky that way," she says. "You can work in isolation. But dance should be more communal. It should flow from people making connections somehow in their lives."

"And from what Michael has said," Philip says, "it looks like you'll be getting ample opportunity to make connections on stage."

Katja finds she is not prepared to make any connections now, would much rather withdraw, she can't help it, all this talk about enthusiasm for the upcoming year only brings back the memory of Hasan and his perennial optimism. She almost wants to cry, but instead has retreated to the safety of silence. But she also can't ignore Philip or even Michael for

44

they have both been so kind to her these past few months and she is grateful for that, this kindness during this period of still fresh mourning has been a comfort to her.

Dave seems to need a little comfort of his own and sidles over to stand next to Philip. "It's nice to see so many of the faculty here speak English," he says.

"Makes you feel at home, does it?" Philip asks.

"Especially since they all have accents. Reminds me of my old ELI," and he sighs. "Though no Spanish accents here, which I sorely miss since it's the only other language I can actually get by on."

"Well that won't help you much here," Philip says.

"I guess I'll have to try to learn some Turkish," Dave says and smiles ingenuously.

"That would be more useful," Philip says.

"And you?" Dave asks Katja. "How's your English?"

Katja looks at him almost as if she does not understand the question, then says, "I speak five languages: Bosnian, Croatian, Serbian, Turkish, and English."

"I'm impressed," Dave says, but, of course, he is impressed with more than her ability in languages. It is, after all, hard not to be impressed by her poise, her dark, sensuous beauty, her deep, sexy eyes. "And you teach in the theatre department?"

"I'm the college's choreographer and dance instructor."

"Actually," Dave says, "my parents were going to name me Fred instead of Dave, thus anticipating my other great passion."

"Which is?" Katja asks.

"Dance."

"And how is Fred connected to that?"

"Astaire, I bet," Philip says.

"You can read my mind," Dave says.

"Unfortunately," Philip sighs, "that doesn't seem to be all that difficult to do."

And though Dave realizes that isn't exactly a compliment, he lets it slide as he begins relating his passion for the tango.

Michael, meanwhile, having rejoined the group, looks over at Philip and says, "If I didn't know any better, I'd think he was Irish." Philip grins but the others look a bit confused and when confronted by looks of a lack of comprehension, he explains, "The blarney stone." But that does not seem to clear up the confusion in any of the women or Meric standing before him so he begins to explain the legend but is interrupted midway through by Bekir's appearance in their group.

"And how is my thespian department?"

"We're in the getting to know you stage without the music," Michael says. "Which is something I actually want to talk to you about."

Bekir looks both amused and intrigued, but that's often the case in his dealings with Michael. "Music?" he asks. "Or getting to know each other?"

"Well, music actually," Michael says. "The getting to know you business will take care of itself."

"And what about music?" Bekir asks.

"Well I'd rather do that at a sit-down sometime."

"You want me to get some chairs?"

"Only if you want to do it here?"

"We could," Bekir says.

"And spoil the reception?" Michael says. "I still haven't had my lunch yet and later there'll be wine, right?"

"Then we should wait till tomorrow," Bekir says. "Your head will be clear then?"

"Like a bell."

"A bell?" Bekir asks.

"It's an idiom," Dave interjects.

"Really?" Bekir says. "I don't follow it."

"The sound of a bell is very clear," Dave explains. "And it carries a great distance."

"Ah well we don't have many bells in Istanbul," Bekir says. "Maybe there are some in areas where there are churches but they do not ring them with much frequency. At least not so often for us to catch this meaning."

"It is, like most idioms, culturally bound," Dave says.

"And you'll be teaching a lot of idioms in the Prep, I suppose" Michael says.

"Ah yes," Bekir says. "The Prep."

"Students love to learn idioms," Dave says. "It makes them feel like they're mastering the language."

"I could use some lessons on idioms myself," Bekir says. "But I hope you'll be too busy with our Prep for that."

"You expect a large group?" Dave asks.

"We had 220 last year," Bekir says. "This year we should have about 300."

"Really?"

"Yes," Bekir says. "At least I hope so. We have hired enough teachers and I would hate to be over-staffed." He smiles. "Did you meet them all?"

"Just a few who are returning from last year."

"Well they are around. Mingle and look for the ones who look somewhat lost. But, of course, you'll meet them after lunch at the departmental meeting part of the agenda."

"How many are there?"

"Fourteen."

"A nice number," Dave says.

"Your dean back in New York tells me you had over a thousand students in your program."

"Yes," he nods. "And over 40 languages and 70 something countries."

"Well here's it's mostly one language but we have some students from other countries here through the Eramus Program," Bekir says. "You think you can accept that challenge?"

"Well it's not as big a challenge as what I left," Dave says.

"Except there you didn't need to know another language other than your own," Bekir says. "But here, you'll have to learn some Turkish to survive." And he smiles. "That's a different kind of challenge, isn't it?"

Dave nods. "I see what you mean."

"Not yet you don't," and his smile broadens as he looks over at Michael who smiles back. "But you will soon enough."

And soon we find them all filtering in to the cafeteria to pass down the line to fill their trays with food, desserts, beverages, bread, and take seats at the tables and continue talking, renewing old friendships, making new ones, gossiping about the changes to come in this the fourth year, and anticipating the increase in the enrollment and their work loads.

Then, after cay or Turkish coffee, they move off to designated classrooms to begin the week long series of departmental meetings, the ordering of textbooks, the revising of curriculums, the scheduling and then the rescheduling of teacher assignments, the shuffling of office space, the indoctrination of the new faculty, the necessary preparation for the next two weeks of student registration and finally the first week of classes. And the excitement mounting each day.

But we won't dwell on this except to drop in on the meeting between Michael and Bekir for the outcome of that influences all that follows.

"So," Bekir says as Michael settles into a chair in his office, "what's this idea you have?"

"Well we plan to do scenes from plays every semester from both the Turkish track students and the English track students but I'd also like to begin work on a large scale production to be done at the end of the year using both groups of students in a bi-lingual production, a musical, actually, with dance numbers, subtitles in both English and Turkish, a large cast, a full-blown production."

"Do you think our students can do this?"

"Yes," Michael says. "Since it'll be a bi-lingual production, we'll play to both their strengths, and we can fully utilize Katja and her dancers."

"What about the music?"

"There are many students here who play instruments and sing in our Music Department. We'll audition them and pick the best to be in our orchestra. And, of course, I hope to get much cooperation from Murat."

Bekir sits back and stares at Michael, a smile forming on his lips as he thinks this could be a great marketing and recruitment tool if successful. "You think you can do this?"

"Yes," Michael says.

"And what play will you use?"

"This, too, must be one of our own creation," Michael says. "So I'm thinking of adapting Shakespeare's *Romeo and Juliet*."

"Shakespeare?" Bekir asks, his eyes widening a bit. "Do you really think our students can do Shakespeare?"

"We'll adapt it," Michael stresses. "We'll keep the basic plot and characters but change the dialogue to a more

49

contemporary usage and add songs and dance to move the plot along. Sort of like what they did with *West Side Story* only maybe using a time period here before the founding of the republic. I'll get Philip to help fashion the script using some of the best student writers. And the acting teachers can help coach the students in both languages. It'll be a real collaborative effort."

"This would be quite an achievement if you can do this."

"Not just me," Michael says. "A lot of the faculty will be actively involved."

"Yes, but you will be the director, so organizing and developing this will mostly fall to you," Bekir says. "This is a big project."

"I know," Michael says. "But I'm confident we can pull this off with your blessing."

"You have it then," Bekir says. "Insallah."

"Yes," Michael grins. "We'll need all the help, divine included, we can get."

And the weeks fly by rapidly, registration is both busy and hectic with more students than they anticipated but certainly not unwelcomed, and before they know it, the first week of classes begins to find Brenda greeting her first class of students in Turkey. "Merhaba," she says, and then gives a somewhat stiff smile. "And that's one of maybe four Turkish words I know, so I certainly hope your English is better than my Turkish. Otherwise you may have trouble in this class." The greeting does not elicit even a flicker of a smile on any of the students' faces, just blank looks as they intently watch her fidget slightly behind the podium with her notes. But the fidgeting does not last long, and soon she has their undivided attention as she begins her lecture on the history of film. And as she speaks, she could be anywhere, these students could be anyone, this moment suspended in time, in place, her life lived in between the here and now and the long time ago.

Deniz spends most of her days organizing the costume shop. She has material to sort, mannequins to position, sewing machines to set-up, and rows upon rows of closet space to partition. There are some students on scholarship who are assigned to her as assistants and, of course, her students must also put in time to help. But the most difficult thing for her to determine is just what she needs to stock. It would help, of course, if she knew what shows are planned and so she decides to speak to Michael about this and she finds him in his office drinking Turkish coffee and making notes on a legal pad in front of him. "Am I disturbing you?" she asks.

"No," and he smiles relieved. "You're actually giving me a great excuse to take a break from this endless paperwork."

"Oh, so you like being disturbed?" she asks.

"From this, yes," he says. "Feel free to barge in here at any free moment and pull me away from these endless reports and projections."

"And what are you projecting?" she asks. "The upcoming year?"

"Yes, more or less," and he leans back in his chair and looks at his cup of Turkish coffee, which has grown rather cold. "Would you like some cay or coffee or something?"

"Oh, so typically Turkish," she says and laughs. "You are adopting our habit of always offering refreshments whenever we meet."

"Well we Italian-Americans do that, too," he says. "You couldn't go anywhere when I was growing up without bringing some cake along so wherever you went, they had to offer tea or coffee."

51

"I guess it's very Mediterranean," she says.

"Yes," and he picks up the phone and calls down to the cafeteria. "Let's hope someone picks up who can handle my basic Turkish." Then he asks, "So what is it? Cay or coffee or something else?"

"Cay, please."

He fumbles through an order and then hangs up. "I think they got it." Then he settles back in his chair and says, "But you didn't come in here for cay."

"No," she says. "I came to find out about your projections for shows so I can begin to prepare."

"Ah yes," and he nods. "Preparation is a good thing."

"So can you help me prepare?"

"What do you mean?"

"By telling me what you're planning."

"You mean the shows?"

"Well, yes," and she laughs. "Aren't I supposed to design costumes for whatever shows we do?"

"Ah, yes, of course," he nods. "The costumes."

"So do you want to tell me what the shows will be or at least give me some hints?"

"Ahhhh," and he leans back further in his chair and just stares at her. Then he says, "I don't mean to be mysterious but I'm still thinking about that."

"Oh," she says. "I see."

"I mean I have definite ideas but maybe it would be best to discuss this at the next departmental meeting."

"Which is?"

"Well," and he shrugs, "we could have one today, I suppose. Say at four when all the classes are over."

"Okay," she says.

"I'll have İrem tell the others and we can meet in an empty classroom." He smiles. "Okay?"

"You're the boss," she says. And the refreshments arrive then and they both sip their respective drinks while eyeing each other.

Later we find Michael eyeing İrem as she works on her course outlines and we see İrem returning his gaze as she sits opposite him in their office. "What?" she asks, looking him directly in the eye.

He seems to snap out of whatever thought is in his head and shrugs. "Nothing," he says. "At least nothing important."

"That was an interesting look for nothing important."

"It's just that I was wondering if you were upset with me for not talking to you about this proposed project first."

"Not upset," she says. "But you do usually use me as a sounding board. That is the correct term, right?"

"Right," he nods.

"And so I was a little hurt maybe."

"Maybe?" he asks, almost tentatively.

"Well maybe more than maybe," she says.

"More like probably?"

"I think more like definitely."

"Ah," he goes. "Then you were seriously hurt."

"You can say that."

"Ah," he goes again, then is silent for a moment while he continues to stare at her. "I apologize," he says finally.

"You don't have to apologize," she says. "Just don't treat me like the others."

"But I don't treat you like the others," he says.

"You did with this project."

"Yes," he says with genuine regret in his voice. "I did. And I'm sorry."

"You should be," she says, and though her tone is light, almost joking, they both know she is deadly serious.

53

"You know," he says after a slight pause, "I don't think of you as being like the others."

"I know," she says. "But I also don't know exactly what you mean by not thinking of me like the others."

"Well you're special to me," he says.

"I am?" she says.

"Yes," he says. "I thought you knew that."

"I do," and she smiles. "But it's nice to hear every now and then."

"And you think because I didn't tell you about this proposal first that you're not special?"

"Well the thought did enter my mind."

"Get it out of there," he says smiling himself. "Immediately."

"Okay, boss," she says. "But you won't let that happen again, will you?"

"No," he says, holding up his hand in the old Boy Scout sign. "I promise."

And though İrem doesn't need to take it that way, she knows instinctively that it is more than a promise. It is, she thinks, bordering on commitment.

And Katja cannot shake the feeling that another promise has been broken. Not by the man who made it, but by whatever guiding principle there is to the universe. For whenever a vow is made by any man in her life, it seems it cannot be fulfilled. Her father, her uncles, now Hasan, the first man she trusted since she was a child. All gone. Disappeared. Never to return.

It haunts her still and the only release she feels is in dance. So after warming her students up, she puts on some samba and demonstrates to her class what it means to move. And as she loses herself in the music, she loses the emptiness that plagues her day, that stains her nights.

And her students watch with rapt attentiveness, mesmerized by the intensity with which she dances. She is not of this world, but of another, a fantasy on two legs before their hypnotized eyes.

"A fantasy," Michael explains to his staff later at their meeting. "That's the way I see this being done. A celebration of love in all its forms. In both languages, with dance and music being an integral part of the production, and the language simplified enough so our students, even the more advanced ones from the Prep who want to be theatre majors, can handle."

"But Shakespeare?" Meric says. "Do you really think they can do it?"

"Simplified Shakespeare," Michael says. "And yes, I do."

"Well I think it's exciting," Deniz says. "And the costumes can be so colorful, and representative of different styles, too, for each age group within each family."

"Yes," Michael says. "That's the way I see it, too."

"And you want me to rewrite Shakespeare?" Philip says. "I mean, for a Brit like me, that's almost sacrilegious."

"Well, you'll keep the plot and the characters but make the language more modern and idiomatic."

"Still," and he sighs, "this is a bit daunting."

"And I'll ask Murat from the Music Department to help with the music," Michael says and smiles. "So we won't be in this alone."

"That's comforting," Philip says.

"And Katja, you'll need to start thinking of dances that could move the action along. I have some ideas already that I'll share, okay?"

Katja nods, thinking she needs projects like this to immerse herself in so she can focus on something other than loss. And her mind starts to drift with images of lovers' ballets while the meeting continues without her.

Murat sits at his desk in his office staring at a drawing on his wall. It is a sketch, really, of the poster for a concert he gave in college done over twenty years ago, with a young man staring off into space where various instruments, musical notes, float suspended in air, and his eyes are gazing lovingly, longingly at the sounds he must hear, the sense of wonder, of awe on the young man's face as he listens to music only audible to him. The face, of course, resembles his, as if foreseeing what would be his role in life. At first it had amused him, but now it saddens him. And though he will not be taking it down, his eyes grow heavy, and they begin to close, there in his office, seated there at his desk.

And Katja watches her students in the dance club try to limber up. There are so few who really have the grace of dancers, but what does she expect. She cannot relate to these young women. When she was their age, she lived and breathed dance. Her body was like an instrument and she constantly practiced at playing it. But her students lack that discipline, all except her two favorite students: Berat and Elena. They seem almost as serious as she was at their age and are lean and lithe the way she was, still is, today. Only now she lacks the intensity she possessed. Life perhaps has robbed her of that. But her hard earned discipline, at least, sustains her.

And the young, the young, they crowd the halls, sit in the classrooms, dance their hearts away. And Katja looks out from tired, wistful eyes remembering her own youth, the boundless energy that once flowed through her limbs that now only ache for the one body that held her so long and so lovingly throughout the endless night.

Watch Deniz peruse magazines, carefully cutting out advertisements of fashion, admiring the lines of bodies, the cut of fabric, the contours of material against shapes, and filing them away for future reference, ideas for costumes, for this year or the next. She cannot always determine what to use or when, for she sees so many shapes, so much color, such a world in transition before her stunned eyes.

"So," Michael says at dinner at his favorite fish restaurant in Kadiköy, The Hamsi Pub, "that's my idea. A timeless *Romeo and Juliet.*"

"Well," Philip says, "it certainly is ambitious."

"Ambitious?" Michael laughs. "That's the understatement of the year."

"Yes, it is," Philip nods.

"But I see this so clearly. I have to do it, you know."

"Well, if you have to do it, don't let me dissuade you. But you know, this is not going to be easy," Philip says.

"I know," Michael says, "but that's why it excites me. The challenge it represents."

"Hmmmm," Philip goes and looks over at İrem. "What do you think about all this?"

"I don't know yet," she says, and then looks at Michael. "But he's the boss and he hasn't disappointed me yet."

"Really?" Michael asks.

"Really," she says.

"Not even once?"

"Well maybe once," she says, "but I'm trying to not hold that against you."

"Was it recently?" he asks a little tentatively.

"Not so recent."

"Were you very disappointed?"

"I think it's better if we don't discuss it. After all, I am trying very hard to forget it."

"Me, too," Michael says. "In fact, I think I've already forgotten it."

"That's rather convenient of you," Philip says.

"I always try to cooperate when someone is overlooking my shortcomings."

"But back to this play," Philip says. "You really expect me to rewrite Shakespeare?"

"You'll have help" Michael promises. "I'll get Murat to write music not only for the dances but some songs, too, to move the plot along. Maybe even use some film as backdrop or transitions. You know, a mixing of different media. We'll get all the departments involved."

"I don't know about you," Philip says to İrem, "but I'm getting a little overwhelmed now."

"And that," she says sighing, "is not surprising at all."

And Michael is off again, painting pictures in the air of how he sees it: a new version of a musical *Romeo and Juliet* with language being the stumbling block to what will eventually be a happy ending. And while he paints his pictures, Philip strains to catch his enthusiasm and İrem finds herself smiling at the grand design while we pull back and leave them to their meze dishes, their wine, a basket of fresh bread, a çoban salad, and grilled fish. A meal. And the beginning of their great adventure.

And finally we end the month with Brenda as she stares at the phone as it rings in her still half furnished apartment. It is long distance, she knows, and it is England calling. Or, to be more accurate, her husband, ex-husband now, though still trying desperately to erase that ex from before the role he so avidly wants to resume playing in her life. Oh Mark, she thinks. Mark, why can't you just go away, though in actuality it is she who has gone away and what she really wants is for him to stay where he is, a few thousand miles away in London in what used to be their flat but is now solely his.

Leave me, she thinks. Leave me to my new adventure and continue playing the misunderstood poet writing your sad, forlorn verses of lost love. She thinks he is only good at love on the page but could never quite make it work in bed. Words, she thinks. Love is just words for him and she craves action.

And as she stares at the phone until it finally ceases ringing, she wonders, hopes that she will find what she is looking for here in this new old world. In this city straddling two continents with over two thousand years of history there might be hidden, somewhere in its bosom, what she is eagerly searching for.

Scene 2
October

Dave finds himself enamored of İrem from the theatre department. It's her quiet efficiency, an almost serenity that exudes from her, that he finds most appealing. And, of course, it helps that she is strikingly beautiful: has full, sensuous lips, deep, dark, mysterious black eyes, black hair that captures the light, and a slender body that moves with poise throughout the day. He catches sight of her in the cafeteria, sipping cay and listening with attentive eyes to whatever is being said around her. And though he doesn't fully understand her relationship with Michael, he decides from all the nonverbal clues of their body movements that it is not sexual and so begins to plot in his mind ways to have more interaction with her. And then, one morning when he comes down to the cafeteria for a late morning snack, he finds her alone at a table drinking cay and reading a play.

"Anything interesting?" he asks as he stops, a cup of Nescafe in one hand, a simit in another, in front of her table.

İrem looks up and for a second does not quite register who he is, then smiles and says, "Just some Chekhov I've read about a hundred times."

"Then it can't be for pleasure," he says. "Is it for a class you're teaching?"

"Modern Drama," she says.

"Of course," he smiles. "I should have guessed." Then he looks at the empty seats at her table and asks, "Mind if I join you? Or would you rather not be disturbed from rereading the play for a hundredth and one time?"

She laughs and puts the play down. "Please do," she says.

And so it begins: the innocent, seemingly harmless chitchat of nothing of any importance, at least that is the way İrem views it, but Dave sees it another way, as an opening to enlarge, an opportunity to exploit, an avenue that lies open now to her heart.

Brenda stands in the shower for a long time letting the water cleanse her. She takes comfort in the way it rolls down her breasts, follows the curve of her hips, her buttocks, soothes the heat in her thighs. She has the blues, she knows, and the shower seems to be her way of washing them away, of giving relief to the aching in her heart, though the relief only lasts just so long, and so long is the time it takes for her to pat herself dry, wrap the towel around her now clean body, and lie down on the bed. Then they come back to rest on her chest, creep up her calves, slide along her thighs, and nuzzle up to that place that misses a man the most. There they are again, the blues, and she feels so empty, so lost, so far from home, she silently begins to cry.

Katja smiles in her sleep and will not wake up. For if she does, she will be in a world that does not contain Hasan and then how will she find happiness? There is only work, there is only toil, there is only the dull pain in her heart. But here, in sleep, there is Hasan. He is smiling, his dark hair is cascading in curls over his ears, on his neck, touching his shoulders, his eyes are twinkling, and his hands, his hands slowly unbutton her blouse. Her breath constraints with anticipation. Her back arches, her breasts rise to meet him, her lips part, her tongue, his tongue, sucking beauty.

And when she finally, reluctantly, awakes, as she knows she must, this world is dull, is gray, is soulless. And she wonders why they had come here, to Turkey, to find such sorrow.

Murat sits in his office and finds it is the only place he does not feel oppressed. It is a haven away from his home and it is here that he can forget that he even has a home, as if this office, this school, is the center of the entire universe and gives meaning to his life. He has respect here, for his knowledge, his talent, his abilities. He can become engaged in meaningful conversations about topics of interest to him and his colleagues. And the students all wish to pursue lives similar to the one he has led. He walks the halls and he is somebody, admired and conspicuous, getting polite nods of greetings from all. He belongs here more than anywhere else, and he knows, deep in his heart, that if he could, he would never leave.

Meric finds a reason, any reason, to pass by the costume shop where Deniz is working to say hello. Sometimes he brings her a glass of cay, or a piece of fruit, or the latest gossip about the students. Other times he invites her to lunch or asks if she'd like to have a drink after work, for he has found out that Deniz likes a glass of wine afterwards to unwind and he, of course, likes a beer.

And Meric charms her with stories about the students or tales of his passion, the art of acting. He describes moments he witnessed on stage, great cinematic moments still etched in his mind, the subtle nuances of an actor's style, his time in New York City studying at The Stella Adler Studio, his classmates, the plays he saw on Broadway, Off-Broadway, in tiny workshops in The Village, his season of summer stock in Michigan, the theatre group he works with in Bakırköy. He recites lines from favorite speeches, gives dramatic readings of poetry, does his best to seduce her with his love of his craft, and finds he falls in love all over with the power of his own performance.

And Deniz finds herself enamored of a passion similar to her own.

"So what do you think of the new film teacher?" Fersat asks Meltem as he sits next to her on one of the benches outside in what is a designated smoking area.

"I like her," Meltem says, flicking ash from her cigarette and then taking a long drag. "Judging from her comments, I think I have a lot of things in common with her. She likes film noir and melodramas and that's what I'm interested in, too."

"Yes, but she doesn't seem too interested in films made from graphic novels."

"Or from Play Station," Meltem laughs. "That disappoint you?"

"A little," he says. "She doesn't seem to get the humor."

"Or appreciate the demeaning way women are depicted there, either."

"It's not all demeaning," Fersat says.

"Not if you're a juvenile boy," Meltem says, teasing him.

"You just don't like it because the women all look like Megan Fox or Michelle Rodriquez."

"You're right there."

"How do you want them to look?"

"Like Saadet Isil Aksoy," she says. "Or, if you want to go American, then Natalie Portman or Kirsten Dunst."

"But they're not film noir types," Fersat says.

"They could be," she says, "if they were cast in one."

"I think our teacher could be cast in one," Fersat says. "At least I would cast her."

"Oh?" and Meltem's eyebrow raises up an inch. "Do I detect a crush on teacher?"

Fersat laughs. "No," he says, "but I do think she's kind of sexy."

"So is she your type then?" Meltem asks playfully, though not as playfully as she had hoped for there is a hint of disappointment in her voice, which she, despite her best efforts, can't seem to hide.

"Not really," Fersat says. "I know Turkish men are supposed to be crazy about blondes, but I prefer dark Turkish girls." And though he doesn't say "like you", it is implied, he thinks, she thinks, and suddenly the air around them seems to change. Then he picks up his camera and, holding it quite gently in his hands, he asks, "Can I take your photo?"

And Meltem doesn't have to say anything. Her smile is her answer and Fersat begins clicking away.

Jennifer knows Meric is flirting with Deniz but thinks as long as he frequents her bed, she still has a hold on him. Deniz is, after all, just competition and Jennifer has dealt with competition before. And though she is old enough to know better, she is still young enough to not be intimidated by a competitor, even one as attractive as Deniz. So as she looks over lovingly at Meric stretched out in her bed and snoring peacefully, she thinks his infatuation with Deniz is a passing phase and if she can control her jealousy, it will soon run its course. She is confident in her hold on him just as she has always been confident in her ability to attain whatever she sets her mind to. This confidence stems from her awareness of just who she is and how no matter what outside forces have tried to mold her, she has always steered her own course through life.

She comes from a typical Midwestern family of good Methodist stock: conservative, Republican, people who have never gone anywhere more exotic than Disney World and who spend most of their weekends at the mall. And though they did not stand in her way when she told them at the dinner table one Sunday that she was going to take a teaching job in Istanbul, they did not encourage her, either. In fact, they were secretly concerned about her choice of country, it being a Muslim one, and they were sure she would be forced to wear a headscarf and thus would come home at the earliest opportunity. They also knew she was a bit headstrong, a trait they attributed to her maternal grandmother who had some French blood mixed in her and had always been a little different than the rest of the family, so they just kept their opinions to themselves and only voiced them when she was out of earshot. But after the first year, they could not contain their amazement that she not only stopped talking about coming home for visits, but she made it clear that she liked Istanbul. And it was at the end of her second year that Jennifer finally felt free of whatever constraints had been tying her to a life like her parents, which she knew she did not want, as she became known in her family circle as the black sheep.

So the black sheep with the long blond hair, who is positive she knows what men really want, slides her hand across Meric's abdomen and down below his waist to where his manhood lies, and finds his response is just what she expected. And she, of course, smiles to herself knowing exactly what to do with it.

İrem enters their office carrying a CD of songs by Chris Rea and puts it on Michael's desk. He looks at it somewhat confused and then looks up at her. She smiles and says, "Somehow this reminds me of you."

He looks at the song titles and though he vaguely remembers a song called "Fool If You Think It's Over" which could be a reminder of his past life, it does not seem to be here which causes him to blink a few times, rub his eyes, and ask, "Any song in particular?"

"No," she says. "Though there are certainly several candidates there, but I think it's more like a complete package idea."

"I see," he says.

"Anyway," and that sweet smile of hers again, "I couldn't help thinking of you as I listened to it and so thought I should give it to you."

"Am I going to thank you for this later?" he says.

"If not," and the smile grows sweeter, broader, "I don't know you as well as I think I do."

He sighs and puts the CD in his book bag then points to the chart on the wall opposite his desk and says, "My latest thinking on our *Romeo and Juliet.*"

She looks at the flow chart of character names with lines drawn to connect relationships and a breakdown of the play's scenes and nods, "It's a beginning."

"I'm beginning to feel the old fire again," Michael says. "That old passion is once again being rekindled here."

"That's good," İrem says. "But I don't think you really ever lose something like that."

"Maybe," Michael says. "But like all things, there are ebbs and tides. But I feel it coming back now with this new challenge."

"Yes, those challenges," İrem says laughing. Then she looks at Michael with much affection in her eyes. "I think there is much more to learn from you. You are a real risk taker."

"Well there's no point in playing it safe," Michael says.

"And do you feel that way about all aspects of your life?"

"I gave up everything in America and came here to start all over again, didn't I?" he asks. "Isn't that risk taking? Especially at my age?"

"You're not so old," İrem says.

"Well not so young, either," Michael sighs.

She looks at him carefully, those dark eyes of hers appraising him again as they often do, and finally says, "I think you worry too much about your age. Those of us who know you, work with you, are friends with you, we don't think of your age at all."

"I am ageless to you?" he asks, a smile forming on his lips, though a bit crooked. "Sort of like the stars. A thing that has always been there."

"You are a star to me," she says, and though she doesn't mean it to be serious, it comes out that way, which surprises them both.

And then he turns back to the chart, not knowing what else to say, leaving all else open, and draws her into a conversation about the play, ideas for a set, a time period to set it in, details to distract them from any more talk of personal matters, details about work to absorb them in something else.

And the students watch Katja as she leads Elena through a dance routine. They are mesmerized by her involvement, her total absorption in the dance and after some missteps by Elena, she, too, becomes at one with the dance steps. The two of them glide across the floor like well-oiled parts of the same engine and everyone in the class applauds them, though one of the male students is a little more enthusiastic than the others for Berat has his eyes trained on just one of the women, and though Berat's eyes are focused solely on Elena, we can't help but notice that all the other eyes in the class stay glued on Katja in tights.

Deniz stares fixedly at the empty canvas in front of her. She knows she wants to fill it but cannot think of how she wants to start. Nothing comes into her mind and she almost loses herself in the whiteness of the canvas before she turns away and begins to dance to the music blaring, The Cranberries singing about a love that just keeps lingering and she begins to sway rhythmically to the music, her short skirt floating above her knees, the sky above dotted with stars, and she feels so alive, so very much a part of the world around her, that she begins to sing along even though she does not know all the words. But who needs words, she thinks, when she has rhythm, when she has the music inside her, life pulsating in her veins, movement and sound and color begin to appear before her eyes, color that takes shape and fills the empty space that once was her canvas but now explodes into brilliant form as a brush flies through the air as she dances, as she twirls, and there is life there, now, on the canvas, and Deniz is in a trance as she creates another burst of vibrant colors in a design on what once was an empty void.

Brenda is standing in her kitchen staring at the contents of her refrigerator. There really isn't much there and she certainly doesn't feel like cooking anything anyway, but the thought of going out again and sitting at yet another restaurant eating alone depresses her. She wonders if there would be anyone appropriate to call and then thinks of her fellow countryman Philip who, she knows, lives alone, too, in nearby Kadiköy. So impulsively she picks up her cell phone and gives him a ring. "Hello," she says after he answers. "I hope I'm not disturbing you."

"No," Philip says. "I'm just walking over to a kebab place to get something for dinner."

"Oh, well then I am disturbing you. You must be meeting friends."

"No, nothing like that," he sighs. "Just my usual self."

"You're eating alone then?" she asks.

"Yes," he sighs. "Caught me, didn't you, leading such an exciting social life."

She laughs. "Mine's no better," she says. "Mind if I join you?"

"For dinner?"

"Yes," she says.

"Be delighted."

"Well then," she says, "where shall we meet?"

"Do you know the Eminönü and Karaköy ferry stop?" he asks.

"Yes."

"Then we'll meet in front of that big theatre, Haldun Taner. That good?"

"Lovely," she says. "I could be there in 20 minutes."

"I'm sure I can rein in my appetite till then."

And Brenda hangs up thinking how easy that was.

Michael is standing with İrem in front of Ali Üsta waiting their turn for a two scoop cone of ice cream and enjoying another warm October evening.

"What are you getting?" she asks.

"Almond and pistachio."

"Sounds good."

"And you?"

"I never decide until I'm standing in front," she says smiling broadly.

"Now who's the risk taker?" he asks.

She laughs and playfully hits him on the shoulder. Then, after ordering, paying, standing off to the side as the line moves, he watches her licking a triple scoop cone of raspberry, mocha, and caramel.

"And what do you want to do now that you have your ice cream?" he asks.

"Well I was thinking we should go over to the tea garden and have some Turkish coffee since it's such a lovely night."

"A brilliant suggestion," he says.

"Of course," she answers.

And as they begin their leisurely stroll toward the tea garden, they both somehow feel strangely at peace.

Dave feels nervous about the evening and wonders why he should but then again knows exactly why: because he has been invited by Jennifer, along with a few of the other Prep teachers, out for drinks in Taksim. And though it seems innocent enough on the surface, the director having a casual night out with some of his staff, he is much too carried away with the thought of an evening out with young, possibly available, women in a foreign city and all the images that conjures in his mind. Could an affair be just around the corner, on its way toward him now, wearing a dress that gently blows above the knees, with clicking high heels and a look of careless abandon in the eyes? But one step at a time, he tells himself. One baby step at a time. And so he waits in front of the 1923 monument next to Galatassaray Lycee looking casually dressy in a white linen shirt, navy blue cotton pants, and Allan Edmund loafers, his heart beating a little too rapidly, his nerves desperately wanting a cigarette that his lungs can no longer handle. And his mind wonders if indeed he needs to put himself through all this for what will be, in the end, a hopeless fantasy on his part, but catching sight of Jennifer walking toward him with Elif and İşmigül next to her makes the breath in his chest constrict.

"Hello, boss," they all say, and as both İşmigül and Jennifer each take him by the arms and lead him into the crowded street, he feels he must be blushing but knows he is happy just the same.

Deniz is twirling under her skylight to the music of Serdar Ortaç when the phone vibrating in her pocket makes her stop. She lowers the volume and answers the call.

"Hi," Meric says on the other end of the line. "Am I disturbing you?"

"No," she says. "I'm just dancing in my room."

"Ah, how timely is my call," and he laughs. "I was calling to see if you wanted to meet me tonight to listen to music and dance, too."

"Really?" she says.

"Yes," he laughs. "I am outside a club now and was hoping you'd like to join me."

And so, of course, Deniz knows where that is and promises to be there within 30 minutes, her heart suddenly leaping in her chest, her skin alive and tingling with anticipation.

Murat finds himself sitting at an outdoor table at a café in Bebek staring at the people at the tables around him. He feels that life is somehow passing him by and wishes he knew how to stop it and catch as much of it as he can. His friend from college, Onur, is sitting opposite him talking about work as if somehow Murat might be interested, but, of course, he is not. His mind is weighed down by this feeling of inadequacy and he does not know how to shake it. Finally he turns to Onur and says, "My life is not the life I started out to have. Somehow, I lost my way."

Onur looks at him, concerned and worried. He has known him for over 20 years and this is the first time he has heard such a remark from his friend. "Is it work?" he asks.

73

"No," Murat says, shaking his head. "It has nothing to do with my professional life. It is my home life. I do not know the people who live in my house."

"Your wife?" Onur asks. "You are talking about Sönmez?"

Murat nods sadly. "Is there anyone else living there?"

"But I thought you were happy," he says.

"It is just appearances on my part," Murat says. "But I think she is happy. She has the kids. They are her life. I am just a necessary part of the family unit she craves."

"When did this feeling start?" Onur asks.

"It has probably always been there. Married life is not exactly what I thought it would be."

"For any of us," Onur says. "But it is a necessary part of life. How else does one have a family? And isn't that what we all want?"

"Is it?" Murat says.

"Isn't it?" Onur asks, suddenly perplexed by his old friend. "I thought you wanted a family, too."

"I guess I was conditioned to think so myself," Murat says, "but now, I look at my wife and she is a stranger to me. And the kids, the kids…" And he falters here, not knowing exactly what or how to say what is in his heart. He just looks out at the people passing by, at the Bosporus stretching out beyond them, and wonders just where his life went and how can he possibly get it back.

"It's not that I'm unhappy I came," Brenda says as she sips her beer and watches the people stroll by on the crowded street full of restaurants specializing in fish. "It's just I sometimes think I'm running away from London rather than coming to Istanbul."

"Ah, well we all must leave behind some things to find other things in front of us," Philip says. "I didn't exactly run away from anything but I needed a change in my life and a different city, a different culture, different people surrounding me seemed like an ideal way to get that change."

"It's just that I had a very messy divorce back home and I needed to put a great deal of distance between me and my ex," she says. "So when I met Bekir at a conference in London and he offered me a job, well, it just seemed the perfect way to escape."

"Ah divorce," and Philip sighs. "I understand."

"You, too?"

"Well not exactly a divorce in any legal sense," Philip explains, "but a break with the past, too."

"I loved him," she says. "I just couldn't live with him."

"An all too common complaint."

Brenda almost hesitates but then blurts it out anyway, sensing somehow she can trust this man to keep her confidences. "It was the sex, really," she says. "Or I should say lack of it that caused the rupture."

"Ah sex," and Philip sighs again. "Then you did right, my dear. Sex at your age, or rather at almost any age, is quite an essential part of a happy arrangement."

"You think so, too, then?"

"Absolutely. We do not live for the mind alone," he says. "There are many muscles and organs that have very specific wants, too."

"That's what I think, also."

"And rightly so."

"But Mark just couldn't understand that," she says. "Mark's my ex-husband."

"I gathered."

"And he's a wonderful man, really. Wonderful poet, wonderful family, wonderful teaching position and publications. It all seemed so wonderful in the beginning."

"You were in Wonderland then, I take it."

"Yes," she says somewhat dreamily. "At least that's how it seemed at first. But then the wonder was gone and only a cold, lonely bed was left."

"Well that is all in the past," Philip says. "You are here now, and are young, very attractive, and I'm sure if you open yourself up to it, you will find ample opportunities to change your life and fill your bed with young, virile men."

"I certainly hope so," she mutters, and drains her beer and signals the waiter for another.

"I love it here," İrem says, looking out at the Sea of Marmara below through the trees shedding their leaves. "Don't you?"

"Yes," Michael says. "It's one of my favorite places in Moda." Then he turns to look for the waiter and says, "Would you like another coffee? I certainly could use another cup."

"You're finished?" she asks. "Shall I tell your fortune?"

"You ask me that every time," Michael says.

"Yes, I do," she nods.

"And every time I decline," he says.

"Yes, you do," she says. "And you make that same face when you do it, too."

"What face?" he asks.

"That face you're making now."

"I'm making a face?"

"Yes," she nods. "And it's always that very same one."

"So," he says, deciding not to belabor the point about which face he is making since he cannot possibly see, or feel, any face at all, "if I decline each time and make whatever face I make when doing so, why do you keep asking me?"

"I'm just an optimist," İrem says. "I keep thinking that one day you'll say yes."

"Is it that important to you? To read my future?"

"It's just a little game," she says, "that I used to play with my friends. And you're my friend so I would like to play it with you."

"So it's just a game?" he says. "Nothing serious?"

"Well I must admit I've gotten pretty good at it over the years."

"So it's not just a game?" he says. "You do take it seriously?"

"Not so seriously," and she smiles. "Of course, I'm not as good as a real fortune teller but I'm pretty good for an amateur."

"Well I really don't believe in these things, especially when it's told by a rabbit like you see around here."

"You don't have to," she laughs. "It's just for fun anyway. And besides, I'm certainly better than a rabbit." He doesn't look too excited by the idea so she adds, "I promise not to tell anyone at school."

He laughs. "I don't think anyone would be that interested."

"Oh I don't know about that," she says. "You're very popular, you know."

"That's because I'm a foreigner and there are very few of us there."

"More this year than last," she says.

"That's because the English track programs are getting bigger."

"But back to your fortune," she says. "How about it, boss. I promise to be discreet."

Michael can't help but laugh. "I don't think at this point in my life there's that much that could be labeled indiscreet."

"So you are ready then?" and her eyes sparkle mischievously.

"Okay," he says, and turns over his coffee cup. "But just this once."

"You never know," İrem says, that smile almost seductive, "but you could get used to this."

"I suppose one could get used to almost anything." And, following her instructions, he rotates the cup three times before setting it down on the table. Then as they wait for the grinds to cool, Michael has another Turkish coffee and İrem some more cay.

Dave has another glass of wine while his "angels", as they are now calling themselves "Dave's Angels", have more drinks, too. Dave notes that Jennifer, like any good Midwestern girl, can handle her beer and he is pleased to note her familiarity with the other two young women who now seem like young women anywhere in the world: laughing, teasing, aware of how they look and that they are noticed by men. And he is flattered to be in the center of their evening out, to be the envy of much younger men at the surrounding tables.

And so he regales them all with tales from his youth, the wild adventures, stories that always feature him in a leading role, for Dave is not just trying to impress but to lay the groundwork for a possible future seduction, though he has little hope of the success of that, but still, being human, has hope, and he cannot afford, at his age, to let an opportunity like this slip away.

Deniz, meanwhile, is being swept away on the dance floor, swirling, whirling to the sounds of Moby's music as it fills her ears, swells her heart, her dress twirling in the air, her thighs so long and shapely spinning in the night, and Meric, Meric is in and out of her line of vision, in and out of what can only be thought of as the presence of her mind.

Brenda's state of mind gains a kind of serenity talking with Philip. It is as if he understands her without needing too much detail, too much exposition. Perhaps it's their shared cultural heritage, though there is at least a generation between them, or maybe a similar experience with ex-partners, though Philip seems a bit hazy on that subject and Brenda is not sure if that is a natural tendency toward reclusiveness or a lack of trust but she is determined to find out.

"I can't tell you how much this talk has meant to me," she says.

"Think nothing of it," he says. "Glad to help."

"You are so understanding," she says. "I guess your experience is similar to mine."

"Well, as I've said before, I wasn't married but was, pardon the expression, a kept man. So when it ended, I had to find someplace to go and a change in scenery was most welcome."

"And that's when you came here?"

"Shortly thereafter," and his eyes glaze over a bit at the memory. "It's been five years now and I am very much adjusted to this life and don't really miss the other."

"Not at all?"

"Just some people, but," and he smiles, "not my ex. And…" and his smile grows broader, "…I don't miss the life there at all. I'm perfectly content to be here. I really love this city." He reaches over and pats her hand. "And believe me, my dear, so will you."

"I hope so," she says.

"You just need to find a man to get your mind off London," he says. "And I'm sure there's one lurking in your future as we speak."

Michael is amused as İrem leans over his coffee cup and begins to see shapes in the grinds that don't indicate anything concerning his future but rather, in his mind, her incredibly vivid imagination.

"I see a woman here very clearly," she says. "Either someone you are involved with now or someone you know and who you will become involved with in the future."

"Are you sure you're looking at my coffee cup?" Michael asks. "Because that sounds like someone else's fortune, not mine."

"Why?" she asks, looking at him with the utmost curiosity. "Don't you want a woman in your life now?"

"No one in the capacity you're speaking about."

"No one?"

"I'm perfectly content with just my cleaning lady," he says. "She's the only woman I know who has been in my apartment since I've been here, besides you, of course, and neither of you would, I suppose, qualify as involvement."

"Be serious," she says.

"I am," he answers. "There is no woman in my life."

"Well it could be a woman you know now who you will one day be involved with."

"No," he says. "I don't see that happening at all."

"Why not?" she asks, and it's almost a challenge as well as a question.

"Because there are just students and some faculty like you."

"And you're not attracted to any of the faculty?"

"No," he says. "Everyone is just too young for me."

"But you're not that old," she says.

"I'm old enough to know what too young is," and he smiles, though there is a touch of melancholy around the edges.

"But there are younger women who like older men," she says, counting herself among that number but not telling him that.

"Maybe," he says, "but I know my limitations. Besides, my cat is more than enough involvement for me."

"But cats are not people."

"How can you say that since you know my cat?"

She laughs and says, "Well I see a woman in your life whether you want one or not. And it looks like she likes cats, too, so you are both going to be happy." Then she looks at him again and adds, "I don't understand why you don't want a woman in your life."

"Having you drop by every Saturday to cook me dinner," he says, "is actually more than enough for me."

"But what will happen if I decide to go away?"

"You're going away?"

"I don't know yet," she says, "but I have been thinking of going to the US to do my PhD."

"You have finally decided to do that?" he asks.

"Not finally," she says. "But I have been thinking about it again. And if I do, who will look after you then?"

"I guess I'll have to find another assistant who likes to cook."

"Is that your criteria for assistants?"

"Well it wasn't until you came along."

She looks at him then not knowing exactly what to say because what she wants to say she thinks she really doesn't want to say or at least shouldn't say though she can't think of a valid reason why not. It seems a little confusing to her then, this fortune telling in regards to him and suddenly she wishes she hadn't suggested it or at least he hadn't given in but she did and he did and now here they are talking about, what seems to her, her value in his life. And he is not, as usual, being very helpful in defining it and she cannot help but wonder why that should upset her slightly but it does.

And Michael, for his part, wonders just what he is doing making light of something that is not insignificant at all but rather something serious, for he cannot imagine having any other assistant than her and the thought of not having her unnerves him, though he would be the last to admit that, especially to her.

And so they both sit there rather lost for the moment over a cup with coffee grinds that have settled into something neither of them quite anticipated, both alone with their thoughts even though they are together.

Murat sits alone in his living room, a glass, a bottle of raki, and a small pitcher of water in front of him. It is two o'clock in the morning and his wife and children are asleep in the back of the house, the kids curled up with their mother, and an empty space on one side of the bed waiting for him. But Murat cannot bring himself to lie in that space. He would rather drink more raki until he falls asleep once again on the couch. This is Murat at home.

Katja visits Michael in his office because he wants them to meet so they can begin to plan which scenes will have songs and dance and which characters will perform them. Michael is, of course, not really prepared for this meeting because he is experiencing anxiety attacks about the thought of İrem leaving for America though he is trying his best to deny that. But Katja has finally been infected not only by Michael's vision of the play but also of a dream of entanglements and obstacles surmounted in two lovers' divergent but similar journey toward a happy ending. And a happy ending is something she, in particular, wishes to believe in. So she comes ready to discuss this with Michael who, though, unfortunately is ill prepared to discuss anything. And though Katja doesn't know it, we know he has other things on his mind to distract him, but first, he must muddle his way through this pre-production meeting with Katja, who Michael sees as a collaborator on his modern epic.

"Your heart is not in this, is it?" Katja asks.

"It's not my heart that's absent but my brain," Michael says. "I just can't seem to concentrate today."

"We can try to do this another time," Katja says. "After all, we do have this semester to plan. It's not scheduled to be performed until the spring."

"Yes, but if we don't start thinking about it now, spring will be upon us and nothing will be done."

"That's optimistic," and she laughs.

"That's one thing I'm never called," Michael says and smiles thinking, I like her laugh. Such a wonderfully sexy laugh from deep down inside her womanhood. And he thinks it's a good thing to hear it again though he knows her grief is still fresh in her heart.

"Well, I was thought to be an optimist, but now…" and a shrug, "I'm not so sure."

"I don't think we can afford more than one pessimist on this project," Michael says. "After all, this play is supposed to have a happy ending."

"And I want it to," she says with more force, more conviction than even she knows she has.

Michael looks at her carefully and intuitively knows she is thinking of all those dark corners in her life. He wishes he could be more upbeat so this enthusiasm she is beginning to show will be reinforced but can't quite rise to the occasion. Later, he thinks, he will find his own enthusiasm again. Later, with İrem sitting across from him and his world once again in balance. Later he will once again be the engine that drives this project, these people, forward. Later.

İrem meanwhile finds herself with a protégé: Pelin. The student follows her everywhere when not in class and once Pelin finds out that İrem had studied in the United States, their bond is sealed. "I dream of studying in America," Pelin tells İrem in the cafeteria at lunch. "I'm just crazy about English."

"But you should finish here first," İrem says.

"Oh yes, I know," Pelin says. "But when I'm graduated, I want to transfer to a US school and do graduate school there," she adds.

"That sounds like a plan," İrem says.

"And I want to study in New York City or in Los Angeles because that's where the best acting schools are. And I want to find a really good voice teacher, too."

"You want to sing, too?"

"I already do," Pelin says, though somewhat modestly. "Sort of, anyway. I sing with a trio of some of the students here in the Music Department. We perform in small clubs and bars."

"Really?" İrem says. "I must come hear you sometime."

"Wait till we get better," Pelin says. "We're still not quite where we should be."

"Well you tell me when."

"But hopefully when I graduate I'll be ready to do an MFA in theatre and music."

"Well there are some very good theatre departments in colleges in other parts of the country, too," she says. "And musical theatre is part of the curriculum, also."

"Really?" Pelin asks. "I didn't think they had theatre colleges anywhere else."

"My old alma mater, for instance," İrem says, "has a very good theatre department."

"Where's that, hoca?"

"The University of Michigan in Ann Arbor."

"Where's Michigan?"

And so İrem explains the geography of America while Pelin listens with rapt attention. "You could always go to New York or LA after college," she says. "But there are really so many good schools to choose from."

"Will you help me decide?"

"Of course," İrem says. "Maybe even next year if I go to America for my PhD, you can come visit me. Would you like that?"

"Oh, that would be fantastic," Pelin says and she almost hugs İrem. "I'm so excited already."

And İrem, in her new role as mentor, can't help but see a younger version of herself in Pelin and thus is excited, too.

Berat has a hard time containing his excitement as he finds himself walking with Elena in Beyazit Square. They stop at one of the cafés to eat some kebab and drink a cola. Then they wander somewhat aimlessly through the Book Bazaar, leafing through the racks of books on display and, though seemingly talking of nothing important, they both manage to find out something very important to both of them: that neither has anyone special in their lives at present. And this, they both silently conclude, is something they intend to rectify.

And so as he walks with her back to the bus station where she will board a bus for Ortaköy before he takes the ferry home to Üsküdar, he sends her an invitation to become friends on Facebook from his iPhone which she promises to acknowledge once she gets home. And though they don't hold hands yet, they have both moved a few steps closer to that in their minds.

Fersat meanwhile has created a new album on his Facebook entitled Turkish Women. And though it contains photos of various women he has photographed on his wanderings around the city, there are a significant number of shots of Meltem: in the cafeteria, walking along the Golden Horn, laughing midair on a swing, eating a fish sandwich at the ferry landing in Karaköy, and gazing in shop windows in Taksim. And as he stares at the photos, he finds he gets lost looking into her eyes.

İrem gets a call from Pelin who asks, "Am I bothering you?"

"No," İrem says. "I'm just reading through my cookbooks looking for new recipes."

"Oh, you like to cook?" Pelin asks.

"Yes," İrem says. "It relaxes me."

"I'd like to cook, too, but you need someone to cook for, don't you think?"

"Yes," İrem nods. "That's always the most satisfying."

"I'd like to have someone to cook for," Pelin sighs. "Do you have someone you cook for?"

"Well I cook dinner once a week for Michael," İrem says, then, for some reason, decides she should elaborate on that a bit. "Besides being colleagues," she adds, "we're good friends."

"Do you like him?" Pelin asks.

"Of course, I like him."

"No," she says, a little hesitant at first. "I mean, do you like him?"

"We're just friends," İrem says, and then thinks how trite that sounds, and yet can think of no other way to call what they are that would make sense to anyone else.

"I don't mean to be rude," Pelin says, "but I just wonder if it happens between people, between older and younger people, that is."

And though neither wants to actually say what this "it" is, they both understand what she is saying. And İrem, sensing that Pelin is on the verge of revealing some hidden intimacy, says rather delicately, "Yes, it can happen between people of any age."

"I think it's happening to me," Pelin sighs.

"Is it mutual?"

"No," Pelin says and sighs again.

"And this person is older?" İrem asks.

"Yes," Pelin says. "And my teacher."

"Oh," İrem says doing mental calculations trying to remember Pelin's class schedule.

"Is that wrong?"

"Nothing is wrong when it comes to the heart," İrem says,

"I don't think it's wrong, either," Pelin says, "but I don't know what to do about it."

"Well, is he interested in you?"

"He likes me, I know, and I think I'm one of his favorite students," and then she sort of laughs, though it is as much from embarrassment as anything else. "I mean, I know I'm one of his favorite students. You can kind of tell that."

"Yes," İrem says. "You can."

"But I don't think he is interested in me the way I am interested in him," and she sighs again. "I'm pretty sure he has a girlfriend. I mean, he must have a girlfriend. He's so hot."

İrem smiles to herself thinking they are always hot when you love them, but the smile is perhaps a little rueful as she also thinks she is not so different than this poor lovesick girl.

Except maybe for the fact that she does not act on her feelings anymore but suppresses them. And being aware of that, she can't help but be envious of this girl.

"I guess there's nothing I really can do," Pelin says.

"Well, not if he has a girlfriend," İrem says. "But perhaps you should find out if that is true first. Don't you think?"

"How do I do that?" she asks. "I can't ask him."

And İrem finds it amusing that Turkish students have no problem asking personal questions of their teachers as long as those questions are not about something that might be personal for themselves. "Just be observant," she says. "You can find all the answers to your questions if you just look for them."

"Yes," Pelin says, brightening a bit. "You're so smart. I'll do that."

"And good luck," İrem says.

"Thanks, hoca. You, too."

And as İrem hangs up, she thinks Pelin has wished her exactly the right thing without knowing. And as she sits staring off into space, all she can think is "Insallah."

Michael sits staring at the glass of whiskey in front of him on the coffee table in his living room. He has not eaten tonight, or at least had any solid food for dinner, this being one of those nights when he feels the need for liquid companionship, though he doesn't really drink, either. He just stares at the glass of whiskey he had poured earlier in the evening and marvels at its color, the way the cat had climbed onto the coffee table to sniff it, then turned away and jumped over to lie beside him on the couch, its head pushing against his leg while he stroked under its chin until it purred itself asleep.

He thinks he is really almost content. Almost. But somehow something he can't quite put his finger on seems missing. And as he looks at the whiskey in his glass, he knows it is not that. For that will not keep him warm at night, nor will it offer comfort or understanding. And though the cat lies sleeping next to him, he knows he needs more. He has, though, stopped believing in attaining it. He has stopped calling out in the night and expecting anyone to be there to hear. But the memory of İrem's fortune is gnawing at the edge of his mind. And though he doesn't want to acknowledge it, it isn't so much the fortune but the person telling it that lingers in the air.

He sighs and would look out the window but the drapes are closed. He thinks about opening them and staring down at the street to see if there is anything there that might amuse him but it is too much energy to get up, and besides it is night and he wouldn't see much anyway. He rubs his eyes and begins to think about fortune telling. He, of course, doesn't believe in it, he actually believes in very little, even not believing in the old adage that things happen for the best because he thinks rather that things just happen and people make the best of them. He knows this would put him at odds with one of his favorite authors, Thomas Hardy, but there is no causality in Michael's world, probably because he does not believe in a god, or any kind of divine operating power in the universe, just chance, blind, random chance. It is the main reason he gravitated toward directing, because he wanted to impose an order on his corner of the universe so he could sleep at night. It had always confused his ex-wife, that is his first ex-wife, who embraced Eastern religious thought, or at least what passed for Eastern religious thought in the California of the 1970s, and who believed devoutly in karma, reincarnation, and followed the advice of mystics and fortune tellers, and who would be more at home listening to what coffee grinds say than he is. Michael only grew more restless during the years, as if tempting lightning to come down from the heavens and strike him into ash. Perhaps, though, if he had shared her views, they might still be together and he would be a father now. Instead he moved through life, and women, making every possible mistake he could without once thinking there would be hell to pay for it, just a profound sense of regret and an emptiness in what passes for his heart.

So this idea of a play becomes for him a way of possibly redeeming himself here in a foreign country where no one knows of the folly of the last several decades of his life. It would not get him into heaven because he does not believe there is a heaven so that is not his aim here, but rather it could, if orchestrated correctly and, of course, changed the current ending of the play, make him feel like he can give a happy ending to someone, even if they are characters in a play. And that, to his current way of thinking, is as close to a blessing as he will ever get.

And Philip is up and out, wandering around the city in the dead of night with only stray cats lying on car roofs or picking through half opened garbage bags to keep him company. But there is something in the night air he finds comforting, his mind a blank slate waiting for something in this dark night to engage it.

And finally, to Berat who sits alone at his desk in Üsküdar staring at the pictures of Elena on her profile. She looks so beautiful, he thinks, especially in ones that catch her staring pensively into the camera's eye, as if contemplating a question that has just been asked before she replies. He has watched her dance so often in class, in the studio with Katja, and is thus so familiar with the lines of her body, her grace, but he has rarely had the opportunity to stare into her face. Even that afternoon they wandered around together through the book stalls gave him little time to actually look into her eyes for longer than a few seconds at a time, but here, now, he finds himself becoming lost as he stares into her face. And those eyes, especially those eyes, seem to hold him in a trance which he finally pulls away from long enough to type a message he will send her, a message telling her how beautiful she is.

His hand moves the mouse up to the send button and his finger hovers over the left side of the mouse hesitating to click on it. It is there now, the open invitation, and he just has to send it out into virtual space to be opened and read. And though he wants to send it, fear mingled with his excitement holds his finger suspended in air. And he closes his eyes and lets his mind go blank for a long, long second. Then he clicks on send, logs off his computer, and goes to bed.

Scene 3
November

Bekir sits in a town board meeting with Mert trying to pay attention to the zoning regulations so they can plot their strategy to acquire more property around the school, but his mind keeps going back to Michael's proposed play for the spring. Shakespeare, he thinks. A full production of Shakespeare with students involved in every facet of the production, with faculty supervision, of course, but total student involvement. A real public relations coup, if they can pull it off, and it would certainly help increase enrollment for the following year as well as be one more thing to make them distinct from other universities. He had not given it serious consideration at first, but now the idea tantalizes him. And he is beginning to calculate in his mind just how much more he needs to commit of the school's resources to guarantee this project's success. And he also begins to envision engaging the film department in the project as well. Why not have them film the production, as well as the planning stages, the casting calls, the rehearsals, with backstage drama, too? It could be two film projects: a documentary on the production and then a filmed version of the play itself.

And as these thoughts run through his mind, he thinks he must share this with Mert afterwards. And so Bekir finds himself the only person smiling as the board meeting continues around him.

Michael is staring at the organizational chart on his wall that clearly defines everyone's role on the production side. He has left empty slots next to the faculty members' names to be filled in with student names who will take leadership roles in the production. Some positions are filled in, like

İrem under his name as Assistant Director and Katja as Choreographer and Murat as Musical Director, but others need to be assigned to faculty members themselves who will not only take on production roles but must begin to select those students they feel who can not only share the responsibility but that they can each work with. It is, he realizes, bigger than he had first imagined, but the concept continues to excite him. This could be larger in scale than anything he did in the US. A bigger success or a grander failure. But definitely a greater gamble than anything he attempted before.

But even as he contemplates his Shakespeare, he also realizes he has two shows to put on at the end of January: one in English and the other in Turkish. These, of course, will not be as difficult to conceive since they are final projects of the acting and directing classes, the students rehearsing their parts in their classes and in the allotted rehearsal time that is part of the curriculum for both the English track and the Turkish track students. He oversees, or sometimes directs, these shows, with İrem acting as his assistant and Meric helping with the Turkish track students, so they are not as complicated as the final show in the spring. But still, he must decide on a set, approve Deniz's costume sketches, and have İrem pick students to act as stage managers, prop masters, stagehands. And the success of these two series of showcases will foreshadow the abilities of his students and staff. So they are all really gambles, after all. And he symbolically blows on the dice before letting them roll.

Dave opens the door to the adjoining faculty rooms where the prep teachers sit, each large room with seven cubicles apiece for the 14 prep instructors, and says his günaydin. All heads pop up and he gets smiles and responses from the almost exclusively female group of teachers who are in various stages of putting on make-up, shuffling papers, reading emails, or text messaging family or friends. And Jennifer, Jennifer looks up from her computer, evidently surprised, but smiles at him, too, and it is a smile not without warmth but, due to his own insecurity perhaps, difficult to read.

So he nods a bit to one and all and then retreats to the cafeteria for his morning cay and pohaca. And as he sits there pondering his next move, Philip comes in from the outside patio where he has enjoyed his sixth cigarette of the morning and joins him. "Having some cay, I see," he says as he sits down.

"Yes," Dave says. "My little morning routine here."

"Yes, I think I might join you if you don't mind."

"No," Dave says. "Please do."

So Philip gets a glass of cay himself and then resettles back into the chair opposite him. "Getting adjusted to life here now, are you?"

"Trying to," Dave says.

"It's a fascinating city," Philip says. "I myself love wandering around and I'm always discovering new archways that lead to new streets winding their way into my heart. This neighborhood, if you love that sort of thing, is a paradise. And Fatih, which is within walking distance, still enchants me."

"Well I really haven't explored that much here," Dave says. "But I do like Taksim."

Philip nods, says, "Yes, lots of pubs there, though a little too crowded, especially on the weekends, for me."

"Some of the Prep teachers have been kind enough to show me around," Dave says.

"Yes, they seem like a nice bunch," Philip says, sipping his cay and clearly longing for another cigarette. "But they're an insular group, like most Prep instructors. Sort of a world onto themselves and not quite part of the college."

"It's like that in all colleges?" Dave asks.

"For some reason, yes," Philip says. "I taught Prep in another college for a year before coming here," Philip says, "and it was that way there, too. I guess it's the nature of the beast. Though the Prep instructors seem to like it that way."

"I'd like to get to know more of the other faculty, though," Dave says, thinking especially of İrem in Philip's own area. "Perhaps I could help with your play."

"Not my play," Philip says. "It's Shakespeare's, though Michael seems to be arm wrestling the bard for control and changing the ending in the process. No tragedies for that man." He laughs. "But you can offer your services to him, if you want. Or see İrem. She always knows who is doing what and is more likely not to be as vague as Michael can be when assigning roles. At least at this stage of the game."

"Thanks," Dave says, thinking he has now the perfect excuse to talk with her. And he intends to exploit that to the best advantage. "Are they involved?" Dave asks.

"It depends on what you mean by involved," Philip says, thinking the answer to that is much more complicated than he could ever possibly explain.

"You know," Dave says. "Involved with each other. Romantically."

"No," Philip says. "They don't seem to think so." And though he doesn't say it, he thinks one day they both will have to analyze just what they are to each other, and will probably both be surprised at what they find. "But it is a rather sort of unique relationship."

"But they're not involved?" Dave persists.

"No," Philip says, his mind drifting away. "Not in the way you're asking." Then he finishes his çay and stands. "Well I must get another smoke before heading back in to class. Care to join me?"

"I gave it up," Dave says and as he watches Philip amble off to the outside smoking area, he begins to formulate his approach to İrem.

Berat and Elena run through their dance steps alone in the studio without the watchful eyes of their fellow dancers following their moves or the supervision of Katja directing them. It is just the two of them, practicing the steps, feeling the ebb and flow of their muscles, now taut, now relaxed, Berat's arms encircling Elena's waist, she pulls away, he follows, this is their dance of seduction, of a longing they feel not only as characters in an imaginary world but as two young people coping with the world they inhabit, a world with prescribed codes of behavior they must try to adhere to, and yet rebel against, their bodies coiling and recoiling as they slide across the floor of the studio, as they maneuver a little awkwardly through a culture in transition, these two young dancers playing at lovers, wanting to move beyond the play and yet being unsure of the steps that haven't been choreographed for them yet.

Katja is not doing very well today. Her heart doesn't seem to be a part of her anymore. It beats, it pumps blood, it keeps her body alive, but it does so with a dull regularity so unlike the heart she once knew. There is no passion, no joy in its work, just the mindless droning of a factory hand. Even as she conducts her classes, runs her dance students through their drills, she feels nothing for the work that used to thrill her so. The only thing that seems to spark her interest is the images fleeting through her head of a lover's ballet. Michael had suggested it and Philip had even indicated a place or two for it to reoccur in the new adaptation of the play while Murat has begun trying to compose a musical theme for the play, and so this, the image of lovers not quite connecting, has resonance for her somehow. And in-between the dull aching of her heartbeats, those images cause a quickening of her pulse, and send the blood cruising through her veins on its way.

İrem comes into the office with a box lunch. "It's a plate of manti I made at home this morning," she says. "I thought maybe you'd forget to eat lunch, as usual, and so could use this."

"Manti?" he says, perking up a bit in his chair. "Really? For me?"

"You do like it, don't you?" she asks, knowing full well he does.

"Yes," he says. "Very much."

"It's still warm but you can heat it up later in the microwave in the prep teachers' room if you wait till lunch. They have one there, right?"

"Yes," he says, opening the container and inhaling the aroma. "This looks great." Then he looks up at her and smiles, "Thanks."

"You're welcome," she says.

"You just keep spoiling me." Then suddenly he thinks of how lost he might be without her and sighs.

"What?" she asks.

"Nothing," he says.

"That sigh was not a nothing sigh," she says. "I know your sighs too well. That was a something sigh."

"A something sigh?" he asks, blinking like a child caught with his hands somewhere they shouldn't be.

"Yes," she says, and stands, arms folded, looking over at him. "It certainly was."

99

"I didn't realize I had different kinds of sighs," he says.

"You do," she says. "Just as you have different ways of avoiding answering a question."

"I do?" he asks, blinking again.

"Yes, you do," she says. "Like now, for instance."

"You think I'm avoiding answering a question?"

"I know you're avoiding answering a question."

"What question?"

"The one asking you what that sigh was about."

"Which sigh?"

"The something sigh you gave about a minute ago."

"I did?"

"You did."

"Funny," he goes, as if lost in thought for a moment. "I don't seem to remember."

She looks at him carefully and then shakes her head. "You've done it again," she says finally.

"What?"

"Avoided answering a question."

"I did?"

She shakes her head some more and finds herself sighing.

"What?" he asks.

"Nothing," she says. Then adds, "Everything." And sighs again.

Brenda doesn't know why but suddenly in the middle of the day she begins to cry. Not outright sobbing, but tears well up in her eyes and she cannot stop them from streaming down her cheeks. She quickly dabs a tissue to her face and makes a quick dash for the ladies' room but bumps into Murat on her way. "Sorry," she blurts out and quickly disentangles herself from his hands as he tries to steady her, and runs off.

But Murat stands there both surprised and confused by the encounter and positive he saw tears running down her cheeks. And he wonders how he should handle this: inquire of her well-being or pretend he didn't notice. A quandary this early in the day.

Fersat sits at his desk on his computer at home in his bedroom while his mother cooks dinner and his father watches TV in the living room. His younger brother is in the next room playing Play Station 3 while listening to Iron Maiden. Fersat has his door closed to keep out all distractions as he posts more pictures of Meltem in his album entitled Turkish Women. The album is really misnamed because there are only a few pictures of other Turkish women in it, most of the pictures are of Meltem and he knows friends are beginning to post comments wondering just what is going on. Is he obsessed, they want to know. Or in love? Is this a new girlfriend? He does not answer any of the comments because he does not know how to answer them. All he can do is take more pictures and post them and want to say yes, yes, yes to all the queries. Instead, though, he just leans forward in his chair and stares at the pictures so intently he does not hear his mother's call to dinner for food is the last thing he hungers for. All his body yearns for is before his eyes.

Katja spends an hour each day after class working on the choreography, drilling Berat and Elena so intensely until all they can think about is each other's bodies. They are incapable of speech, but intimate just the same, for they speak through their fingers, their toes, their muscles so in tune with each other that they are beginning to have one body, Berat holding Elena briefly here and there, brushing against each other, biting their tongues, and praying the hour doesn't end.

And Katja begins to live her love through them, almost feeling Hasan in the same room, dancing through them with him, her lover again.

Deniz is most alive in her studio, filling a canvas with color, watching it take shape before her eyes, the music blaring, the light streaming down through her skylight bathing everything in a warm glow. She does not think when she paints but surrenders to some inner passion that takes hold of her brush to find its own outlet. And though she always has a plan, a concept in mind when she designs costumes, her painting is totally instinctive, her brush having a mind of its own and her hand just follows it. Her painting always seems to surprise her and those surprises delight her so. And this is something she has a hard time explaining to someone like Meric who is very much concerned with what he produces, the means for him only something to suffer through to reach the final product which he always has envisioned before he even begins. They both seem to be interested in two very different things.

Meric speaks of his childhood in Adana, playing sports, hanging out with his friends, and his life suddenly changing when he discovered movies, not just the movies that played in the local cinemas, but movies that a teacher he had lent him on tape: movies from the golden age of Hollywood, the 30s and 40s, and then the exciting discovery of films of the 60s and 70s with the start of the independent filmmakers. His ideas, his dreams, his goals, constantly changing and the actors he sees now—Brad Pitt, John Malkovich, Sean Penn, George Clooney, Johnny Depp—suddenly have become his idols and he knows what he wants to become, what kind of roles he wants to play, the people he must portray.

He, of course, is result oriented, is obsessed with the final product, and Deniz, feeling no need or desire to explain herself, to say that the paintings are just a byproduct but not the end product of her real ambition which is just simply to astound herself with whatever it is on her canvas when she finishes. Instead, though, to appease him, she talks about her work as a designer which is, she concedes, result oriented, because she must satisfy the vision of a director with his concept of the show. And there they meet, in her work in the theatre, which is, she cannot tell him, only something she does to be able to have the freedom to paint.

But because she wants to meet him somewhere, she uses the theatre as their common ground, their shared space, for she decides he is too much fun, too appealing, not to have a shared space.

Pelin haunts the theatre, the cafeteria, the acting studio, always on the lookout for Meric, seeing who he talks to, what he laughs at, where he smiles. She is at times invisible to him, standing amid groups of students, sitting at tables, lost in throngs of people on ferries, strolling on streets, milling about in stores, lounging at tables in cafés. But she is there, her eyes fixed on him as he moves throughout his day, his evening, a specter just outside his line of vision, watching, waiting, staring, recording all she sees in her mind's eye.

İrem is sitting in the office making a prop list for the two evenings of performances in January. They are actually not full-length plays but two evenings of selected scenes from various plays that the students have been working on in their scene study classes. The sets will be simple enough, but the props needed are fairly extensive. And, of course, she must confer with Deniz about costumes for the actors. It is all very exciting for her and working closely with Michael is her idea of heaven. And even though he isn't in their office at the moment, just being there, working on a project for him, surrounded by little mementos that belong to him, like his

103

subway map on the wall and a map of the LA Freeway system opposite it, a picture of his cat tacked on his cork board along with a card that shows a pig sailing down a highway, and the charts of his projections for the plays, the class rosters, the cups with pens and pencils, and his apple and jar of hazelnuts, a small metal dinosaur, all these simple things that she finds endearing, are waiting there for his return, just as she waits, there, in their shared office, staring at his desk.

Philip finally finds Brenda in her office and suggests a tea break. "If you're not busy, that is," he says.

"No," and she smiles relieved to be pulled away from her desk. "I'd love to."

And as they enter the cafeteria, they do not notice Murat who is standing shivering slightly outside on the patio in the chilly November air, for Brenda is too self-conscious to look around and Philip is too distracted by his craving for a cigarette to bother scanning the tables for any familiar faces. Instead he asks, "Do you mind if I pop out for a quick smoke? Or you can join me, if you like."

"I don't smoke," she says, "but the air might do me good."

And as they pass out onto the patio, they find Murat standing by a table next to theirs. And once eye contact has been established, it is only natural for him to join them, though he feels a bit awkward since this is the first time he's actually seen Brenda since she bumped into him crying, but since she seems unaware of the fact that he saw the tears, it isn't as awkward for her which makes it easier for him. Philip, of course, is totally oblivious and so Murat has another cigarette while trying hard not to study Brenda too carefully.

"You don't smoke?" Murat says to Brenda when she politely refuses his offer for a cigarette.

"No," she says. "It's one bad habit I've never acquired."

"Ah, well I hope the others were more fun," Philip says.

"I suppose that depends on one's point of view," she says.

"Well I was hoping yours," he replies.

"Then yes," she says. "They were mostly more fun."

"Mostly is good enough for me," Philip says.

"Me, too," Murat adds, though he isn't exactly sure if he isn't intruding on something private between them, but the smile she gives him puts his mind at ease.

And Brenda does smile at him, thinking he is an attractive man and it's always best to smile at attractive men, especially when she is feeling so low about men in particular these days. And he smiles back which helps to make her feel sexually attractive again after such a long spell of disappointment and self-doubt, which characterized her marriage. And she finds herself playing with her hair as she asks him about his classes.

"They're going well," he says, "though I wish the students were more interested in the history of the music rather than the anecdotes I tell them about the composers. But this group this year seem brighter than last year's students, which is always hopeful." He then takes another drag on his cigarette and is careful to exhale away from her face. "What about your group?"

"They're attentive," she says, "but not very inquisitive. I'm disappointed in the lack of questions my lectures seem to generate."

"They're shy about using their English," Philip explains. "At least in the classroom. I find I have more conversations with them in English out here while smoking. I refer to it as my English Smoking Club."

"Yes," Murat nods. "I think you're right about that."

"Pity then," Brenda says, "that I don't speak Turkish or smoke."

"Well," Philip says, "you can always cultivate one of those two, though I think smoking is easier but learning Turkish might be more beneficial in the long run."

"How is your Turkish?" Brenda asks.

"Abysmal," Philip says, "if you consider I've been here now for five years. Lots of vocabulary but little command of the syntax."

"Perhaps I should engage a tutor," she says.

"I could help you," Murat offers, surprising himself. "I mean here at school, or after classes, if you'd like."

They look at each other then, both aware somehow of something more being offered, unsaid, but certainly implied, and neither knowing exactly how they feel about that, if they feel anything at all. But both, for reasons neither fully understands, are willing to find out.

"Okay," she says. "But I'll have to have some way of repaying you."

And though he doesn't offer any solution, he thinks it's best left unsaid.

"I'm sorry to leave you alone to do all this tedious work," Michael says as he returns to his office to find İrem still making lists.

"Oh, I don't mind," she says.

"Really?" and he looks skeptical. "Anyway, let me buy you dinner as a reward. That is, if you don't have any other plans."

"That'd be great," she says. "But I must warn you, I'm pretty hungry."

"Me, too," he says. "But you sure you don't have other plans?"

"No," and she smiles. "I have no other plans."

"Well," and he grabs his coat from the rack on the back of the door, "let's blow this pop stand then."

Dave is standing outside the school debating about what to do for dinner exactly when Katja comes out wearing her leotards under a loose fitting skirt and sweater. "Hi," he says.

"Hi," she answers.

"You look a little lost," he says smiling. "Been a tough day?"

"Yes and no," and she returns the smile but it's a little weak along the edges. "Just contemplating what to do for dinner."

"Oh, is that all?" and he laughs. "Here I thought it was something more serious."

"Well," and Katja's smile starts to fade, "dinner is pretty serious stuff when you live alone."

"Tell me about it."

"Do you have this problem, too?"

"Frequently," he says. "It can be one of the loneliest times of the day. But," and here his smile turns on the old charm, "if you have no plans tonight, how about solving this problem by joining me?"

"Is that an invitation?"

"You bet."

She looks at him for a moment, then seems to come to a decision in her head and says, "I'm dressed rather informally so it can't be any place fancy."

"We could go to Taksim," he says. "There are many informal places there."

"And they serve alcohol, too," she says.

"My thoughts exactly."

And she brushes back her hair and says, "Then what are we waiting for?"

And off they go looking for a taxi.

Philip meets Brenda for dinner on Bağdat Street. "Well there certainly are several choices here for coffee at a Starbucks," he says. "But where do you recommend for dinner?"

"There's a nice kebab place that isn't expensive we could try," she says.

"Do they serve beer?"

"Yes, they do."

"Then that sounds divine."

"You're certainly easy to please," she says laughing.

"When it comes to food anyway," he says. "I'm a bit more picky with the beer, but I'm sure, this being Turkey, they'll have Efes on tap."

And as they make their way to the restaurant, Philip can't help but notice how different the crowds walking up and down the avenue are than in his neighborhood of Kadiköy. "A bit upscale here," he remarks. "And quite trendy, too."

"Yes," Brenda says. "It's a great street for a woman to lose herself trying on shoes."

"Something I've always found fascinating but never could identify with myself."

"You mean you don't like trying on shoes," she teases.

"Right," he says, stopping to light another cigarette. "I think I own two pair myself. One black, these here on my feet," he says, pointing down. "And the other brown." He stops and reflects for a second. "I did have a pair of boots once but I fear I have left them somewhere in London."

"You poor boy," Brenda says, consoling him. "Not even a pair of slippers?"

"Ah yes," he says. "I have one pair of those at home here. Do they count as well?"

"We are speaking of anything in the category of footwear," she says, "so yes, they count."

"Three pair then," he says. "And they're brown as well. Very comfortable, too. A bit of fleece lining, you see."

She laughs and then stops in front of a kebab house called Günaydin. "How's this?" she asks.

"Good Morning," he says. "I'm not sure this is appropriate for this time of day but I'll overlook the hour if you will."

"Then we have arrived," she says and patiently waits for him to finish his cigarette before entering.

Meanwhile Deniz and Meric are sitting in a rather noisy bar in Taksim drinking: she white wine and he beer, while nibbling on mezes of eggplant puree, deep-fried oysters, and suçuk with fries.

"They say these are good for one's sexual prowess," Deniz says as she pops an oyster into her mouth.

"Really?" Meric says, his eyes widening a bit. "Perhaps we should order another dish."

"But they should be raw," she says, laughing. "I'm not sure they work like this."

"Ah well, I'm young yet and don't really need such aids," and he winks at her.

"And you feel that is necessary to tell me," she says.

"I think it's important to fill you in on all my vital statistics," he says.

"Oh?" and her eyebrow rises over her right eye. "And do you have a resume to offer for me to peruse in my spare time listing all your experiences, your strengths, weaknesses, bad habits, etc.?"

109

"I could supply one, if you need," he says. "With references, of course."

"Of course," she says. "At least three."

"Not more?"

"Well, more is always better, but let's not overdo it."

"Oh, I don't want to overdo anything," he says.

"Not anything?" she asks, that eyebrow rising again.

"Well, nothing that isn't requested," he says.

"And you think I need to know all this?" she asks, a playful glint in her eyes.

"Most definitely," he says, gravely serious in tone. "I don't want to make any promises I cannot keep."

"And you are a man of your word?"

"I have been trying to tell you that for quite some time now."

"Hmmm," she goes. "This is all very interesting. I will have to take it under advisement."

"But hopefully you won't delay too long," he says. "You know the old poem about gathering rose buds while you may because otherwise they begin to wilt so it's especially prudent to enjoy them while you can."

"In season, you mean," she says.

"Exactly," Meric says.

"And is this the proper season?"

"As far as this particular rose bud is concerned," and he grins.

"Hmmm," she goes. "I think I need to dwell on that while having another glass of wine."

"And more oysters?" he asks.

"Yes," she says. "I think we need more of those, too."

And whether one would see Meric as a rose bud or not, he certainly feels himself to be blooming.

Pelin, meanwhile, hovers in the background, her mouth watering for more than oysters, her heart beating wildly against her chest as she watches a seduction in progress she wishes was her own. And yet as she sees Meric, in her mind, becoming half of a couple, she is only more acutely aware of how alone she truly is.

Murat sits alone at a tavern in Bebek, drinking raki and watching people walk by on the street outside. He can't help but remember how he used to sit here, at this very same tavern, with Sönmez drinking raki while she drank beer and they would invent stories about the people passing by and laugh uncontrollably, touching each other under the table and whispering into and licking each other's ears. They couldn't wait to get home in those days to rip off each other's clothing and make mad, passionate love on the floor, in chairs, across the kitchen table, and finally end up in bed where they would sleep wrapped in each other's arms, their legs intertwined, until morning. He can't help but wonder what happened to those days, those nights, and thinks it isn't just the children, that there had to be some underlying cause before that. But no matter how much scrutiny he applies to his memories of those times, he just cannot see any indication of where it changed, what went wrong, what missing ingredient there might have been in their chemistry to cause this reversal. Just how did he happen to find himself here alone, drinking raki, and whispering to no one?

Michael watches in amazement once again as İrem charms the waiters at his favorite fish restaurant, The Hamsi Pub. They are usually very solicitous of him since he is a regular customer but she always utterly captivates them all, their eyes constantly settling on their table to see if they need anything, refilling the water glasses and the wine glasses before they are even half empty, bringing over a second basket of fresh bread, deboning the fish, and blushing slightly when she speaks to them in that casual manner of a lifelong friend. He can't help but think she is very sophisticated and credits that to her experience living alone overseas as well as here in Istanbul, far from her family in Izmir. And though he hates the thought of her leaving him, he knows she is a star in the making, destined for bigger things than staying here to work under him. And that thought saddens him and dims the glow he has been feeling in his heart.

She, however, looks at him for a moment and then asks, "What?"

"Huh?" he says.

"What are you thinking that's made your mood change?" she says, her head tilted slightly, a look he can't quite recognize in her eyes.

"Nothing," he lies, then shifts in his chair. "Well, yes, actually maybe something."

"Go ahead then," she says. "I promise not to bite."

"You bite?" he asks.

"Only people I don't like," he says, "so you have nothing to worry about."

"That's good," he says, sighing with mock relief. "It certainly wouldn't do for a constructive working arrangement."

"I think we have more than a constructive working arrangement," she says.

"We do, of course," he says, a little surprised by her perception but then realizing she always surprises him by her ability to read his thoughts.

"Yes," she says. "I admire and respect you, and hope to learn a great deal from you. But I also like you very much and always think of you as my friend."

And here the terrain becomes a little difficult for him, that no man's land that stretches out between colleague and friend, working relationships that grow deeper than that, deep enough to develop into evenings like this, ones he finds he cannot bear to think will end, but knows instinctively they must. But boundaries have been crossed, barriers erased, and she has become an important part of his life here, and that frightens him a bit.

"Did I say something wrong?" she asks, staring at him with those eyes that appear older and wiser than he had previously thought, or at least had not consciously acknowledged.

"No," he says.

"Then what is it?" she asks.

"I was just thinking about the play," he lies again, and thinks he should perhaps feel guilty about this deception, but knows no other way around a conversation he would rather not have at present.

"What about the play?"

"Just images," he says. "You know, these images I have keep interrupting my thoughts, bringing disorder to my days."

"You're obsessing about the play," she says. "Didn't you once tell me that when you start dreaming about your work, it's time to quit?"

"My Uncle Mike used to say that actually," Michael says.

"Do you always quote your Uncle Mike?"

"He was my favorite uncle," Michael says.

"And what did he do?"

"He worked as a supervisor for New Jersey Bell," Michael says. "Which is, of course, not the same thing I do. Except maybe they're both related to communication."

İrem studies him carefully and then says, "So you don't plan on quitting, I take it."

"The thought never entered my mind."

"So maybe you'd like to share some of these images with me?" she asks.

"Not now," he says. "Now let's just have some more wine. I'd rather forget work right now and just enjoy a pleasant evening with you."

"What a splendid idea," she says and reaches over for the wine bottle but before she can touch it, a waiter comes out of nowhere and pours them each another glassful before retreating again.

"So," he says lifting his wine glass, "to a good year ahead and both of us getting what we wish."

And İrem taps her glass against his and adds, "Insallah."

Dave leans back in his chair content as the waiters begin clearing the table. "Well," he says, "this was certainly much better than eating alone."

"It seems to me the food always tastes better when shared, don't you think?" Katja asks.

"Yes," he says. "And that was especially true tonight."

Katja laughs. "You are a flatterer, I think," she says.

"Yes," he acknowledges, "but not in this case. With you, there's no need to flatter."

"That's very sweet of you to say," she says, but her smile is not as bright as he had hoped. Instead there's that tinge of sadness tugging at its corners that no one, including Dave, can seem to wipe away for more than an instant, a fleeting second, the blink of an eye.

Dave reaches over to the wine bottle and refills both their glasses. Then, having second thoughts as he looks at her sad, tired eyes, he says, "I really shouldn't encourage you to drink any more. You look so tired that perhaps some coffee would be a better idea. Or," and he smiles tenderly her way, "maybe we should call it a night and you should go home to get some rest."

"No, I'm okay," she says, her head slowly rising so that her eyes can see into his. "I'm just not getting a lot of sleep these days."

"Anything you want to talk about?" he asks.

"I don't know if I can, but," and she smiles tenderly his way, "I really appreciate the fact that you asked."

"Hey," he says, "we are becoming friends, aren't we? And isn't that what friends are for?"

"You are too kind."

"No," he says. "I am not too kind. I try to be kind enough."

"Well, you are successful," and that sad smile again. "At least where I am concerned anyway."

And they sip their wine, sit in silence, each lost in thought. He gazes at her, her face turned away slightly, her eyes off in some distant memory, her full lips partially open, her face so beautiful it takes his breath away. There is so much to fall in love with, he thinks, and then slaps himself in his mind to keep himself grounded in reality. Trouble, he thinks. There is too much trouble here, too much work, the recesses too deep for him to fathom, and so he tries hard to avoid the pitfall, looks away from her strong cheekbones, the length of her neck, the way her hair falls effortlessly onto her shoulders. And he lets the silence speak volumes for him, for her, for them.

Brenda feels extremely comfortable with Philip, safe and secure, an older man from her own country who exudes empathy toward her, not sympathy which she would not appreciate, but empathy which is quite a different thing, the ability to look at life and her situation from her perspective and thus understand her. And she does not find him unattractive, though she is not necessarily attracted to older men, or at least not a whole generation ahead of her, her father's generation, and there have been men from that generation that have aggressively flirted with her, even going so far as to ogling her on the tubes, or on the street, or even while at a restaurant with Mark, but she has never really seriously considered a relationship with someone that old, though Philip is certainly cultured, intelligent, and handsome, also unattached, though there seems to be something not quite right with the picture, as they say, and so before she starts thinking about the possibility, she must first clear up this mystery.

"I really enjoy your company," she says, though thinks that's a rather lame way to start a flirtation, and realizes just how out of practice she is in this potential dating game.

"Yes," he says, "and I enjoy yours."

"It's just that I haven't really felt comfortable with men since my divorce," she says. "Actually it probably goes back further than that. I was never really very good at dating even before Mark. And he certainly didn't help increase my confidence since the lack of physical compatibility has almost made me self-conscious with men."

"Well it seems to me you're best out of that marriage. You're sure to find someone who can stimulate you here."

"You think so?" she says.

"Oh yes," he nods. "You're charming, quite beautiful, intelligent, with a stable job and income. Believe me, you're quite the catch."

"Really?" she asks. "I just never seem to think of myself that way."

"But you are," he says emphatically.

"And you think men will find me attractive?"

"Of course they will."

"Do you find me attractive?"

"Well I would," he says, "if I were so inclined that way. But," and he smiles, "I'm not."

"Inclined what way?" she asks, slightly confused by that expression.

"Inclined toward women," he says. "But, you see, I prefer the other gender."

"Oh," she says, almost embarrassed at her own stupidity. "I didn't realize."

"No?" he asks, almost as surprised as she is. "But I thought you knew. It's clear if you've read my CV. I mean, it's what I write about."

"Oh, well I haven't read it," she says. "Nor have I read anyone's, actually. Oh, how silly of me."

"No," he laughs. "No harm done. But again, to answer your question, yes, I would find you quite attractive if I were so inclined. So I really wouldn't worry about finding men here. They will, I'm positive, come flocking soon enough."

"You really think so?" she asks.

"Yes," he says. "As soon as you open yourself up to the possibility. You know, begin to dress a little more provocatively and start flirting with the single men. And go to clubs and such where you'll meet them."

"I'd feel a little awkward doing that here," she says.

"Well I'll accompany you, if you'd like, so you'll be safe. Would you like that?"

"You wouldn't mind?"

"Of course not," and he smiles. "I'm not actively on the prowl myself but I certainly have no objection to window shopping."

And Brenda can't help but laugh.

Meric has Deniz twirling on the dance floor, doing shots of schnapps in beer, and laughing at his impersonations of Turkish pop stars. She thinks he is perhaps the funniest, most charming man she's met in a long time and finds her sides hurt from laughing, her legs ache from dancing, her head is spinning from the alcohol. And when she finds herself out on the streets of Kadiköy with him in the hours long past midnight, eating Anatolian style food in a place called Ali Rıza, she is hungry for more than the white beans and pilaf on her plate, and he navigates the way to his apartment in Acibadem where he slowly undresses her, caressing the nipples of her breasts, burying his head between her legs, her mouth sucking in air, and the night closes around them and only their breathing, their sighs, cries of delight, follow them to morning.

Pelin is on the street below, watching the light turn on, then off in Meric's apartment, her heart breaking in pieces in her chest. She has trouble breathing as she starts what seems to her the longest walk in her life back to the bus depot, and home to her lonely bed.

Murat is numb with raki as he fumbles with his keys in the lock, bumps his way into the apartment, collapses on the couch, his jacket dropped on the floor, his shirt partially unbuttoned, his shoes lost somewhere in the hall. He wishes he had someone to hold his head so it would stop spinning but there is no one there, just the darkness, the couch, the sound of someone crying. And as he falls off into a troubled sleep, he is suddenly aware the person crying is himself.

Dave dreams of doors closing, footsteps on the stairs, a car door shutting somewhere on a street long, long ago. He is standing in his living room, a glass in his hand, music coming from a far wall, a clock dropping digits on a nightstand that stands forlornly beside an empty bed with sheets as cold as a January morning in a room he hesitates to enter. And the loneliness that plagues him from house to house, state to state, now country to country, is what he wakes to, along with his stifled sobs, on another chilly morning, in another bed, alone.

Katja tosses and turns in the night. Her dreams are so vivid, the faces that surround her, the arms that hold and comfort her, so real, she surrenders to the illusion. There is Hasan, his dark, curly hair falling across her face as he holds her ever so tightly against him, cradling her in his arms and whispering, "I love you" in her ear, and slowly, ever so slowly, rocking her to the rhythm of his breathing until her breathing matches his, their breathing becoming one breath, they becoming one person, there in the night, in their bed, a haven safe from the world of screaming women, frightened children, from dark men in dirty military uniforms banging on doors outside. And the fitfulness of her sleep dissipates and the world is once again full of hope and peace.

But this does not last for Hasan is ephemeral, a ghost in the night, and he disappears as the night progresses, a vapor, no longer a presence in her life. And the terror returns, her heart, her breath constricts, and she shrivels up into a ball in the center of the bed, hoping to withdraw so far inward that the fear will not find her.

Brenda wakes to the phone ringing. She can see by the Caller ID that it is London calling. It is three am there and she knows it is Mark. Another restless night for him, she supposes, and more tortured love poems that he'll send in an email and that she will delete without reading. She wishes it would end but knows it will not, not for a long time yet to come, for he is relishing his pain too much, and then feeds on that pain to write more poems. He will continue till he gets a book out of it, she supposes, which will bring him many female admirers who will wish to soothe his pain away.

She waits for the phone to stop ringing, then turns it off. She closes her eyes and turns over in the bed. She pulls the comforter up around her shoulders and wills herself back to sleep.

Philip sits on his balcony looking out as dawn lights the street below. He has a glass of cay in his hand, his robe pulled tight against his body, his slippers dangling from his bare feet. He thinks he should get dressed soon, and go out for his morning stroll. This is his favorite part of the day when the city is not quite awake but still a bit groggy in the day's first light. He likes it groggy, its citizens not up yet, though Istanbul, unlike London or New York, is not wary of strangers, and though aware of the foreigner among them, lets him roam about its ancient streets unmolested, undisturbed.

Michael sits in silence on a bench by the shore watching the ships that lay out on the water, motionless and dark. He likes watching the ships, the gulls as they glide and swoop out over the sea, their cries like babies calling out for attention. He has not slept much in the night, having risen way before dawn to shuffle around his apartment, make notes on the play, dwell on the images in his mind. He thinks it is past Thanksgiving back in America, and his brothers had celebrated yet another holiday without him at the table, drinking wine and trying not to talk with his mouth full. He missed the holiday again this year, as he missed the others last year, as he'll miss the ones yet to come.

His eyes, though, are almost vacant, yet a spark glows there, somewhere, in that part of the eye that sees either the future or the past, depending on who is looking and the circumstances surrounding their gaze. With Michael, though, here, the circumstances are primarily pensive and thus he is lingering in the past, both distant and only just recent, images circling around in his brain, of faces, both lovers and friends, and some names he cannot quite recall, and others he would like to forget. And those eyes grow heavy, there on the bench. And he closes them as he feels the breeze on his face, hears the gulls in his ears.

And finally to İrem who is up in her kitchen making menemen, adding a touch of crushed red pepper, and tiny bits of meat and green peppers. She will taste it in a minute to make sure there is enough salt, then scoop it into a container to bring to Michael at school, a surprise in his day. She knows he will be there, even though it is a weekend, annotating his script, staring at his charts, nibbling on a pencil as he leans back in his chair, and feeling a gnawing in his stomach because he has, as usual, forgot to eat. She knows his habits, his routines, and though she doesn't want to change anything about him, she does want to make sure he eats. And they will eat together, this morning, as she helps him work on the play, and slowly, very surely, remain a part of his life.

Scene 4
December

December is, as we all know, a cold month here in Istanbul, as it is most places north of the equator. There is no snow yet, but there are also no lines standing outside Ali Üsta for their ice cream, though people still wait inside for some, and the tea gardens with outdoor tables have thick plastic walls and a roof with portable heaters going as they stay open for business now. People sit huddled inside the ferries and steam heat rises from the radiators, the days are shorter, the nights longer, and though students and faculty alike still go outside onto the patio or the street to smoke a cigarette, the conversations are shorter as well.

"You busy?" Dave asks while standing in the doorway of the theatre department office.

İrem looks up from the sheets of paper laid out on her desk, smiles, and says, "Well that depends on how you define busy."

"Well not busy enough that you can't spare some time for a cup of coffee to discuss some possibilities for work in New York if what I hear is correct and you're intending to go back for your PhD?" Dave asks. "I think I may know a few people who could help."

"Ah well, if put that way…" İrem says, "though actually I haven't finally decided if I'll go, or even if I want to study in New York or California, but I am leaning that way and will make some applications this January."

"That's what I like," Dave says, "a woman who keeps her options open."

İrem laughs. "Only a woman?" she asks. "What about a man?"

"Him, too," Dave grins. "If one were here."

And so they both adjourn to the cafeteria for coffee and since it's late afternoon already, and most faculty and students are on the way home, he suggests continuing the discussion at dinner. "That is, if you have nothing else to do and don't mind," he says. "And don't let the fact that I'm new here, far, far from home, with no one else to have dinner with, influence you at all."

"Well, put that way," and she laughs. "Okay."

And though the dinner is rather harmless, the conversation revolving mostly around grad school and some contacts he knows in a few Off-Broadway companies, Dave feels he has made some progress in getting to know her better and though he plans no attempt at seduction here in Turkey, he thinks if she does indeed go to New York to study, well, he might as well leave some options open himself.

Murat stares at his notes for class. His semester has been divided into a study of distinctive musical styles and this month it is jazz. He has supplementary material from Nat Hentoff and Leonard Feather as well as some radio interviews of various artists from Studs Terkel's program and, of course, lots of music to listen to and some film clips to watch. But somehow his mind is not focusing on the lesson, even though this is one of his personal favorites. He just keeps thinking about Brenda in her office down the hall and wondering if he should stop by and chat. He sees the tears in her eyes that day when she inadvertently bumped into him, the pain, the loneliness, and wonders if his loneliness, his pain, might not mesh with hers, might not somehow blend into something else, a balm perhaps, a means to an end, for him, for her. And it is with that thought in mind that he pulls himself up from his chair and traverses the distance between his office and hers and stands in her doorway, leans against the doorframe, and smiles.

"How are the classes going?" he asks.

She looks up, startled at first, then smiles at a friendly face. "Oh, you caught me daydreaming," she says.

"About anything good?"

"Aren't all daydreams good?" she says.

"I don't know," he says. "I don't seem to daydream much myself these days."

"No?" she asks.

"No," and he sighs. "Brood, maybe. But that isn't really the same thing."

"No," she says. "I don't think there's anything good to be associated with brooding. Do you?"

"I agree," he says. "But unfortunately, it's what I'm left with now."

"Are you brooding about school?" she asks, and then wonders if maybe she shouldn't delve into his personal life, but then again, she thinks, he did mention it.

"No, not school," he says. "My life," and he sighs. "I'm at that stage in life where one looks back with regret and broods over how you can change that into something a bit more positive."

"Regret?"

"Yes," and that sad smile that seems so much a part of him now. "I think often that somehow I only achieved part of what I set out to do. That somehow I am only half complete. Do you know what I mean?"

"I'm not sure," she says. "Could you elaborate?"

"Maybe it's nothing more than a clichéd midlife crisis," he says, "but as I look at myself, I am only happy here, in my professional half of my life. But when I look at my personal life, well, I think I am not looking at myself. It is as

126

if I am looking at a film I am watching about someone else, someone who looks and behaves like me, but is not me. There is not anyone I would want to be." He laughs suddenly, but it is a strangled laugh, caught somewhere in his throat, and it pains him as he tries to let it out. "I don't know why I'm saying this," he says, "but somehow I thought maybe you would understand." And he looks at her then, his eyes holding hers. "Do you understand?"

"Yes," she says, and then realizes that by saying that, she has somehow opened a door, a door she will not be able to close, and that both frightens and excites her.

And he stands there for a long moment looking at her seated behind her desk, feeling somehow connected and yet still apart. "Perhaps," he says slowly, cautiously, "you'd like to have dinner tonight. Perhaps we could talk more about this. If you'd like."

And she nods, hears herself saying, "Yes," feels the door opening wider, and wonders if that is to let something in or to let something out. Or maybe, she realizes, to do both.

Katja loses herself in dance. It is as if some other person is in control and she is just an instrument of her emotions, her desires. She glides across the floor, the principal dancers following, her movements so fluid, so graceful, they are all in awe of her. The lover's dance has become a tango, and she guides her two principal dancers, Berat and Elena, through the movements, they desperately trying to stay with her, her body so alive with sexual energy, they almost lose their control, stumble beside her, a wild, sexual animal on the prowl.

And afterwards, as their reward, she takes them to dinner at a place in Taksim, and though they are excited, eager to talk, she is a subdued animal, a lioness resting after the hunt, her belly full, her appetite whetted, her mind at rest.

Dinner is at his place, and Meric attempts to cook some kofte, to make a salad, to slice the bread, but Deniz is more interested in a meal of a different nature, and before he can even light the stove, she is unzipping his trousers, pulling him toward the bedroom, for a feast of their own. And Meric, used to improvisation, is more than willing to eat his full.

Michael sits at his favorite fish restaurant, The Hamsi Pub, and cannot help but notice the waiters' disappointment that İrem is not sitting opposite him. But such is life, he thinks, though he understands why they feel let down, for he, too, finds İrem a great deal more attractive to sit opposite from. Instead he listens to conversations in Turkish all around him and wonders where İrem could have gone since she had already left by the time he returned to the office and he has to admit to himself that he was not only surprised but disappointed, too.

"Alone tonight?" Naım asks, and when Michael nods, he looks over at Memati, the other regular waiter at the restaurant, and they both exchange a meaningful look that Michael can only interpret as "poor soul." And he feels very much like one himself. And he can't help but think this is what it will be like if İrem goes off to the US for her PhD. There will be the occasional dinners with Philip, meetings with his other friends in Istanbul, but generally speaking, there will be a void in his life if she is gone. For she accompanies him to the opera and concerts, they go to the cinema together when there is that rare American film he wishes to see, but more often than not, they watch a DVD at his place after she has cooked a meal for him. There are the lunches at school together, the ride home on the bus and ferry together, three or four dinners together during the week, the shared office, the in-jokes they share, even lately the occasional trip to the Mediterranean during the summer and the time they met in Ephesus when she was home during vacation in Izmir. And the trips they have talked about taking together to London to catch some shows will never happen now, nor the planned trip to Vienna for opera season. No, his life will change drastically if she goes, and yet what did he expect? They are friends, after all, but what life could he have with her, or, to be more accurate, what life could she have with him? She has youth and a future lying out before her, and he has only the past behind him and a limited number of years left. Her future lies beyond this present and this present is all the future he has left.

So he takes another sip of his wine and gazes out the window to the street outside. And he watches people stroll by for a long time before signaling the waiters for another bottle while thinking the night isn't going the way he had planned.

"My life," Murat says, "is just not the life I envisioned twenty years ago," he says. "When I go home, I feel like a stranger in my own house. It is as if the only Murat I know is the one at school, or sitting here talking to you, but not the one who lives in that house." He looks deeply into her eyes, and Brenda finds herself falling into their pools, as he asks, "Have you ever felt so disconnected yourself?"

"Yes," she says. "Though not in the same way exactly. But I often felt like I was sleepwalking in my marriage. That I was in a dream I could not wake from and that dream was like an alternative world I had somehow, without knowing how, crossed over to and could not find my way back."

"So what did you do?" Murat asks.

"I left him," she says quite simply, but realizes, of course, it was not so simple, that no act of regaining one's freedom ever is.

"And you feel like you've gotten your life back?"

"Not yet," she says. "But it's a start."

"How long were you married?" he asks.

"Two years," she says. "Though when I think about it, it seems so much longer. I guess because I've known him since graduate school. Seven years in total."

"And it changed after you were married?"

"Yes," she says. "He was so romantic before, writing me poems, popping up unexpectedly with flowers, a dinner invitation, carriage rides through the park, long weekend holidays at some coastal hideaway, and the sex..." and she looks off to some long ago memory of flickering candlelight, half empty wine bottles, violins weeping in the background, and her heart cracks a little recalling, tears welling in her eyes. "But that all changed, of course, after we were married. Oh, there were still the poems, but his love became just words, words on paper, but nothing in bed."

"I'm sorry," Murat says, those deep, dark eyes holding hers. "I know it is difficult to speak of these things, but if it is any consolation, I truly understand."

"Do you?" she asks. "You don't think I'm shallow, do you? That I gave up a marriage because of a lack of sex?"

"No," he says. "I think you are quite brave to do it. To know what you wanted, needed, and to act decisively to attain it."

"My parents, my friends, all think I acted too rashly, that I should have been more understanding, more patient, with him." And there's wildness in her eyes as she looks at him. "But I was suffocating," she adds. "I felt like the air around me was gone and I could not breathe."

"I feel that every night when I go home," Murat says, "so I envy you for breaking free."

"It wasn't as hard as it seemed at first," she says. "But afterwards, there's this loneliness, this emptiness inside."

130

"Ah, but I have that now," he says. "It couldn't be any worse if I, too, broke free. I imagine instead it would be better."

"Then what's preventing you from doing it?" she asks.

"The children," he says. "They are so young, and I feel responsible." Then he sighs. "But it is ironic, too, because it is the children that changed everything. Because of them, I have lost the person who was my wife."

And they sit then, both drawn closer by a shared sense of loss and loneliness, and both strangely comforted knowing they are not alone.

Fersat captures Meltem in his camera's eye: her smile, her laugh, the way her eyes will suddenly darken with clouds he cannot see beyond, the vacant look that appears as she gazes out a bus window, the dreaminess in those eyes that look out to the sea. It is her eyes, the way her mouth turns, the line of her chin, her hair rustling in the breeze that captivates him and enchants his camera. And she, the budding actress, delights in being the object of his undivided attention. She begins to play different roles for him, letting her personality shift from moonstruck girl to sophisticated lady to world-weary veteran to vixen to sphinx. And though he captures every look, every gesture, the one role that eludes his camera is the one role his heart yearns for the most: a woman in love with him.

But Meltem, though she doesn't show it, is already rehearsing that part in her head.

Deniz's eyes are open and Meric's are closed as they make love, and though Deniz takes the tightness in his face as a sign of concentration, she does wonder what he sees behind those eyes. Is it her face he makes love to or some other memory or fantasy, this being so new and that concentration being so intense as to close her out. For with

131

her, her eyes are wide open, taking in every detail of the here and now. She has thrown herself into this love affair much like she does with her painting, with complete abandon, and that creates a sense of reckless adventure which is not only exciting but completely intoxicating. And like a drunk, she cannot absorb enough.

Meric, for his part, hovers over her, his eyes open now, looking through her, his mouth on hers, his tongue down her throat, her tongue is sucked up and swallowed, his breath is her breath is his breath is hers, his hands are all over her body, his finger is working its magic, his tongue, his tongue is everywhere, and then something harder, something she has not felt in a long time, something that is male and hard and demanding, and she cannot resist, cannot stop this penetration, this long, hard, gentle, soft, overwhelming penetration, and she gives herself up to it, there on the pillows, on the floor. And it blends together, music in the background, incense burning, candles glow, and the steady movement inside her, it all takes her away.

Michael sits in his living room, a drink of whiskey in front of him on the coffee table, untouched but comforting by its presence. He might drink it, he thinks, but then again he might not. It is still open for debate. But in the meantime, he sits in semi-darkness, only a reading light glowing in the corner by his reading chair, a book lying on the armrest, *The Charterhouse of Parma*, which he has begun rereading, and the cat prowling restlessly at his feet.

He looks down at the cat, sees a whiff of cat hair on the floor near it, and says, "Because of you, I had to buy a vacuum cleaner. You know that, right?"

The cat ignores him. Purrs as it rubs up against his leg, then moves off noiselessly to sleep on his reading chair, oblivious to Michael's restless mind and the images that flash through it, of faceless lovers embracing, then drifting apart. And though he doesn't quite understand how it happens, or even how to consciously acknowledge it, the female lovers all begin to take on a face, a face he begins to recognize, and then he closes his eyes to such images, shuts off his mind, tries vainly for sleep.

Dave stares at his computer screen, at an email he has composed, a new email, to a woman, an invitation for dinner on Saturday night. It is to Katja, of course, and though he knows he is perhaps pushing his luck, he still feels a strong desire to reach out anyway and see where it leads, what he might grasp. And in the reaching, his finger hits the send button and lets whatever will follow, follow, for he has, he reasons, nothing to lose.

İrem has been up early in the morning and out to the markets in Kadiköy, buying fresh tomatoes, cucumbers, red onions, a head of lettuce, lemons, some seasoning, especially a packet of sea salt and parsley, cornmeal, a large sea bass, some hamsi, some fruit for dessert, and together with a baking tray, she finds she is ready for the dinner she has planned. And though she can't wait to call him, she spends the rest of the morning rereading the play and making notes. Then, at 11am, she dials Michael's number on her cell.

"Hi," she says. "I didn't want to call too early because I wasn't sure when you get up."

"I've been up," Michael says, "mainly because I haven't gone to sleep."

"You haven't slept?" she says.

"My mind's too active, I think," he says and sighs. "It's been like this forever. I can't remember the last time I actually slept an entire night without waking up."

"This is not good," she says. "You need your rest. That's why you always look so tired at school."

133

Michael shakes his head to clear it and then says, "Surely you didn't call to check up on my sleeping habits."

"No," she says. "It's about our dinner tonight."

"Right," he says. "We're still on for dinner?"

"Of course," she says. "Why wouldn't we be?"

"I don't know," he says and thinks he's letting his insecurity get the best of him. "My mind's not working properly this morning. This is Saturday, right?"

"Yes," she says. "And I thought I'd cook fish. That is if you don't mind."

"You want to make dinner?"

"Yes," she says. "That's what we usually do, isn't it?"

"Of course," he says, and slaps himself softly so she can't hear. "My mind again."

"Anyway, I have everything I need: fish, salad, herbs. How's around four sound?"

"Sure," he says, a little overwhelmed by the prospect, but definitely not opposed to the idea. "What do you need from me?"

"Just your kitchen," she says laughing. "And you can supply the wine, as usual."

And as she hangs up, she wonders why that seemed more difficult than it should have been.

Murat finds he thinks about Brenda all morning and then, before he hesitates, he impulsively calls her on her cell. "Hi," he says. "It's Murat."

"I know," she says.

"You do?"

"Caller ID," she says. "Very convenient when you don't want to necessarily answer the call."

"Ah yes," he nods. "But you answered."

"Yes," she says. "I was hoping you would call."

"Really?"

"Yes, really," she says and finds she is actually blushing. "Is that wrong?"

"No," he says, his heart racing a little faster than it already was when he began the call. "I wanted to call earlier but wasn't sure I should."

"I'm glad you did."

Then they both just breathe into their respective phones, neither knowing just how to continue but both knowing not only that they want to continue but that the other person wants that, too. Finally he blurts out, "Can I see you tonight?"

"Yes," she says.

"When?" he asks.

"When do you want to?"

"Now," he says. "Right this minute."

"Can you get away?"

"Yes," he says. "I won't even be missed."

"Then come," she says. "Come as soon as you can."

Deniz wakes first this time, in the afternoon, and props herself up on her side and gazes over at her sleeping lion, for that is how she sees Meric now, as her big, insatiable lion. He lies there, on his back, his mouth partially open, snoring peacefully, a sexual animal at rest. She thinks of waking him, but then changes her mind for she finds she is hungry for something other than sex, some nameless desire that pulls her from the bed and so she rises.

She goes out naked to his kitchen, opens the refrigerator, and takes out some yogurt, a spoon from the drawer, and sits naked cross legged on his living room floor and begins eating while surveying the room. There is not much furniture in the apartment; it looks more like a college dorm room with a couch, a desk and chair with his laptop, a TV screen, DVD player, and stereo components on a stand that looks like he bought at Ikea. There is the rug she is sitting on and, of course, some DVDs, plays, scripts, and Stella Adler's book on Method Acting on a small three-shelf bookcase. She smiles to herself thinking it isn't really someplace a person lives, just a resting place in between other resting places.

After finishing the yogurt, she rises again and goes back into the bedroom, quietly slips back into her clothes, and tiptoes out to his hallway, puts on her boots, and silently closes the door behind her as she leaves.

Berat holds the door open for Elena as they enter the restaurant and she smiles slightly at this act of chivalry. He is, she thinks, a bit old fashioned, but that pleases her. It is so different than the last boyfriend she had in Kiev who was always looking over her shoulder at other women and walked through doorways expecting her to follow. This respect Berat shows for her puts her in control and she finds it makes him even more attractive to her. As in dance, she takes the lead and he accompanies her which only allows her to be more creative in where she will lead him.

Fersat cannot take his eyes off Meltem, his camera suspended halfway to his face, his mind's eye snapping away instead at pictures that will forever be engraved in his memory. And Meltem, aware of her power over him, hovers in the center of his eye.

Jennifer gets a call from Meric apologizing for not returning her last two calls with the excuse that he's been too tired lately from school. "But what are you doing now?" he asks.

"Nothing special," she says, a little hesitantly, almost hurt that he calls on a Saturday afternoon asking about a Saturday night when he's been avoiding her all week long at school. "Just the usual weekend chores: laundry, shopping, some preparation for the week, things like that."

"Any plans for dinner?"

She almost lies and says yes, but then thinks of the old expression "cutting off your nose to spite your face" and changes her mind. She wants to see him, to reclaim her position in his life, his bed, so why pretend otherwise. "No," she says. "I don't."

"Then why not come over here?" he says, his voice low, soft, almost a caress. "We could make something together. Like we used to do."

And she has no will power, no pride. She knows what she wants and she also knows she knows what she cannot resist. "Okay," she says. "I'll be over in an hour."

Dave prepares dinner for Katja at home. He bakes a whole chicken, makes a green salad with tomatoes and cucumbers, and mashed potatoes. He has ice cream and some pastries for dessert along with drip coffee and herbal tea. And, of course, there is wine, and as he pours some into her glass, with Chopin playing softly in the background, he cannot help but be struck once again by her beauty. Her eyes are so clear, almost innocent, but that tinge of sadness still shades them and touches his heart.

They eat, though he can't help notice that she seems to have trouble finishing things as if the very act of chewing required more energy than she possesses, and food is moved around on her plate more than consumed. And though he tries conversation, it, too, is mostly left unfinished. He briefly considers it is the food, the subject of conversation, the length of his hair, his cologne, but, of course, knows this was a bad idea, there are depths here to her sorrow he will never be able to comprehend, and so he lets the meal grow cold, the words disappear in the air, the wine stay untouched in her glass. And as the evening ends, as it surely must, he thanks whoever is listening that he doesn't have to see her

137

home. And he sits alone in this apartment he temporarily calls home and finishes what's left in his glass, the bottle, as the evening closes around him, and he thinks perhaps he is over his head in the pursuit of Katja but his loneliness had outweighed his caution. No, he thinks, there is nothing to lose with her that he already doesn't have and so his thoughts begin to drift toward İrem where he thinks he might have a better chance at finding what he is looking for.

Pelin sings in clubs with her trio of musicians. She sings sad, heart-felt torch songs, most of which she learned from listening to Julie London and Peggy Lee CDs. And she sings these songs hoping Meric will one day walk through the door of a club she performs in and hear her, for now she sings for him.

İrem takes over his kitchen and Michael, a glass of wine in hand, leaning against the doorjamb, watches her amazed. She seems so at home there, slicing things and taking charge of the pots and pans, the oven, that he begins to realize how much he has grown accustomed to watching her in this kitchen, doing the things she is doing, preparing a meal to share. And because he finds himself loving watching her, he also begins to feel dread sneaking its way up his spine and laying siege to his brain. This is dangerous, he thinks. He could easily fall victim to melancholy once she is gone, seeing her there every evening, every morning, a life together that almost was, eating meals, working on plays, sharing ideas, stories, in this kitchen, at that table, in this apartment.

"What are you thinking?" she asks after she slides the baking tray with the sea bass on it into the oven to bake. "You seem lost somewhere."

"No," and he bucks up, forces himself to confront the present instead of imagining a future with only her memory.

"I'm just enjoying watching you cook," he says, "and maybe, for a minute there, it brought back some past associations and I got a little lost."

"Ah, past associations," she says and smiles. "Were they pleasant ones?"

"The ones conjured up watching you were," he says.

"Then I'm glad I was the cause," and that smile again, partially seductive, causes him to look away and reach for the bottle of wine on the kitchen table. He pours a glass for her, and then refills his own. She senses the shift in his mood and instinctively understands what he, with his ghosts from the past, his fear of the future, must be going through. So she touches her glass to his and says, "To only pleasant memories tonight."

"Ah," he says, straightening up. "Yes."

And they both take a healthy sip of their wine and look into each other's eyes. And İrem sees the future, while Michael sees danger and wonders if he's strong enough to heed the signs.

She knows what she is doing is dangerous, is wrong, is something she would not want done to her, but she can't help herself. Brenda is drawn to Murat, feels a connection, and knows she must follow her heart in this regardless of the moral dilemma it puts her in. So as soon as she opens the door and sees him standing there, she reaches out for his face and pulls him to her, their mouths open, gulping in as much love as they can, hands groping, the door closing behind him, her dress hiked up, his pants unzipped and down around his ankles, and they make love standing up in her hallway before they even say hello.

Jennifer wastes no time in pulling Meric toward the bedroom and he is more than willing to follow. And once there, she takes charge of his bed, the one place she feels she has undivided command of his attention, and begins to remind him of why he cannot possibly live without her and he, of course, remembers and thinks how lucky he is at this time in his life to have two women who completely satisfy him. Now the trick, he realizes, is to keep them both. And he does his best to remind her, too, just how much she needs him.

Afterwards, she can't stop herself from bringing up a topic briefly discussed before. "I make you happy, don't I?" she asks.

"Of course," he says.

"You like my being here then?"

"Yes" he says, and puts his arm around her hoping that will end the conversation and he can get some needed sleep.

"Then why don't we live together?" she says. "It would make things so much easier, don't you think?"

"Is that really necessary," he says, thinking he might not get that needed sleep after all. "I mean, what's wrong with the way things are now?"

"It would be more economical," she says. "One place, one rent divided by two."

"But we'd need a bigger place," he says. "And I like it here."

"I thought you loved me," she says, and pulls out of his embrace, and looks closely into his eyes.

"Of course I do," he says, thinking how relative that word has always been to him all his life. "What does that have to do with living together?"

"Everything," she says.

"It is that important to you?" he asks.

"Yes," she says. "It is."

And there it is: a line drawn in the sand. And Meric wanting nothing more than to sleep for at least a hundred years to get his strength back, finds he must either cross it or eventually lose this woman. "Well then we'll see," he says in an attempt to avoid the unavoidable. "We'll see."

And though Jennifer backs away from the issue this time, she knows she must persist, perhaps more subtly, to make this her home.

Murat finds that school is as good an excuse as necessary to come home later and later each evening and to disappear for hours on end on Saturday as well. Of course it isn't schoolwork that consumes him but Brenda and though he feels like the illicit man in an illicit romance, he really doesn't care how it would look but only in how it feels. And to be with her, not only for the sex, which there is in abundance, but for the long talks afterwards, the sense of finally having someone to share his life with, that gives him such pleasure, he cannot resist.

Brenda, for her part, feels this is more like her idea of a marriage than the marriage she left. And as she lies naked against him in her bed, her hand lightly gliding over his chest and abdomen, she wonders if it is Murat she craves or just the idea of a man, any man, who could make her feel desired again. And Murat certainly does that, she thinks. And for that she will be eternally grateful. And to demonstrate just how grateful she is, she slides down to below his waist and takes his manhood in her mouth till he claws at her back to pull her up to him, and works all her loneliness away.

İrem begins getting regular invitations to dinner from Dave on Friday nights. And though she accepts some almost half-heartedly, she finds the conversations innocent enough to be distracting since at first they mostly discuss school and their students. But soon, to keep her interested, Dave begins to discuss her possible pursuit of a PhD in America, keeping the focus on New York as the desired location, and dropping

141

names in theatre departments he supposedly has influence with at Columbia, NYU, and Stony Brook. This is all in the guise of helping her not only with the application process, but in getting settled in New York. "It is the place to be," he says, "if you are serious about the theatre."

İrem, for her part, feels slightly guilty for some reason and thinks it is absurd because this is a Friday night, not a Saturday, when she would normally have her dinner with Michael. Besides, this is related to her future plans and she cannot help but think Michael would understand that and approve. So they eat, though he can't help but notice that she seems a little distant so he keeps steering the conversation to New York and his supposed contacts in theatre there. And the picture he paints of the life he could introduce her to in New York is mostly fabrication, but İrem does not know this, will not know it until after she is settled in the city and he is the man he envisions she cooks for, spends time with, and eventually, in his mind, shares his bed. A goal, he thinks, not unrealistic as he continues to lay the groundwork of his planned seduction.

İrem begins to imagine a life in the city, the plays to see, the classes to take, the people to meet, and these Friday evenings begin to take on a significance she hadn't at first anticipated. And Dave, sensing that, keeps spinning his web in the hopes of making these evenings a part of his/her routine here. And Dave begins to display parts of himself to İrem in the hopes that she will begin to be attracted to him beyond his helpfulness if she does decide to go to New York. And the best way, he thinks, is to expose his creative side to someone who is involved in the arts. "With me, I find release for what I feel in the writing," Dave says. "I don't have as much time as I did when I was younger for it, but I still manage to put some time in."

"What kinds of things do you write?"

"Stories mostly, though for the last few years they've really been no more than character sketches. I've tried to write a novel but I just can't seem to go the distance."

"Who do you write your stories about?"

"Students, and sometimes other teachers. But generally students. I only deal with foreign students and immigrants so there's a lot of source material there."

"Will you write stories about the students here?"

"Maybe," and he smiles. "But right now I'm more interested in some of the teachers." İrem almost blushes, he thinks, but she averts her face and he cannot be sure. Then he says, "Perhaps you'd like to read some of my stories sometime. That is if you don't mind my showing them to you."

"No," she says. "I wouldn't mind but I may not have time to read anything until after we're finished with the play."

"There's no rush," he says. "I have some on my computer and some much older ones on my external drive. I'll sort through them and send you a few."

And though he doesn't think he's any closer to her yet than he wants to be, he knows he's not farther away, either.

Michael, meanwhile, begins to notice a void where one did not exist before and memory, and past experience, reminds him to expect it to grow.

Katja has a void of her own that begins to feel more and more like home. For it is only when she surrenders to the illusion of Hasan holding her that she finds comfort and peace from the memories that haunt her so. And she slips into a deep sleep without dreams of mourning women in black and mass graves where houses once stood. A

143

beginning, she thinks, of the life that now awaits her here in this country she is trying so hard to make her own.

For Michael, it starts with a phone call, as regular as the sun in the morning and the Bosporus rolling by every day, from İrem on Saturday morning. "Are you there?" she asks.

"I would have to be," he says, "to answer the phone."

"Just making sure," she says, "because I've been shopping."

"You have?" he says.

"Yes, and I think we'll try something different tonight. That is," and she smiles into her end of the phone, "if you don't mind being my guinea pig."

"I think," Michael says, "being Italian, I would prefer being called something else."

"That is the wrong term?" she asks, momentarily confused.

"No," he says, realizing once again there is a cultural difference at work here, "it's a kind of joke, a word play."

"A word play," she says.

"On guinea," he says. "That sounds like a slang term for an Italian."

"It does?"

"Well, yes," he sighs. "But no matter. It's not important."

"But I didn't mean it that way," she says.

"I know. Forget it. I'm looking forward to being your guinea pig."

"Are you sure?"

"Positive," he says.

"It's a different fish dish," she says. "And I'm going to try making homemade soup."

"I'm all yours," he says.

And İrem, for a second, has to think about that, while he wonders, having said it, if he isn't playing with words himself and meaning more than he is saying, or meaning what he isn't saying, or possibly saying what he is meaning but pretending it means something else.

It's when he leaves that Brenda feels even more alone again. But he has to go back, having come in the morning, spent the whole afternoon, and only left after dinner, to go home, or at least to go back to the place that is supposed to be his home, though he feels more at home with Brenda than he has ever felt with Sönmez, except maybe in the early years, long before the children arrived, and he began to feel like a foreigner in his own bed.

But Brenda feels the loneliness descend again and calls Philip to fill what remains of her evening with company.

"Ah," he says. "I thought perhaps you went back to England on the weekends."

"No," she says. "I've been preoccupied."

"In a pleasant way?" he asks.

"Very pleasant."

"Well good for you," he says. "And now you've gone slumming by calling me."

"No," she says. "I've missed you. What are you doing?"

"Star gazing," he says.

"Can you see them in the sky there?"

"Not in the heavens, but here on earth."

"Beg your pardon?"

"I'm sitting in a bar observing the stars of youth."

"Oh, how lovely," she says. "Can I join you?"

"You're welcome anytime."

And once she writes down the address, it's only a short cab ride away.

145

Meric takes Deniz dancing. It is one of those bars along what is affectionately known as Bar Street in Moda· and a place he frequented as a young college student so it has nostalgic appeal for him. He is, in his way, trying to have her get to know him, to see the many facets of his personality as well as the places that have significance in his life. And this, a step backward into his past, is part of that process. Besides, dancing was part of his courtship with her and so he knows she will enjoy it.

And Deniz does, of course, losing herself in the rhythm, the band's sets of an eclectic mix of both American and British rock of the 70s and 80s and Turkish rock of the 90s. It is music they both grew up listening to and so there is a myriad of emotions it conjures up for her as well. And they dance, dance, dance the night away.

"Dance has been everything to me," Katja says to her dancers. "It has kept me grounded in all my moments of despair. And," she sighs helplessly, "there have been too many of those. And it has given me a language in foreign lands when I had no common language other than dance. And it can give you all that same ability to communicate no matter wherever you go and whoever you are with."

And her dancers nod in agreement and begin to move through the steps she shows them to express the love inside the words of the play they will perform. And Katja feels her love flow outward as she guides them in her studio, inside her heart.

Michael puts his fork down, leans back in his chair, and lets out a deep breath. "God," he says, "that was delicious." Then he looks at İrem sitting opposite him, beaming with pride and yet something else there in that look she is giving him that makes his heart stop. And he finds himself reaching for the bottle of wine to pour himself another glassful, something, he realizes, he is doing with even more frequency now than before. And if he thought about that, which he is trying very hard not to, he could be worried.

"You know," İrem says, "I could teach you some of these recipes so that you could cook them yourself."

"I'm lousy in the kitchen," Michael says. "About all I can do is grill a hot dog or make scrambled eggs. That's why I ate out so much before you started cooking for me."

"But some of these recipes are pretty easy," she says. "I bet you could make some now after having watched me cook for so long."

"But why would I want to learn to cook when I have you around?" he says, and then suddenly gets a premonition that the conversation, and the night, might be taking a different course than he expected.

"Well I won't always be around," she says. "As a matter of fact, I'm seriously applying to grad schools in America next month."

"You decided?" he says, and feels something funny happening in what he believes to be the pit of his stomach.

"Yes," she says. "I'm ninety percent sure."

"Ah," he goes, and tries to think of something else to follow it but his mind is a blank.

"So I'll be needing your recommendation soon."

"Sure," he nods.

"Actually the Prep Director, Dave, has been very helpful. He knows some people at Columbia and NYU and Stony Brook University in the Fine Arts departments. And, as you know, I want to concentrate on schools in New York but will also apply to California, too."

He nods some more and thinks he must look like an idiot because he is beginning to feel like one. The world is changing, he thinks, and there's nothing he can do about it since he has no right to think it shouldn't change. He's had a good run these last few years, and now the run is soon to be over. And though he has a premonition of the gulf soon to appear in his life, in their relationship, he ignores as best he can the glimpse of the emptiness that awaits him. Then he says, "Well I know you'll get accepted. You're an excellent candidate."

"You think so?" she asks, looking directly into his eyes for the first time, he realizes, since she started this conversation.

"Yes," he says.

İrem continues to look at him for a long moment. There seems to be something she wants to say that keeps nagging at the corners of her mind but for some reason she cannot quite find the words to say it. Instead all she can think to say seems rather inadequate to her, but she says it anyway. "I worry about you, though," she says. "Who will look after you when I'm gone?"

"Oh, I'll manage," he says, trying to be flippant but feeling hollow inside instead. "After all, I got this far in one piece."

"I'll worry anyway," she says finally. "It's a habit I fell into knowing you."

"Well you can always call every now and then to check up on me," he says.

"Yes," and there's a seriousness to her tone that he doesn't quite recognize. "I will."

And they stare at each other for a very long moment before Michael breaks the spell by reaching for the bottle of wine again and pouring more into both their glasses. "To your future," he says, raising his glass.

And though she smiles and touches his glass, she doesn't verbally respond. And Michael, many hours later as dawn breaks outside his window, will still be wondering about that.

"I don't know what I'm doing," Brenda says. "All I know is I can't help myself."

"Well," Philip says, growing somewhat reflective, especially after three beers, "he seems nice enough. And he's unhappy in his marriage, you say."

"They don't sleep together anymore, or at least that's what he claims." Then she sees in her mind's eye the ferociousness with which he attacks lovemaking, the almost desperate appeal in his eyes, and finds she believes him. "Or if they do, there's no physical contact at all."

"But there had to be at some point," Philip says. "After all, there are three children involved."

"The last was a total accident, he says. A one night drunken attempt on his part to get the spark back. Apparently she just laid there. A sort of zombie, in fact."

"Well, some people find that appealing," Philip says smirking. "No one I know, though."

"Nor I."

"So what do you propose to do about all this?"

"Continue, I suppose," she sighs. "I just don't seem to have the will power to stop."

"Interesting," Philip says, looking at her appraisingly.

"And besides," she adds, "I think I really like him."

"Always a good thing when one is involved in a relationship."

"I'm not sure it qualifies as a relationship yet," Brenda says. "But it does have possibilities."

"This gets more interesting by the minute."

"You're enjoying this, aren't you?" she asks and can't help but smile.

"Immensely," he says. "I'm living my life vicariously through you at the moment."

"Don't you want to live your life on your own?"

"I don't have the energy any longer."

"That's sad," she says.

"No, just a phase, hopefully, I'm going through."

"That doesn't sound like any fun," she says. "Aren't you allowed a second act?"

"Oh, I've already had that," Philip says rather wearily. "A third act, too, I might add."

"My, but you've been busy."

"Of course, I'm always open for an encore at some later date, but, as of now, I'll just sit back, be your cheering section, and watch you get your second act."

"That's very kind of you."

"Yes, it is, isn't it?" and he smiles and raises his beer mug to toast her. "To reprisals," he says. "May they be long and satisfying."

And they touch glasses, and drink.

And finally that night to Murat who stands in the doorway of his bedroom and looks down upon the sleeping form of his wife and three children, all comfortably enclosed in the blankets and all somewhere deep into their own private dreamland. Sönmez looks content with their infant son in her arms, a smile of satisfaction on her lips, and surrounded by the other two girls. There is no place for him even if he wanted to join them, and that both saddens him and gives him a sense of justification for what he has been doing before coming home. He has, he reasons, been driven to infidelity, and here is the proof. And though the couch is not the best place to sleep for his back, it is preferable to lying on the edge of an already crowded bed.

So he backs up and goes out to the kitchen, takes the bottle of raki, a pitcher of water, and a handful of ice cubes out to the living room and mixes them all together in a tall, thin glass reserved for his drinking. And though he would rather be someplace else now, at least he finally knows where that someplace else is and who resides there. Now, if only he could find a way to get there.

But first, he takes a long sip from his glass, closes his eyes, and only sees Brenda spread out naked before him. He sighs. And then he drinks again.

And the year ends for the college staff at a restaurant in Fatih that sits on a hill overlooking the Bosporus rolling by. This party at first saves Meric the agony of choosing who to spend the evening with since both Jennifer and Deniz are there, but only complicates it further when he realizes he must dance equally with the two of them and so gets little opportunity to sit. And the women, both dressed to advantage and both blessed, as far as he is concerned, with boundless energy, keep him on the floor all night.

Philip, too, seems to be doing his version of some 80s pogo dancing while Brenda tries to keep up but finds her laughing gets in the way and Dave pulls İrem out to join in the horon that Bekir has requested be played.

And then to Michael who, though he doesn't smoke, feels he needs some night air to clear his head from all the alcohol he has consumed and to give his legs some rest from the dancing he always feels compelled to engage in whenever music and whiskey and women are all present in one place together on a beautiful night. So he wanders over to the far end of the patio, thus avoiding disrupting what appears to be a somewhat intimate conversation between two shadowy silhouettes on the other end, and gazes up at the sky, hoping to see stars. He sips the whiskey in the glass he's holding and almost doesn't see Katja standing in the shadows until he almost bumps into her. "Ah," he says, pulling himself up into what he hopes is an erect position, "taking the air?"

"Yes," she says.

"I would think you'd be out dancing," he says. "It is a night for it."

"You seemed to be doing enough for both of us," Katja says.

"Ah well," and he sighs, "I have been but these old feet need a bit of rest. They are, after all, not as young as my heart."

Katja smiles at him. "Still," she says, "they weren't doing too badly for old feet."

"There's some life in them yet," he concedes. "But yours are much younger than mine and trained for this kind of activity. So why aren't they out there with the rest of the faculty?"

"They will be," she says. "Soon. But first I thought a little night air would be refreshing."

"Yes," Michael nods. "My thoughts exactly."

And they stand together for a while, both gazing up at the sky, Michael sipping his whiskey and letting the taste soothe him and keep his mind from wondering just who İrem is dancing with now and Katja trying to not see Hasan in her mind's eye, but trying to concentrate on the stars above. And though they don't speak, they somehow find comfort in each other's company. Finally, though, Katja rubs her arms and looks at the patio door.

"I think it's time to go back in," she says. She starts for the door but when Michael doesn't follow, she turns back to him and asks, "Are you coming?"

"In a bit," he says.

And it's then she thinks she sees a sadness almost as deep as her own in his eyes. And though she almost asks, the two faculty members, who it turns out are Murat and Brenda, in the shadows emerge distracting her. There are nods, and Katja follows them back into the restaurant while Michael wanders off to some tables and sits on a chair staring out at the Bosporus below.

Back inside things are really heating up between Jennifer and Deniz who seem to both be aware that they are competing and find they are both aggressive, competitive animals. The dancing, then, takes on a fairly suggestive, erotic tone and other faculty members are drawn in: female members becoming bolder, male members becoming aroused. A controlled wildness seems to spread across the floor, the air charged with sexual energy, and husbands and wives, boyfriends and girlfriends, and unattached members of both genders begin competing with each other for the floor. And İrem sees the physical manifestation of Michael's theme for the play being acted out in front of her eyes and turns looking for him to see if he sees it, too. But he is, of course, nowhere to be found in the room and once she realizes this, confusion, then mild panic, takes over her.

Dave, meanwhile, draws Katja out onto the dance floor and she loses herself in the dance, forgetting about everything but the music, the gypsy flavored beat, her body taking on a life of its own, and Dave almost stands still watching. He thinks he would like to have this woman, though he knows it is almost an impossible wish, but cannot refrain from wishing it anyway.

And in the hundred or so people at the party, more than half are out dancing but Murat and Brenda only see each other. And Philip, surrounded by a few of the Prep Teachers, is pogoing away. Only İrem seems somewhat lost all of a sudden and walks the room looking for Michael. Then she spies the patio door and on a hunch, goes out to find him sitting on a chair gazing out to the Bosporus below. "There you are," she says.

"Ah," he goes. "I've been found out."

"Were you hiding?" she asks, trying for a playful tone to hide what she senses is real concern.

"Not really," he says. "I just needed some fresh air and to give these tired old feet a rest. And then, sitting here, I sort of got lost while watching the water roll by." He smiles at her, though thankfully, because of the dark, she does not see how melancholy that smile really is. "It's a fitting way to end the year, you know."

"Aren't you cold?" she asks.

"I hadn't noticed," he says, "until you brought it up, but yes, it is a bit cold out here."

"Then why don't you come back inside?"

"Hmmmm," and he stands, though a bit reluctantly. "Might as well," he says. "After all, I'm all out of whiskey here."

"Well you can't let that happen, can you?"

"Not on New Year's Eve."

And as they both head back in, they almost hold hands, or at least the impulse is there in each of them, but not knowing how the other would feel about it, they resist and just walk back side by side without touching until they come to the patio door where they bump into each other, and both over apologize. And as they enter, a feeling lingers in the air between them of a missed opportunity. And neither knows just how to handle, or even explain, that.

Meanwhile the rivalry between Jennifer and Deniz is taking on a new twist as the two women become more and more fascinated with each other and begin dancing around

154

Meric rather than dancing with him and find themselves dancing together and being fascinated with their own aura and sexuality. Meric tries for some control but is virtually ignored on the dance floor as the women focus on themselves.

And the midnight hour comes, there are bells to be rung, whistles to be blown, horns to blare, and much hugging, kissing, laughing, as the hundred or so people gathered there embrace the new year. And the music continues, the dancing resumes with Bekir taking the lead, and for another few hours the party rages on, but somewhere, in the noisy celebration, a pair slip out unnoticed by the rest, and Murat and Brenda disappear to her place to bring in their own new year. And as the crowd dwindles, Meric finds himself alone, the two women abandoning him to fade into the night, and Dave, being a gentleman with ulterior motives, escorts Katja home and settles for a polite kiss on the cheek, while Michael is led away by İrem and safely deposited in his bed where he slips off to dreamland still in his suit and İrem finds she hesitates slightly before easing herself out his door and down the steps to a waiting taxi in the street.

And finally we find Philip, with a toy horn in hand, doing what is for him a rather complicated dance step all the way home.

And the sun rises on this new day, just like any other, and lets the New Year in.

Scene 5
January

The sun on New Year's Day finds the world slightly changed for a few people and life seems to hold a different sort of promise this early in the year. Jennifer, for one, wakes to discover Deniz in bed with her, sleeping rather peacefully, her long, black hair spread out on the pillow, her mouth slightly open, her skin still glowing from the night before. Jennifer gazes at her in wonder, in awe, remembering how beautiful she looked on the dance floor, how attractive, alluring, she was, how she blotted out all thoughts of Meric, of any man, how giddy they both became, the cab ride here, their hands, fingers restlessly exploring, their tongues, the smoothness of their skin together, the knowledge each intuitively possessed of the other, the taste of champagne kisses, the dizziness, the intoxication, the endless pleasure they felt.

And so her hand lightly glides its way across her cheek, down her neck, Deniz's eyes opening, the smile as Jennifer's hand continues its journey down to where it now belongs, and Deniz's arms encircle her, pull her toward her on the bed, and there is a gasp, though neither knows just whose, since it belongs to them both, and the morning is even better than the night.

Brenda wakes to find Murat no longer in bed and she thinks that last night must have been a dream, and she closes her eyes against that thought, but they pop open again as she hears noises coming from outside the bedroom, water running somewhere, a man's voice humming a tune, and she rises, grabs her robe from the back of the door and makes her way to the kitchen to find Murat, standing naked at her counter, brewing coffee and slicing an onion. He turns to face her then, smiles, and says, "How's an omelet sound?"

And Brenda can't believe how good the thought of an omelet in the morning is to her right now. And she laughs, brushes up against him, her robe opening, and says, "Later," and her lips touch his. "Much later, dear."

Michael wakes with a dry mouth in a rumpled suit and sighs. The cat, which has been sleeping rather peacefully in his socks drawer, looks up at him and yawns. "Right," Michael says. He then sits up in what could only be called a slumped position and begins shedding his clothes. Once free of all the garments, he lies back down on the bed and waits patiently for either energy or death, whichever comes first. Neither arrives, just the cat, which curls up next to him, begins licking his forearm in some sort of grooming ritual, and then sighs, rests its head on his arm, and falls back asleep.

Great, Michael thinks. Just great. And he closes his eyes, lets out a deep breath, and falls back into fitful sleep.

Dave sits in jockey shorts, tube socks, and an old t-shirt at his desk writing an email to a former girlfriend back in New York. It is a sort of New Year's greeting, but it doesn't seem to come out right no matter how he phrases it. He squints as he reads it, takes a sip of his morning coffee, and winces when he realizes it's cold. He gets up, ambles out to the kitchen and reheats the coffee in the microwave. Then he sips it again. But the coffee, hot or cold, does not provide any inspiration.

Jesus, he thinks. Life was much simpler when he was younger. Or maybe it just appeared so.

İrem has not slept well and now, in the morning light, stares at the clock waiting for an appropriate hour to strike so she can call Michael. She doesn't know exactly why she is so concerned, except that she sensed something different in his drinking last night that she hadn't noticed before, an abandon that has not been evident to her until now, and it has begun to worry her. She cannot help but feel protective of him and yet logically she knows this does not make sense. And now, with her applications to universities in America almost complete, she can't help but wonder what will happen when she eventually leaves. And so, with these conflicting thoughts running through her head, she picks up her cell phone and calls him.

"Hi," she says when he answers. "Happy New Year."

"Is it?" he asks. "Already?"

"Since midnight last night."

"And didn't you wish me that then, too?"

"I did."

"I thought so," he says and sighs. "For a minute there I was afraid I was having a senior moment."

"You're not so senior," she says.

"No?"

"At least not when you're dancing."

"Ah yes," and he sighs. "Dancing. That explains the aching in my feet."

"Are you ready for the first breakfast of the New Year?"

"You mean like now?"

"Yes," she says. "Unless you have other plans."

"No," he answers. "No other plans."

"Then how about in 30 minutes."

"Make it an hour. I'll need at least that long in the shower to feel alive again."

And as İrem hangs up, she can't help but wonder why she's doing this.

Katja's dream: she wakes in the morning, sunlight filtering through the lace curtains in the bedroom, the aroma of freshly brewed coffee, strong and black, freshly baked bread, and eggs frying in butter, caressing her nose. She rises, her nightgown falling to her knees as she stands barefoot in the bedroom, then walks quietly, her bare feet making no sound, out to the kitchen where the eggs are frying in a skillet on the stove, the bread, still warm, lies sliced on the table, coffee is in two mugs, the steam still rising in the air. There are apricot preserves in a small dish next to the bread and a bowl with deep, dark honey, sliced tomatoes, Kalamata olives in an opened jar, and Hasan's scent in the air, lingering by the stove, as if he were just there but has stepped out momentarily, behind a door, perhaps, in the cupboard, lying in an opened drawer, under the table, leaning back in a chair, smiling at her. He is here, he is here, she knows, but just out of sight, lurking in a corner, playing some game with her, waiting to step out and spread his arms open to receive her, just behind the door, around the corner in the living room, under the stairs, by the opened window, next to the lamp. He is here, he is here, she knows, if only she can find him, can see him, can be held once again in his arms. Here. In this empty house. In her empty heart.

Philip sits at a café sopping up the last remnants of an omelet with his bread and sipping his morning cay. He thinks he really needs to go home but for some reason doesn't want to. At least not yet. He has been out all night and all morning and though he thinks he really should get some sleep, he isn't really tired. Not in the sense anyway where sleep is needed. Instead he thinks there is too much to see yet on this first day of the New Year. To feel, to embrace, an epiphany is waiting just around the corner for him to experience, to blunder into and to somehow be changed. Into what, or who, he isn't quite sure, but he knows it is out there waiting for him and if he can just keep wandering around this day, the first day of transformations and resolutions fulfilled, it will find him, a man on the prowl.

Meric calls but no one answers, the phone ringing in some room somewhere he is no longer able to go. He cannot quite comprehend what has happened. How did he, who not so very long ago had two lovers, end up now with none? He keeps replaying New Year's Eve in his head and it mystifies him every time. What did he do wrong? What should he have done right? How did he end up going home to an empty bed? And, most importantly, what should he do now? He lies in bed staring at the ceiling but there are no answers staring back.

Jennifer and Deniz lie in bed in each other's arms so intertwined as to be one body, not two. Neither has ever felt so complete as they feel now, and so much at ease. They have both heard the expression, like all women, of finding your better half, but this is something different, something else, it is like finding yourself in someone else, of not another half or even a twin, but staring into your own eyes, of touching your own body, of seeing yourself in yourself anew. And they cannot get enough of this revelation.

And slowly they turn to each other, instinctively sensing what the other is feeling, and lose themselves in themselves once again.

Brenda rolls over in bed and watches Murat slowly get dressed. She has begun missing him as soon as he said he had to go and watching him like this is painful but she cannot take her eyes off him as long as he is in the same room. He senses her eyes and stops buttoning his shirt as he turns to return her gaze. They stand frozen in time for a very long moment, then he says, "I really have to go."

"I know," she says.

"I don't want to."

"I know that, too."

"But I promise I'll be back tomorrow."

"Yes," she says. "I know."

And they stare at each other again, the pain of separation almost unbearable in each pair of eyes, until she raises the sheet at the edge of the bed and he unbuttons his shirt, unbuckles his belt, climbs back inside the bed, her, and they both lose sight of the world outside once again.

İrem brings over eggs and tomatoes, some fresh mozzarella cheese, green peppers, and suçuk she bought earlier in a market in Kadiköy. Though she is one of those Muslims that does not adhere strictly to all the rules of her religion which makes it easier to deal with Michael who follows no rules of any religion and is, quite possibly as far as she can tell, a true agnostic, she does draw the line at his preference for ham, or any pork products for that matter. But to accommodate his taste buds, she adds the mozzarella to make her own version of menemem according to tastes they both share. He, of course, watches her while drinking coffee laced with Bailey's Irish Cream, a bottle of which he found on a shelf in Rind, his favorite liquor store in Moda. It is, for him, a perfect morning, and she tries her best to ignore the laced coffee and concentrates on cooking.

After they eat, they settle in the living room and Michael plays disc jockey, shuffling through the hundreds of CDs he owns to play music he feels is appropriate to bring in a new year. That includes *"Start Me Up"* by The Rolling Stones, *"Top Hat, White Tie, And Tails"* by Louis Armstrong, *"My Way"* by Frank Sinatra, and, in a nod to her, a cut from the Chris Rea CD she bought him called *"Let's Dance"*, which he does, pulling her up onto her feet and twirling her around his living room. She is not sure what the proper response to this should be but she has to admit to herself that he does make her laugh. And it is in this way he manages to avoid thinking about the dreaded topic of her leaving. Instead they eventually talk about the play and as İrem shares her insights from watching the dancers on New Year's Eve, Michael can't help but wonder what he will do when he finally does lose her.

Bekir goes over the plans for the end of the school year celebration that includes a film festival of student-produced films from the Film Program and the musical of *Romeo and Juliet* from the Theatre Department. There will also be their first graduation ceremony since the university was founded. This is the all-important year for that reason and he needs to make sure it is a total success if he wants to ensure his contract will be renewed for another two year period. So he begins meeting with his department heads and anticipating the end of semester projects from all the departments.

The meeting with Michael goes smoothly for the two end of semester productions will be presentations of scenes the students are working on in their acting classes. So the conversation doesn't dwell on them but on the year-end production of *Romeo and Juliet.*

"I'm very happy with the concept," Michael says. "Of course, it's still just a work on paper, and won't be a tragedy but Philip has to really start fashioning the text with his student writers, and Katja has some great ideas for the dances and we'll be borrowing music from different genres so it'll be an exciting show."

"It won't be a tragedy?" Bekir asks.

"No," Michael says. "I want it to have a more positive message about accepting differences in culture, language. The lovers here will represent a bringing together of people rather than being victimized by the feuding."

"And the actors?" Bekir asks.

"Well we'll hold auditions naturally, but I have some ideas already since I've worked with many of these students for three years now and have sat in on some of Meric's classes so I have a feel for those students, too."

"Even in Turkish?" Bekir says, smiling slightly.

"I can judge the talent even if I don't know what they're saying," Michael says. "Living in California trains you that way."

Bekir laughs. And he thinks the programs are now beginning to mesh in ways he had not originally anticipated, but in ways that will make the college even more attractive to future students. And his smile lasts the entire day and into the night and once home, his wife finds him dancing in the living room to an old Black Sea song.

Katja stays late at school in the dance studio working on a new concept for a solo lover's dance. It is part ballet, part modern dance, all twisted, contorted yearning and after an hour or so of strenuous working and reworking of the movement, she huddles in a corner of the studio shivering. There is so much she has left of herself on the dance floor, so much longing in every part of her body, that she begins to weep.

Deniz is at home in her studio, winter's light filtering down from the skylight, a slight chill in the air, but her body hot, her passion flowing through every muscle as her hand clutching her brush slashes through the air attacking the canvas with such energy that colors explode, collide, mesh with each other in such a way as to startle and excite her.

Brenda squirms in her chair as Murat's hand glides along the inside of her thigh as they sit side by side reviewing the list of musical themes for the proposed film projects submitted by the senior class students. He pretends to be engrossed in the selection but his mind is totally focused on where his hand is and what it is doing there, and he takes extreme satisfaction in hearing her sharp intakes of breath as his hand probes and strokes and wonders if he could separate himself long enough to risk rising and locking his door to take her there on his desk.

İrem sits next to Michael on his couch in his living room hunched over the coffee table mapping out the schedule for the semester end presentations together. It is their ritual: Saturday afternoons spent working on the theatre programs, she taking over his kitchen and cooking dinner for both of them in the evening, and afterwards watching a DVD together while he exposes her to the many films she knows absolutely nothing about, then just listening to music and talking about nothing and everything as the night slowly evaporates and they enter what Michael refers to as The Frank Sinatra Hours. It is her favorite day/evening of the week and she wishes it never ends.

Tonight they watch John Ford's *The Quiet Man* and afterwards she slices some oranges and apples, lays some hazelnuts and pistachios in a dish, and he opens a bottle of wine and pours them each a glass. He settles back in an armchair while she sits opposite him on the couch. Miles Davis' trumpet floats through the air and the night steadily closes around them.

And Michael finds he does not hunger for whiskey during those nights, is just satisfied with wine, sharing the films, the music, the conversation, and looking into her open face, the tilt of her head, those deep, dark eyes, and watching the cat snuggle up to her on the couch, rest its head against her thigh, and purr itself to sleep. And though he does not want to think it, he envies the cat. And he, too, wishes the night would never end.

Philip sits in the bar listening to the conversations around him, not understanding the words but enjoying the sound nonetheless. He doesn't feel a need to speak himself, just sips his beer, watches people at the surrounding tables, and feels blissfully at peace. There is a heated argument at one table between two fairly drunk men, both with scruffy beards and shaggy hair, as if auditioning for a movie about disaffected youth from the late 60s, another low-key seduction at a table in the corner between two slightly older customers who are much better dressed, a group of six mixed couples of friends having a very animated talk about something one of them said earlier which has produced quite a bit of laughter from the others, and one other lone customer sitting at a table near the entrance who keeps looking at his watch every half minute or so, obviously waiting for someone or wanting to appear waiting for someone, but who does not make eye contact with any of the others.

And, of course, there is Philip, alone, aloof, seemingly disinterested but keenly aware of everything around him. Enjoying himself immensely as he writes his Istanbul book in his head.

Dave cleans and cleans again the apartment throughout the night in anticipation of İrem's visit the next day. He had hoped for a Saturday night dinner with her but is content to settle for a Sunday lunch. Any meal, he thinks, is a good sign and it is good signs he is looking for. And he thinks that after this month he will have to begin sharing her with other people: her actors, Michael, Philip, all the pressures of a play that will soon go into rehearsals in April, but more group planning will be necessary in February when they come back from their break, and so he must take advantage of the time left to him for her undivided attention. And weekend dinners, lunches, meetings of any sort are all he has open to him to make any headway into her heart. And into her heart is where he very much wants to go.

Jennifer watches Deniz sketch her portrait in charcoal on her drawing pad and can't help but laugh. "How do you do that?" she asks. "I always wanted to learn."

"It's easy," Deniz says, and then begins teaching her about perspective. Then she grins. "I have so many things to teach you."

"Can you teach me to paint?"

"You want to learn?"

"Yes," Jennifer says. "I want to paint like you."

"Then you must turn off your brain, open your heart, and let the brush speak for you."

"That's the trick?" Jennifer asks.

"That is not a trick," Deniz says. "It is a way of life." Then her smile turns both seductive and serious. "Do you want to learn it now?"

And Jennifer begins to understand. "Yes," she breathes. "I want to embrace it."

And Deniz opens her arms to receive her.

Dave opens the bottle of wine and pours them each a glass. "I really shouldn't drink too much," İrem says. "I have work to do tonight yet."

"On the play?" Dave asks.

"Yes," she says. "Michael and I are beginning to work with Philip on the chronology of the scenes."

"Aren't you following the play's scenes?"

"Not exactly," and she laughs. "Michael has his own ideas of how the story should go and he is only in partial agreement with Shakespeare. You know he plans a happy ending, don't you?"

"Yes," he smiles. "I've heard the rumors."

And then İrem begins to explain in further detail about Michael's concept while Dave finds a tinge of jealousy creeping into his heart. "You work very closely with him, don't you?"

"Yes," she says. "For the last four years. The first year it was just the department chairs and some hand-picked faculty and support staff laying the groundwork for the university and for some reason, after our initial interview, he accepted me as his assistant. He sensed that I had the ability and, though at times I didn't think I was capable of administrative work, his faith in me never wavered."

Dave almost asks what other things Michael feels about her but then hesitates, realizing he must move slowly here, she is attached to him in ways he doesn't quite understand, nor does he think she does. He watches as she brushes back a few strands of hair from her face and looks somewhat wistfully toward the window. He can't help but admire that face, the clean lines of her cheekbones, the softness in her eyes that can turn introspective as they seem to be doing now, the highlights in her hair, her swanlike neck. He realizes that waking each morning to that face would be infinitely better than what he wakes to now, an empty pillow, a futile struggle to rise from an empty bed and face another cold dawn. But he also realizes that he is entering the last six months of his stay here and just what are the realities of entering into a relationship with her here and now. Would it not be better to continue to lay the groundwork for a possible seduction of İrem in America? And just what does he want anyway? Just what are his intentions?

And as he stares at that face turned absently toward his window, he thinks that he, too, should not drink so much this afternoon.

Drinking is something Michael has been doing on and off for several decades now and even though he at times, though somewhat less frequently now than in past years, has thought he should really stop, he never seems to. It is like breathing for him. Something he does without thinking, which is a blessing, really, because if he thought about it, he might be forced to contemplate change. But now, as he stares at his computer screen while trying to write a recommendation for İrem, he thinks he is sliding into patterns he really should try to avoid. And though he knows it is all tied into his latent feelings about her, he thinks he must somehow get beyond them.

He must now write her recommendation. He has dreaded this moment and now it is here and though he wants the best for her, knows there is nothing possible between them, he still had harbored a desire to have her stay longer, to be with him still, to prolong the contentment he feels whenever she is in the same room, the same school, the same city. Pure selfishness, he knows. And as he begins to write a glowing letter of recommendation for her to attach to her online applications, he feels something drain out of him, and realizes it is the blood in his heart. And though there is a glass of whiskey sitting right next to his computer screen and in easy reach of his somewhat shaking hand, he knows it is a poor substitute for blood. But it is a substitute nevertheless.

Murat thinks that his relationship with Brenda is the first time in a very long time that he has felt he has a relationship with anyone again. What he has with Sönmez is a poor substitute for what he needs, what he desires. And only with Brenda does he feel alive and satisfied. And as he watches her dress, fastening her bra, rolling up her panty hose, slipping on a dress, his heart breaks.

Philip stares at the words on paper and, though he does not quite think he has the tone exactly right, he does think he has found patterns of speech he can use for the lovers that will play to young audiences anywhere. And he finds, as he always does, that he is attracted to these characters, that they breathe for him, are becoming real for him, are not just Shakespeare's but his, too, now in an intimate way. And that is the wonder of it all, he thinks. The wonder that characters created over 400 years ago can still speak to people today, can still respond to changes imposed upon them by time, by circumstance, by a new hand tinkering with their particulars without really changing their essence. A miracle, he thinks. Not in any supernatural sense, but in the quality of the writing, and in his ever respectful, always obliging hands.

And he pushes the pad away from him on his desk, closes his eyes, and smiles.

Meric comes into Michael's office and sits down, his smile waning somewhat, but trying to keep that smile on his face nonetheless. "You have a minute?" he asks, then shakes his head slightly and adds, "Not a minute, really. More like 10 or 15."

Michael looks up from the mess on his desk, the pile of production notes he has been trying to organize amid all the other copies of attendance reports, grade sheets, and supply requests. "Sure," he says. "What's up?"

"I need to talk to you," Meric says. "Get some advice." Then he looks over at İrem's desk and adds, "Alone."

Michael senses an almost desperate tone in his voice and a wildness about his eyes that troubles him. He shifts in his chair and says, "She won't be back for another hour. She's teaching now. But, if you want more privacy, why don't we meet later after classes when no one is around?"

"Yes," Meric nods. "Later. That's better." And he stands as if to go but hesitates, as if rooted to the spot. "Thanks," he says. "Thanks a lot." And then he tears himself away and is gone. Michael looks at the empty doorway and becomes lost in thought,

For some reason she cannot quite identify, İrem feels somewhat disoriented when Michael tells her he is staying late to confer with a colleague. She doesn't know why that should unsettle her but it does somehow, and though she knows she cannot expect to be a part of all aspects of his life, she does feel she should not be excluded, either. And so it is with this illogical feeling of rejection still hovering over her, that she accepts an invitation to dinner from Dave, who is ever ready to capitalize on her availability.

Dinner is at a restaurant Dave has discovered through guidebooks of Istanbul that is known for its candlelight settings and cozy, private tables. And though it is perhaps a little too romantic a setting than he had intended, he does not regret the choice but decides to subtly use it to his advantage. İrem, though, is totally oblivious to its charms. Her mind is still on Michael and she finds she must make an effort to channel its direction anywhere else.

"So," he says, after the waiter pours the first glass of wine into each of their glasses, "are you excited about the prospect of studying in the States?"

"I would be, I suppose," İrem says, "if I hadn't already studied there. But I do admit there are things that excite me about both New York and California."

"New York's a great city culturally," Dave says, deciding to focus on the coast he lives on. "You'll have lots to see and do outside of your studies and all relating to theatre and the arts."

"Yes," she says. "I know."

172

"Do you know many people there?" he asks, almost casually, a little too casually, but she doesn't seem to notice.

"No, but I'm sure there will be other people in the program I'll become friendly with."

"Of course," he says. "Some of my closest friends are still my university friends." Then he picks at the bulgar on his plate and slices a piece of the chicken sis before carefully, almost daintily putting it in his mouth. After chewing and then swallowing, he says, "I'll be back in New York myself and if you need anyone to help you get settled in any way, you can always call."

"Thanks," she says. "I may do that."

"Please do," he says, then adds almost innocently, "And if you need a place to stay while looking for an apartment of your own, I have a guest bedroom at my house you're welcome to use."

"That's very kind of you," she says, "but Columbia has housing available for grad students, and I have already requested a room from them."

"That would be more convenient," he says. "Anyway, I can always pick you up at the airport when you arrive. I know it's better to have a friendly face meeting you rather than coming alone to a new city."

İrem looks at him closely, and then says, "Thanks again. You are being most kind."

"Think nothing of it," he says as his gaze returns to his plate. "I'm just returning the Turkish hospitality I received here."

And they both continue eating.

Murat stares at the food on his plate but can't seem to work up any appetite. He watches his oldest daughter play with her food and almost envies her. She is at least involved in some way with her meal while he cannot even look at his.

173

But it isn't the food, he realizes, but the table he is sitting at, the room he is sitting in, the people that surround him. And yet these children are his own flesh and blood, the woman sitting opposite him is his wife of twelve years, the only woman in his life for over twenty. His entire adult life is connected to hers in ways he cannot possibly untangle, and yet he feels no emotional connection at all. What he feels, he is almost ashamed to admit, is much darker, even slightly malicious. He wishes it weren't so, but it is, and he is too tired and obsessed with someone else to deny it. For all he can think about, all he desires, is to sit at another table, in another room, with another woman, the woman he is falling hopelessly in love with: Brenda.

"I don't know where to begin," Meric says as he shifts uneasily in his seat outside on the patio opposite Michael at The Belfast in Moda.

"The beginning's always a good place," Michael says.

"It's just all becoming jumbled up in my head."

"Well," and Michael sighs, "drinking probably won't help to unjumble it but it'll probably make listening to it easier."

"I just need to tell someone," Meric says, and his eyes have a lost, almost childlike quality to them. "I think in the telling I might be able to understand this better myself."

"That could work," Michael says and then smiles as Osman brings over his glass of whiskey and a beer for Meric. "You don't know how badly this is needed right now."

"That's pretty much what everyone says who sits here," Osman says.

"Yes," Michael nods. "It would be."

Meric looks over at Michael's glass of whiskey and says, "What are you drinking?"

"Irish whiskey," Michael says. "What else could be more appropriate at a bar called The Belfast?"

"Does it taste like scotch?"

"Better," Michael says. "Or at least in my opinion. And besides, it was the Irish that invented this stuff so you must honor that memory as best you can."

"Can I try it?" Meric asks.

Michael waves his hand magnanimously through the air and watches as Meric sips his drink.

"That's good," Meric says.

"Have I ever steered you wrong?" Michael asks.

"Maybe I should drink one of those myself."

"It gives more lucidity than beer, which, in my mind, has always added a sort of fog on the evening."

"I'm all for lucidity tonight," Meric says.

"Then it's the Irish for you, too," and he signals Osman to bring one for Meric as well. "And some water, too," Michael says. Then he adds to Meric, "You don't want to dehydrate. It leaves a nasty hangover otherwise."

"I feel like a walking hangover every day," Meric says gloomily. "At least ever since New Year's."

"Has this anything to do with resolutions?" Michael asks. "Because if it has, I'm moving to another table."

"It's women," Meric says. "They're messing with my brain."

"Oh," Michael sighs. "That." Then he takes a long sip of his whiskey and says, "Perhaps we should ask for the bottle the way they do in all those Westerns."

"What Westerns?" Meric asks.

"Or Humphrey Bogart movies," Michael muses. "They always leave the bottle for him."

Meric looks at him a bit quizzically, then decides it's some kind of cultural difference and goes back to his preoccupation with women. "I just don't know what to make of it all."

"Join the club," Michael says. "It's an open membership."

"It's just that I thought I had it all under control," Meric says. "But then I realized I was totally lost. I mean, one day I have two women and then the next day I have none. But they have each other." And he looks at Michael at that point and asks, "Does that sound right to you?"

Michael squints a little and then asks, "Come again?"

And Meric begins his story, leaving nothing out but getting the timeline a little blurred. However, by the third whiskey, it doesn't seem blurred to either one of them. And Michael lets out a long sigh as he picks up the fourth drink Osman has laid before him and thinks he knows so little of the people who are around him but wonders if that isn't a good thing after all.

"What do you think I ought to do?" Meric asks.

"I don't know," Michael sighs again. "This seems a little beyond me. I mean, I've always had trouble when I was involved with just one woman, but two, well I wouldn't have been able to handle that, what with the different birthdays, all those names to remember of their friends, family, it would have been too much for me. And this lesbian thing, it's not something I have much experience with. I mean, of course I know gay people, lesbians, in the theatre, especially when I was acting, they were everywhere, and I have friends, of course, who are gay, but I was never involved with anyone of that persuasion, or at least I don't think I was, so this is really not something I can relate to." He looks at his whiskey and contemplates the color, the simplicity of it, and then lifts it to his mouth and drains the glass, looks over for Osman to signal for a refill, then back to Meric, and sighs again. "Not much help, am I?"

"I guess I didn't really expect any help," Meric says. "I just wanted to tell someone. It was like this constant pressure in my head."

"And is it gone now?" Michael asks.

"I think so," Meric says. "But it could be the whiskey makes it feel gone." Then he shrugs and sighs himself. "I guess I won't know until tomorrow."

"Ah yes," Michael says and looks off somewhere to where the street would be, just outside the thick plastic covering the outside to keep the heat generated by the portable heaters inside. "Tomorrow," he mutters. "There's always that."

And they both silently drink whatever is placed before them and try not to think of anything else.

Of course the semester end projects are something to think about, as well as the exams, the attendance reports, all the necessary grading, but for the performance grades, something all the students are required to do in some capacity, whether it be an actual performance or technical support, that is in full swing and occupying all the minds of our principals.

Brenda has scheduled two evenings of short films, mostly music videos and commercials, of the third and fourth year students, as well as ongoing exhibits of student photography, Murat has his recitals, and Michael and İrem have two evenings of the acting and directing classes performing scenes as their final projects. There are also exhibits of sketches of scene designs, costumes, and a Sunday afternoon of cabaret performances. Overall, two weekends filled with activity and a festive mood prevails.

"What do you think about doing something special for Valentine's Day?" İrem asks while marinating chicken in Michael's kitchen.

"Come again?" Michael says, not quite sure he has heard right, and if he did, if it means what he thinks it means, what he hopes and also fears it could mean. And if it does, he thinks he'll need more than what's in his glass to answer.

"At school," she says, looking up from the chicken with a bottle of soy sauce held tantalizingly over the poultry. "In the spring semester."

"Do something at school?" he asks, still slightly bewildered but realizing it is not what he thought at first and is thus both disappointed and relieved. "In the spring?"

"Yes," she says. "Like a cabaret performance."

"Cabaret?" Michael parrots.

"Yes," İrem says. "I've been talking with Pelin who performs in clubs with a trio of musicians from the Music Department at school and well, I thought it might be a good idea for them to create a show specifically for Valentine's Day which will be a kind of preview of our show based on **Romeo and Juliet**." Her head tilts, her eyes hold his, and she says, "What do you think?"

"Well," he says, "it's a thought."

"And maybe we could even use them in the show, like the dancers. You know, commenting on and complementing the action."

Michael looks at her for a long moment and then slowly begins to nod. "You know," he says, "that's a really terrific idea."

"You think so?"

"Yes," he says, and then leans back against the wall and sighs. "But we'll have to have some input into the songs they

178

sing," he says, "because we'll want to use most of them in the show."

"I already have some ideas as to where they'll go," she says.

"You do, huh?"

"I've been giving it a lot of thought."

And as he listens to her start to describe the song placements, he begins to wonder just how he'll survive once she is gone.

And Michael looks at İrem and wonders just what he is doing in this world. For the world is tilting, and he has no handle to grip, no toehold, no wall to lean against as things start sliding off the edge and he watches Dave whispering something in her ear and there is a smile on her lips, her eyes are partially closed, and Dave's arm is around her shoulder, his hand resting with such authority on her bare skin, and Michael's breath seems lost, it has gone somewhere on its own and he starts to gasp, his mouth open, groping for oxygen like some crippled beast in the forest, thrashing alone in a pile of leaves, his fingers clawing at the sheets as his eyes pop open, his body twists and turns, a dream, a dream, only a dream, but oh so real, the pain, the hurt, the confusion, oh so very, very real. And Michael stands, still somewhat shakily on his feet, and finds his way somehow to the kitchen, to a glass, the bottle of whiskey on the counter, and a drink, to steady his nerves, to calm his beating, aching heart.

Meric finds himself wandering around Bar Street in Moda, drifting into one bar after another, having a drink, listening to the music, trying to keep himself distracted from the thoughts that constantly prey on his mind, looking at women with such hunger in his eyes that it scares them. And the confusion, the desperation, drives him on.

179

And in another part of the city, the two women, Deniz and Jennifer, sleep in each other's arms, dreaming no dreams for nothing in sleep could be as good as it is when they are wide awake.

Brenda meanwhile stands in the hallway brushing her hand across the suede of Murat's coat, breathing in the scent of his cologne on his wool scarf, and draping it over the coat on its hanger before putting them both in her closet, closing the door, and slowly walking toward the bedroom where he will join her as soon as he finishes opening the bottle of wine he brought. And the night, the night has just begun for the two of them, here in the one place they both feel at home.

Dave sits at his computer writing emails to people back in America. Earlier he had updated a photo album on Facebook about his Turkish experience adding pictures of the students in the Prep Program and the teachers, too, but looking at some of the comments made from friends back in the States made him quite melancholy and a bit homesick. So he finds himself writing long letters waxing sentimentally about the past and New York in particular, and even finding he misses the snow. This his friends will find strange since he has only complained about snow his entire adult life but now, so far away from all that is familiar, he even misses shoveling his driveway. And if he took a few seconds to think about it, he would realize just how absurd that is. But he is too lost in this longing for the familiar to stop to analyze any emotions or thoughts he might be having. He just keeps imagining the world he left behind and begins, in his head, a countdown to his eventual return.

Katja's mind is on Hasan. It seems to be always on Hasan, in one way or another, whether he is first and foremost in her thoughts or lurking just below the surface, ready to appear when some trivial thing sets off a chain

180

reaction of associations that brings him back to life. She thinks she needs to be free of him, to move on toward something else since all the wishes in the world will not, cannot bring him back, for wishes are such useless things, but breaking free of his memory is still so hard to do, for she lives here in his country, in the city he brought her to, at the college where they had worked together, in the apartment they had picked out, amid the furniture, the prints on the walls, the pots and pans in the kitchen, that they had purchased, sat in, gazed at, cooked in. And the bed, the bed is where she lay held in his arms, his scent still clinging to the sheets, the pillows, that scent overwhelming her still.

And as she moves listlessly through the apartment, she knows she cannot be free of his memory for she still clings to it, will not let it go.

Philip wanders through the city at night without any definite plan as to where he goes or what he sees but aimlessly roams the streets open to whatever lies around a corner, down a narrow, cobblestoned street. He isn't looking for anything so much as he is open to letting something find him. And though his life is not unfulfilled at present, he finds he wouldn't mind a bit more diversion if he is lucky enough to stumble upon it.

And finally to İrem who is vacillating by the phone wondering if she should call Michael. The semester is over, the grades are in, and it is only Friday night, not Saturday, and so there is no reason to call, just this nagging feeling that she should. For she would like to see him, to cook him dinner, drink some wine, sit in the living room and talk about nothing, about everything, and know everything is all right, just the same, even though she knows it is changing and there doesn't seem to be anything she can do about it for she is the one who has changed it. The ball is moving down the court and she can really do nothing more than follow the ball wherever it might lead.

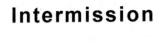

Intermission

The intersession finds Philip off to Sinop on the Black Sea. He is visiting friends and thus gets a guided tour of sorts along the decaying walls and along the beach, listening to tales of Temel, the perennial Black Sea character whose misadventures constitute folk wisdom here. Later, as evening descends, they sit in a seaside restaurant next to a large plate glass window overlooking the sea, and eat grilled fish and çoban salad. He feels at peace here and entertains the thought of teaching in a community like this, away from the distractions of the city, where he could concentrate on his writing. A different sort of life, he thinks. Almost like retirement. And wouldn't that be nice, he thinks, if he could actually afford to do that.

İrem is watching her mother cook Albanian liver and can't help asking how she gets it so tender. "It's because I don't wash the liver before cooking. You mustn't wash it, you know. But if you do, then you must make sure it is dry before you cook it. That's very important."

İrem nods, thinks maybe she should take notes, then decides not to. She can remember this and file it away along with all the other recipes she has stored for use in the future.

"I don't know why you're learning more recipes if you're going to go to America," her mother says while wiping her hands on a towel. "Who will you cook for there?"

"Oh," İrem says, wistfully, "maybe I'll meet someone to cook for."

"If only that were true," her mother sighs. "I wish for that every day."

"Every day?" İrem says.

"Yes," her mother says. "It's what every mother wishes for, you know. We all want to see our children happily married." Then she looks at her daughter and says, "And you're not getting any younger, you know. You are 32."

"Too old to get married?" İrem says, though not seriously thinking that.

"Well you are less desirable as you age," her mother says. "This is a known fact."

"I don't know that."

"And you don't even have a boyfriend," her mother continues, ignoring her. "No one really to cook for."

"I cook for Michael," İrem says.

"He is not a boyfriend," her mother says. "He is just your boss."

"My friend," İrem corrects her.

"Boss, friend, what difference does it make? He is still not your boyfriend." And her mother sighs dramatically. "I just wish you'd meet someone. And how will you do that going back to America to school?"

And İrem, though she doesn't agree with her mother's assessment of her situation, begins wondering about the answers to those questions herself.

Michael stares at the wall in front of him instead of at his notes on the desk. The wall seems easier to deal with since there are just two maps hanging there to bring back memories of the past: his New York City Subway Map and his map of the LA Freeway System. He often, when his mind tends to wander, stares at one or both of these maps and travels along familiar paths. He fluctuates between which city he'd rather be in but, then again, he often fluctuates between which country he'd rather be in. Usually it's Turkey but occasionally he gets homesick sort of for New York, especially the theatre and seeing foreign films with English subtitles on bigger screens than his TV at home, and jazz clubs. With LA, it's the weather and eating homemade potato chips on the Santa Monica Pier, that is if they still make them there. It's been so long since he was in LA that the LA he remembers is the one from the 70s and 80s when he was eking out a living as an actor and teaching theatre history part-time at a community college. There were years later farther north: other colleges, other shows, faces, names, women loved, lost, addresses scratched out in books. Somehow, though, they run together in a tie dye mosaic while the early years are etched far deeper in his mind.

The good old days, he thinks. Or at least the old days. His youth, his first love, his passion, the madness of dancing on the beach at night with his actress wife, who was moonlighting as a topless dancer in a strip club, wearing a G-string and bikini top to Steely Dan's Black Cow, drinking bourbon from the bottle and wishing the fear he felt that it would all somehow end in the morning would go away. But it never did go away, and his ex-wife, the life, the beach, even the bourbon, all recede in his mind.

Michael sighs in his office, an old man with fading memories, and a hunger to taste salt sea wind in his open mouth again.

Brenda sits in her mother's flat listening to her go on about how she shouldn't be so hasty in divorcing Mark. "He's a good catch," she says. "A good position at university, well respected in his field, a real gentleman." Then she adds, "And he still asks about you."

Brenda would like to reply but all she can think about is how cold and wet it is in London and how much milder the weather is in Istanbul. She also can't help but think of Murat, too, and knows, of course, that is what she really misses, not

186

the weather. And the sigh that escapes from her is misinterpreted by her mother who thinks it is for Mark. But Brenda's mind is in another time zone in a city divided between two continents, just like her heart.

Murat meanwhile sits on the opposite side of the school building from Michael staring at his own wall and trying to erase memories from his mind. He can't help but wish he could somehow start over. Go back to those university days when life was full of possibilities and he was not tied down by all his responsibilities. What if he had met Brenda then? he thinks. What if he had gone to England to study and met her there? A whole new life unfolds before him in his imagination, ignoring the fact that there is a 12-year gap between them and she would have been in grade school when he was in college. But imaginations don't need to pay strict attention to reality and so he loses himself in his fantasy and begins to construct instead an alternate reality that will one day become a scenario not just in his head but on paper. A life for him to live vicariously through music to a film he will see in his head. And this thought frees him from himself. And he smiles alone in his office watching his movie in his mind.

Fersat still cannot believe he is living the life he is in. Every morning he wakes up to a text message from Meltem which begins their constant messaging all day long. Most days he sees her but even when he doesn't, they are in constant communication via texting, WhatsApp, and Facebook chatting. This is what it is to have a girlfriend, he thinks. This is what it is to have Meltem in his life.

Both Deniz and Jennifer decided to go on an island vacation together and they lie on the hot sand now, sharing the same blanket, rubbing lotion on each other and basking in the warmth of the sun and their own company. Jennifer still cannot quite believe that she is so much in love with another woman but has learned to stop questioning it and to just enjoy the feeling she has every time she is with Deniz. And Deniz, of course, is smart enough to know not to mention past lovers, both male and female, to her so that Jennifer will still bask in the newness of the experience. They can, of course, talk of Meric, since they both shared him for a brief time, but neither feels the need to do that. He is like a distant memory to Jennifer, and Deniz has relegated him to her attic of ex-lovers and feels nothing when she sees him hanging doglike in her peripheral vision at school. She isn't that much older than Jennifer, only three years, but she has had so much more experience that she feels quite the elder. But she also knows that she feels something slightly different for her, this blond Midwestern girl. And though she has been in love before, she has never truly loved anyone. Until now, she thinks. Until right now.

And as she rubs sun tan lotion on Jennifer's back, she feels quite possessive. And this, she knows, is a different feeling than she has ever had.

Meric wanders Bar Street in Moda completely lost, without purpose, stumbling into one bar after another, having a drink here, a drink there, losing himself in the crowds of people, too dazed to know exactly what he is looking for but instinctively knowing he is indeed looking for something, for someone, to clear up the confusion in his mind. And then, quite impulsively, he calls Michael who he knows lives somewhere nearby. "Hi," he says when Michael answers. "It's Meric. Are you up?"

"Well if I wasn't," Michael says, rather wearily, "I am now."

"I'm on Bar Street," Meric says. "You want to meet me for a drink?"

Michael looks at the clock on his nightstand which says a few minutes before midnight, sighs, and says, "Sure, why not?" He puts the book he was reading aside, John Reed's account of the Mexican Revolution, and dislodges the cat from its cradle on his left arm and stands. "Where should we meet?"

"How about The Belfast?" Meric says.

"Okay. I'll be there in about 10 minutes." Then he stretches, ambles into the bathroom to comb his thinning hair, rinses his dry mouth, and before putting on his shoes, he finishes the glass of whiskey that sits rather forlornly on his nightstand, and pulls on his coat. The cat doesn't even stir from the bed. "Right," Michael says. "I'll miss you, too."

And he is off.

Pelin finds herself forlornly wandering Kadiköy hoping to catch a glimpse of Meric but having no luck in finding him. She knows instinctively that he is here somewhere, either in the bars singing along to the music or else on Bar Street drowning his sorrows. She doesn't know why he is so obsessed with those women but then again thinks she is no one to point fingers since she has her own obsession to deal with, but whatever he had with them is obviously over so why doesn't he have the good sense to open his eyes to other possibilities? Why can't he seem to move on? Men, she thinks. They must conquer but cannot understand rejection.

Brenda sits in the same pub she used to frequent when in college waiting, like back then, for Mark to appear. She thinks it is probably a mistake, this meeting, for what could they possibly have to talk about, it's been over a year since they've seen each other and their lives have not exactly run in parallel lines, but like a loose tooth, she can't help but keep touching it till it eventually falls out.

So even though it wasn't intended, it seems fitting that it takes place, this meeting of Brenda's with her ex-husband Mark. So she meets him in the pub, the air is heavy with the aroma of various beers, ale and memories, so many memories, a cloud on their eyes.

"Your hair," he says after settling in opposite her, "it's shorter."

"Just something different," she says. "You know me, I like change."

"Yes," Mark says, nodding sadly, thinking, perhaps, he, too, was part of her changes. "I remember that."

Suddenly Brenda feels so sad, so heavy in the chest, a weight she had not anticipated that she cannot quite bear. And she smiles quickly, a smile to mask what she feels, a sudden, false smile that does not go undetected by Mark.

"Are you well?" he asks, his voice tender, the voice he uses for readings, his eyes soft, so sensitive there in this dusty light, so like a photo on a book jacket. "Are you happy, there, in Turkey?"

And she nods her head, says, "Yes, I am happy," to this man, this man who was her husband, her first real love, her ideal, the only man she ever thought, at one time not so very long ago, she would ever live with, and wonders, with what must surely be some variation of regret, what happened to the years, over a decade ago to only a little less than two years ago to now. Who has changed, she wonders, this man, my first true love, or me? And, of course, she knows the answer--she has changed, she is no longer the girl mesmerized by the poet, the girl he thought he loved, was probably never the girl he thought he loved, though she did truly, in her way, at one time for quite a few years, want to be.

Mark talks about his life, mutual friends she has stopped contacting, about London, his plans now, an apartment he is thinking of buying, of his teaching, of his soon to be published book of poetry, his scheduled readings, "One is this coming Saturday. Maybe you could come, if you'll still be here."

But she says she can't, must get back to Istanbul, classes to begin soon, syllabi to write, scheduling to do, a lie, she knows, but as she says it, she realizes that she really wants to be back in Istanbul, away from London, his readings, her mother, the friends she might bump into if she stays any longer, and the longing she feels as she thinks about Murat sitting in his office, waiting for her.

And though Brenda listens, smiles, laughs at a joke, sees him still so animated, so soulful, his brooding eyes, his boyish charm, and thinks, I still love this man, but I could never be with him again, here, in London, in a life that could not be her own. And as she sees her life unfolding a few thousand miles away in another time zone, she bids this love, this man, farewell.

And as she finally leaves the pub and feels the cold winter air on her hot cheeks, tears come to her eyes. And later, in her mother's car alone, parked on a side street before driving back to her mother's flat, she cries for all that she has lost, all that she is losing, all that she has gained, all that still awaits her back in her newly adopted city, back where her heart now belongs, back to a man who makes her feel whole, to a life that is hers for the giving, the taking, the loving, the living, again.

"I just don't know," Meric says sometime after the second drink and in the middle of the third. "I seem to be slipping and I don't know how to stop."

Michael nods, not knowing what to say and hoping Meric doesn't expect an answer because at this hour and in the state he's in, Michael finds himself all out of those.

"You know what I mean?" Meric says. "You ever find yourself feeling like this?"

"Not so much anymore," Michael says, "but certainly when I was younger."

"And how did you handle it?"

"Poorly, I'm sure," Michael says. "Like I handled most things when I was young."

Meric looks off, his eyes glazed by drink, and wonders what time it is. And though he feels like he stares into space for hours, it is only a few minutes until last call is announced.

Last call, though, does not necessarily mean last drink, for the two of them could, if they want, adjourn to the inside of the bar where, behind closed doors and warmed by central heating, they might continue to drink with the others who do not want the evening to end. But instead, they meander down the street to one of the many little convenience stores open till close to dawn and buy a bottle of Jameson and climb the stairs to Michael's apartment where they find themselves sitting on the floor by the stereo listening to old Tom Waits CDs and making a rather large dent in the bottle before Meric drops off to sleep and Michael sits staring rather dully at the wall.

Katja spends the break in her studio, avoiding contact with any of the other faculty members who have remained in Istanbul during the intersession, and concentrates on working on the dances for the play. She could have returned home to Sarajevo for a holiday but decided against it, knowing that there she would be wrapped in the grief of her aunts, her own grief added to it, how could she ever break free of that? No, she thinks, it is best to stay here amid the memories of Hasan and let her pain be engulfed by her work.

Berat wanders around Kiev holding Elena's hand like a puppy on a leash. He is so smitten with her that he barely sees the churches she points out, the house where Mikhail Bulgakov lived, the cafés she frequented, the restaurant she loves. He could, he realizes, live here if she wanted, or live in Istanbul with her, or go to London or Paris or any of the places she wants to visit, to live, to dance, just as long as she is always holding his hand like now and leading him through life.

Dave finds himself surrounded by friends at a restaurant all celebrating his return for this all too brief holiday.

"And you like it there?" George asks.

"Yes," Dave says. "It takes a bit of getting used to but there's a certain charm to a city that's 2600 years old."

"What do you miss the most, though?" Jenny asks.

"Going to the movies," Dave says. "They don't get that many foreign films and when they do, the subtitles are in Turkish, not English, so that rules me out. And the same goes for theatre. There's nothing in English so I miss going to shows. They do have a vibrant arts scene there but not with the diversity in cultures and languages like we have here."

"What about the food?" Andres asks. "What do you miss the most?"

"Nathan's hotdogs," Dave says grinning. "And Chinese food."

"There are no Chinese restaurants there?"

"I guess there are some, though I haven't found one. But even so, it's not like here where we have one every other block, like pizza places. There it's kebab places."

"I'm sure there's a MacDonald's, though," Andres says. "They're everywhere."

"Yes," and he shakes his head almost in disbelief as he adds, "But Burger King is more popular for some reason. The Whopper has a distinct advantage over the Big Mac. And there are the ubiquitous Starbucks, of course."

"Well at least you're not denied your morning café latte," Helen says laughing.

And they all join in as more sangria is poured into glasses and more tapas arrive to the table. And Dave feels a warm glow spreading throughout his body as he surveys the table, his friends, the laughter like a balm soothing the loneliness he felt so far from home. But as the evening eventually ends, he finds himself sitting alone on the Long Island Railroad, staring out at the darkness beyond the window as Queens rolls by outside on his way eastward toward his dark, empty house and another night, whether here or in Istanbul, lying alone in his big, empty bed.

Jennifer and Deniz still find themselves going to bed early in the evening and rising late in the morning, spending much of their time engaged in pillow talk after long sessions of lovemaking that never seems to grow old. "I love your hands," Jennifer says as Deniz glides her fingers along her skin, making her tingle with anticipation.

"You do, do you?" Deniz says and then lets her tongue circle Jennifer's nipple for a long, deliciously agonizing moment. "Is that all you like?"

And Jennifer pulls her head closer, locks her mouth onto Deniz's and they cling to each other as they both almost lose consciousness before they end hopelessly deflated in each other's arms.

"I'll never get enough of you," Jennifer sighs.

And they both drift off to blissful sleep.

Brenda returns earlier than expected and the first thing she does from the airport is call Murat. "I'm back," she says.

"Where are you?"

"At baggage claim at Ataturk Airport."

"Do you want me to come get you?"

"It'll take too long," she says. "Just meet me at my apartment."

"I'm on my way."

And as Brenda's bag comes around on the carousal, she can't help smiling to be home where she now belongs.

İrem can't help thinking of Michael and so decides to call him from Izmir. "Hi," she says when he answers. "How's Istanbul?"

"Still here," he says. "At least last time I looked out the window. But I suppose it could be gone now. You want me to go look?"

"No," she says. "I'm sure it's still out there. If not, I would have heard something on the news."

"Right," he says. "There's always that." Then says in spite of not wanting to, "You coming back soon?"

"This weekend. School does start again on Monday."

"Right," he says. "It certainly does."

"You'll be hungry, won't you, when I get back?"

"You mean in wanting something to eat?"

"What else?" she asks.

"Well there's spiritual as well as emotional hunger," he says. "I could be in need of feeding those."

"Hmmmm," she goes. "I'm not sure I can satisfy those with Albanian liver."

"Liver, you say," Michael says. "That's supposed to be good for you, isn't it? Something to do with nutrients, I think."

"And it's tasty, too," she says. "And reportedly boosts energy."

"I can always use a boost there," he says. "And this is what you were thinking of making when you return?"

"That was the game plan."

"Well far be it for me to derail any game plans."

"Then how about Saturday when I come back?"

"My heart is beating faster already in anticipation."

And after she hangs up she thinks she will miss this man more than she realizes if she goes to America, except, of course, that she is now realizing it which more or less means she knows exactly just how much she will miss him.

And Michael, on the other end of the disconnected line, thinks he isn't kidding when he says his heart beats faster with anticipation. But he also knows it's not for the liver. No, not for the liver at all.

Part II
The Spring Semester

Scene 6
February

Michael wakes up, looks at the clock, and sees it is only 4am. He doesn't know why it is only 4am, thinks it is somewhat unfair to be only 4am, especially since he had gone to bed only an hour ago at 3am, and feels it should be, by all that is right and fair in the world, at least 6am, but his eyes do not deceive him. It's only 4am and he has been what could loosely be called asleep for only an hour. He sighs, rolls over onto his back, and stares upward to where the ceiling should be, would be, if only he could see in the dark. He hears the cat make what sounds like a groan and then is aware of it creeping slowly in his direction across the bed. Once it reaches him, it leans as close to his face as possible without actually touching it, sniffs a bit, then plops down beside him. It rests its head on his arm, sighs, and falls back to sleep.

"Lucky you," Michael murmurs and closes his eyes.

Brenda cannot keep her eyes closed. Instead she stares at Murat's sleeping form next to her and almost pinches herself to make sure she is not dreaming. But she is awake, he is there asleep, having told his wife that he had to go to Ankara for a few days and she being too involved with the children to miss him. And so they have these few days, these all too precious nights together. And Brenda cannot keep her eyes closed, cannot keep her hands from straying over his body, cannot contain her excitement as his eyes open to stare into hers, and his mouth, his mouth finds hers, their bodies melt into each other's, and Brenda cries out in the night as he enters and drives away all thoughts of sleep for both of them this night.

Philip sits by his window staring out at the street below as dawn slowly, steadily lights his world. He had fallen asleep a little before midnight but had awoken an hour or so before dawn, his mind filled with images of frolicking lovers, which could, under different circumstances, give him reason enough to curse Michael and his play, but instead he finds he is becoming enamored of the characters as they begin to take shape in his mind. So he sits by the window and imagines them down below, fumbling their way toward love on narrow Istanbul streets. And the play finally begins to take shape in his mind's eye.

Jennifer avoids asking though she knows the answer to her question preys on her mind. She hates herself for feeling any jealousy and knows this is something she must learn to deal with, to conquer, if she is ever to have a healthy relationship here in this new old world she has elected to live in. And it is that fact, her living here in a foreign country with people who speak a language she still, after four years now, cannot quite fathom, that is at the root of her problem. She was never jealous back in the States with boyfriends she had there, but here, first with Meric and now even more intensely with Deniz, she is haunted by this jealousy that gnaws at her in every waking hour, in dreams during sleep. Perhaps, she thinks, it is because there is so much she still does not understand about these people, this culture, that fuels her insecurity. Or maybe it is because she has never been in love with another woman before, never felt so totally in someone else's grip, so powerless at times when Deniz just stares at her, and completely defenseless when Deniz touches her body, her fingers, her tongue, are the masters she is enslaved to. With Meric, the jealousy really stemmed from competitiveness, but with Deniz it is so far beyond that, to some inner turmoil that torments her. Just the thought of her with someone else, with anyone else, man or woman, drives her to despair. For she now cannot imagine a life without Deniz in it, she would be too empty inside.

And Deniz, for her part, is beginning to lose any recollection of anyone before her. Jennifer is all she desires, all she, for the very first time in her life, truly loves.

Meric finds himself still adrift. It is even worse now, he thinks, since he sees both Deniz and Jennifer almost constantly during the day, their paths crossing even while he tries unsuccessfully to avoid them. It is almost a plot, he thinks, then abandons that line of reasoning as totally absurd. Just bad luck and poor timing.

So he tries vainly to submerge himself in his classes, devoting more and more time to his students in the hopes of distractions. And Pelin, taking advantage of his increased availability, seeks his advice about her interpretation of songs she has chosen for her Valentine's Day show.

"I want to sell the story behind the songs," she says. "I need to find the emotional truth in the lyrics."

And Meric huddles with her in his office, analyzing the words, suggesting which ones to emphasize, where the stress should come, how to color her vocal tone to match the emotion required. It is like a private acting lesson and though he revisits the song lyrics discovering emotions he himself can identify with, Pelin is just content to be in the same room, sitting side by side, her knees lightly touching his, her hands brushing against him occasionally, the air filled with electricity that thrills her so.

İrem finds herself distracted easily. She doesn't know why this is since it so rarely happens but her mind keeps drifting away from her. It is as if she is overworked and needs a vacation, but, of course, that is not the case for she does not feel overworked, nor does she need a vacation since she has only recently returned from a mini-holiday during intersession and has been looking forward to the start of this semester for quite some time now. For now she and Michael will begin seriously working on ***Romeo and Juliet*** with casting to begin next month and rehearsals to quickly follow. And yet, even though she feels thrilled by that prospect, her mind keeps slipping away from her at the oddest moments and she often loses track of conversations she is supposedly involved in.

"I don't understand it," she says to Michael over coffee in their office, "but I have trouble focusing these days."

"Really?" he says, looking somewhat surprised at his usually unflappable assistant. "How can that be? That's going against type."

"Oh," she says, an eyebrow rising. "Am I a type to you?"

"Not in a bad way," he says feeling somewhat defensive and wondering why.

"Is there a good way?"

"There is if it's a good type."

"And I'm a good type, am I?"

"That's always the way I see you."

"And what is my type exactly?" she asks, though at this point not really sure if she wants to hear the answer.

"Well," he says, growing cagey on her, "that's not so easy to describe."

"Try," she says.

"You're putting me on the spot," he says.

"Well you're the one who brought up this type business."

"Only because you said something so out of character."

"And I'm not allowed to deviate from my assigned role for you?" she says and feels angry for some reason she cannot quite grasp.

"I didn't say that," he says but then thinks that perhaps he did, or at least implied it, and then thinks that he should learn to not let his mouth speak faster than his brain can think, though that does seem to be a recurring problem for him throughout his life.

"You didn't?" she asks, an aggressive tone, which is quite uncharacteristic, in her voice. "It sounded like you did to me."

"Well it's just you're never distracted," he says. "That's usually me in this relationship, so I was kind of surprised is all."

"I'm surprised, too," she says, "which is why I said it. But I didn't expect to get typecast after saying it."

"I'd never typecast you," he says, and it is with so much sincerity that she is taken aback slightly, then touched even.

"That's reassuring," she says and they both sit staring at each other for a long moment, neither knowing exactly what to say next.

Then a couple of students come in to see Michael and the moment, whatever it was, could have been, is lost forever.

Berat and Elena, ever since sharing a hotel room together in Kiev, are now more seriously involved with each other than ever but that, of course, leads to complications neither had consciously considered before, namely religion. "It would be important to my family if the woman I married was a Muslim."

"And are we going to marry?" Elena says, looking at him.

"I don't know," he says, suddenly confused and embarrassed at the same time.

"Well if you don't know," she says, "then talking about religion is a little premature, don't you think?"

"I guess," he says, then shifts in his seat in the café they are sitting in and stares off in the distance. He thinks he has not handled this correctly, but does not know how he should have handled it, or if he should have waited a little longer before broaching this subject. All he knows is that he cannot think of anyone else but her, cannot even imagine being with anyone else, and yet is now unsure of just what she feels. It seems the only time she is not a mystery to him is when they are dancing but knows, of course, they cannot spend their lives doing that.

And then Elena tosses back her long blonde hair, stands, and says, "I must be going. But don't worry," and she smiles mischievoiusly. "It's not to church."

And as Berat watches her go, he thinks dancing is so much less complicated.

Sönmez watches Murat as he tries to explain himself. "It's just that I feel out of place here," he says. "As if I'm not needed, am an extra appendage in this home."

"I don't understand how you could say that," Sönmez says. "Without you, there would be no home."

"Because I pay all the bills?" he says. "Is that what you mean?"

"It is more than that," Sönmez says. "You are my husband and the father of these children. How could we exist if not for you?"

"But I don't feel as if I matter here," he says. "What do we talk about? What do we do? We never even sleep together anymore."

"Is that my fault?" she asks. "Have I banned you from our bed? Or do you stay away yourself for reasons I don't understand?"

"There is no room for me there," he says. "The children sleep with you."

"And can we not move them?" she asks. "Are they permanently fixed there?"

"They seem to be permanently attached to you."

She looks at him for a long moment with eyes that are impossible for him to read before she says, "And these children you speak of, are they not yours, too? Did you not want them also?"

And here he feels somewhat trapped by two people: the Murat of his youth and the Murat he has now become. And torn between the two halves of himself, he struggles to find what he wants, what he needs. And Sönmez stares at him for a long time, afraid of the questions she has not asked.

And both stand so very close to each other but are so very far apart.

Dave looks at the calendar and sees that Valentine's Day is upon him and he has no one to send flowers to, or at least no one who expects flowers from him or would even be receptive to the gift. And here he is, he thinks, alone in a foreign country with four more months to go and no prospects of someone making that time fly by. He thinks of Katja but then decides that would not be appropriate, especially since he senses from her changing moods that she is really still in mourning. Then he thinks of İrem but feels it is too soon to make that gesture. Better to wait till he has her in New York and Michael is no longer around, because though he does not know the full extent of their relationship, he knows enough to know as long as Michael is in the picture, he will always be on the sidelines. And as for Jennifer, he has given up any hope of attracting her. So he calls a local florist back in New York via Skype to arrange for flowers to be sent to the woman he last slept with there in the hopes that that might be rekindled upon his return.

Then he looks through his wardrobe to pick something to wear to this evening's cabaret performance so that even though he may not have a woman, he can at least look like he should have.

Philip wonders how he'll make it through this evening of love songs being billed as a cabaret performance by students from the Theatre and Music Departments but, being a loyal supporter of all things related to the university, he dusts off his one decent sports coat, the only pair of dress pants he has that goes with it, and thinks about shining his shoes. After a moment or two of inner debate, he decides to let one of the many hustlers with shoeshine boxes to have the pleasure of earning five Turkish lira to shine them for him. He also, with considerable less debate, elects not to wear a tie. This, of course, is a foregone conclusion since he does not own a tie, but even if he did, he wouldn't wear one. There is, after all, a limit to his commitment to the university.

And so before boarding a bus to go to the evening's festivities, he opens a bottle of Efes and takes a very long swallow. Listening to love songs sung by twenty year olds does require some liquid fortification.

Brenda enters with Philip but finds her eyes travelling across the room to where Murat is sitting, legs crossed, his suit fitting him like second skin, a glass of wine before him on one of the small round tables that are dispersed around the largest of the rehearsal rooms which is decorated to look like a New York City nightclub. And for this evening, beer and wine is being served to the faculty and staff and older students, while fruit punch is available for those abstaining from alcohol. There are also some bowls of crackers, cheese, sliced suçuk, assorted grapes and orange slices, nuts, chips.

Brenda does not have to say anything to Philip who knows she will want to sit at Murat's table so the two of them take beverages from one of the several students decked out as waiters and waitresses and join Murat.

Dave is seated at a table nearby with a few of the Prep teachers but his eyes roam restlessly around the room, without really knowing what he's looking for, but looking just the same. And though he does not catch any eyes of faculty members, there are quite a few Prep students giggling behind their cupped hands to shield the obvious crushes they have on him.

Michael enters alone, İrem meanwhile in another smaller rehearsal room being used as a dressing room to give a final pep talk to Pelin who is more nervous than normal. He seems tired somehow, bags under his eyes as if he were planning a trip, and fatigue tugging at the corners of his mouth. It is only the sight of wine on a tray that seems to partially revive him and Michael takes a glass before settling at a table to wait for İrem to join him. He is too tired to scan the rest of the tables but if he did he would notice the many groups of couples, Berat and Elena as well as Fersat and Meltem among them. Instead he gazes into his wine glass as if that were the evening's scheduled entertainment and awaits enlightenment. It does not come.

Katja does come, though, and she crosses to his table and asks, "May I join you?"

"Of course," he says.

"Where's İrem?" she asks after settling in.

"With Pelin, I think. Her protégé, you know."

"This was her idea then, I take it."

"Yes," Michael says. "She sees it as a sort of coming attraction for the play. Many of the songs sung here tonight will be worked in somehow. And, of course, you'll have to come up with dances to go along with them."

"That's a good idea," she says. "Do you know which songs yet?"

"Actually that's for the three of us, plus Murat, to decide. So let your imagination run wild tonight."

İrem comes in then and sits on Michael's other side just before the lights dim. Meric is following her and slips in to the seat next to her, trying very hard not to look over to the table where Deniz and Jennifer sit. Instead he looks over at Michael who seems to be mesmerized by the wine in his glass but who is in actuality trying very hard not to notice just how close İrem's knee is to his.

And it's then, while both men at this table are trying so hard to not look where they are being irresistibly drawn, that a spotlight illuminates Pelin in a rather slinky black dress with a slit up the side that reveals, to Meric's surprise, a very shapely leg. The trio behind her smoothly begins the intro to ***"I've Got You Under My Skin"*** and Pelin's voice begins its seduction of the audience while her eyes linger for a beat or two longer than expected on Meric whose eyes wander up from her leg to her face and are left dazzled by who he feels he sees for the very first time.

And the evening continues with many old standards sprinkled in among the pop songs Pelin sings and both Dave and Michael find themselves transported across time: Dave to memories of Broadway shows he has seen and the variety of women that he saw them with; Michael to his first wife, a singer/actress who performed in clubs herself and sang many of these same songs, some dedicated to him. And Dave finds himself slipping toward depression since he is so very much alone now, while Michael feels the sadness that always hovers close by descend once again upon his shoulders causing him to slump a little further down in his chair.

The others, though, are not moved to melancholy but rather find themselves edging closer to the person sitting by their side: notice Meltem leaning in to Fersat and Elena's hand squeezing Berat's, and Brenda finds it difficult to keep her head from resting on Murat's shoulder while Deniz's hand slides along Jennifer's leg under the table which is unseen by all but hardly unnoticed by Jennifer.

Only Katja and İrem seem to be in a state of emotional limbo: Katja repressing thoughts of Hasan and trying to stay focused instead on deciding which songs would work as dances for the play, and İrem concentrating on Pelin's performance while trying hard not to notice Michael's changing mood. But neither, however, is as successful as they hope.

And Pelin ends the evening with the Cole Porter song *"Night and Day"* and manages to look at Meric often enough to give him no doubt that she is indeed singing to him. And now that he knows that, he must decide what to do about it.

Murat follows Brenda home and before she can get her key out of the door, he has her against the wall, her panties on the floor, and he is thrust deep inside her. Her tongue is in his ear, her legs straddled around his waist, her breathing in short, sharp bursts. And he carries her that way into the bedroom and Valentine's Day ends there, amid damp sheets, many hours later.

Fersat sits with Meltem in her parents' house looking at photographs from her childhood, their knees touching under the table, her mother's eyes on him the entire time, but somehow they are both content to gaze at pictures, drink cay, and breathe the same air till it is time for him to go.

Deniz holds a sleeping Jennifer in her arms, inhaling the scent from her hair, and feeling as if this apartment she lives in is finally a home.

Meric does not know what he should do. He does know that Pelin is definitely trying to tell him something and that if he listens, he will end up in bed with her, but that is a little more complicated than he wants since she is a student, he is her teacher, and no matter how he looks at it, from whatever angle he chooses to use, it somehow does not seem right, or at least ethical, and though he thinks that that is probably the same thing, he is trying very hard to keep them separate in his mind. He wonders under what circumstances it would be okay for a teacher to become involved with a student, for he surely knows that it has happened in the past, but he thinks he is perhaps not the best person to be considering this. And it is with that thought firmly lodged in his head that he decides to give Michael a call.

"Are you busy right now?" he asks.

"That depends on how you define busy," Michael says.

"Are you free to talk?" Meric asks.

"We're all free to talk in a democratic society," Michael says, "though I do notice that there are some restrictions here which I, as a resident alien, seem to somehow be excused from."

Meric's head seems to be spinning slightly since this conversation is not going the way he had anticipated. "Can you talk with me tonight?" he finally blurts out.

"You mean like now?" Michael says.

"Yes," Meric nods. "I know it's late but I really need to talk to someone who can offer me advice."

Michael's eyes roll to the back of his head as he thinks this is about women, of course, and he feels so inadequate lately to be offering anyone advice about them, but knowing Meric, it won't make any difference anyway. "Where are you?" he asks.

"Close by," Meric says. "I can be at the Belfast in ten minutes."

"Great" Michael says and sighs. "Okay, I'll meet you there."

Then after they both hang up, Michael looks over at the cat who is sitting in front of him expecting a treat no doubt and says, "Duty calls, partner." The cat's eyes blink but he does not budge. Michael sighs again. Then he opens the kitchen cabinet where he keeps the cat's food and extracts a container of treats. "Here," he says as he puts a few down on the ground in front of the cat. "Why should you be any different than anyone else?"

And he grabs his coat and is off thinking at least there will be alcohol there and that is his treat, he supposes.

Philip, meanwhile, sits at his window watching the street below. There is movement by what he perceives to be a house of ill repute on the corner and that always piques his interest. He wonders if he shouldn't go in sometime, just to see what it looks like inside, how things are done logistically, though not for any entertainment value himself, but purely for research and to satisfy his curiosity. There is a book in that house, he thinks, and perhaps he is the one to write it since it holds no other value for him than strictly literary value. Stories, he thinks. There are stories there between those four walls on those three floors. And his mind races a little faster thinking about what those stories could be.

İrem sits thinking about Michael. She doesn't know why he seems to be on her mind so much lately but there he is firmly wedged in and refusing to budge an inch to let another thought enter. It's his expressions, she realizes, that she now finds hard to read, whereas in the past, she thought she could usually ascertain what was on his mind. Now he is becoming a mystery to her. Even tonight, at the cabaret show, he

212

seemed distant and preoccupied and when she had tried to engage him in conversation about which songs he thought appropriate for the play, he seemed to be baffled by the question and confessed that he wasn't really paying attention but that his mind was on something else. Something else? What else could he be thinking about if not about the play?

And now when she would like to call him to find out, she must deal with Pelin instead who wants to meet her to ask for advice. And so reluctantly she buttons up her coat and leaves for Bar Street in Moda to play mentor to her protégé.

Meric is on his second drink by the time Michael arrives. And though Michael has every intention of catching up soon, he dreads that wild look in Meric's eyes.

"I don't know what to do," Meric says. "I'm so confused."

"Well when in a bar," Michael says, "the best thing to do is drink."

"Not about here," Meric says. "About my situation."

"Which is?" Michael says looking around rather anxiously for Osman so he can order a drink and only feeling somewhat relieved when Osman brings him a glass of whiskey without his even asking for it. "Bless you," Michael says to him. "You're a true Saint Bernard."

"What's that?" Osman asks.

"A bringer of mercy." Michael answers, thinking it's best to leave out any reference to a large dog. Then he turns his attention back to Meric and says, "Where were we?"

"Talking about my confusion."

"Right," Michael nods, taking a long sip of his drink. "Which is?"

"About a student."

Michael shakes his head slightly as if to clear it and then says, "You're confused about a student?"

"Well really about my feelings for a student."

"You have confused feelings for a student?"

"Sort of," Meric says, losing heart slightly to go on with this but thinking that since he's already started, he might as well continue. "I think I have feelings for her," he says. "Or at least I think I could have feelings for her since she has feelings for me."

"Ah," Michael goes. "I see."

"Do you?" Meric asks. "I mean, has that ever happened to you?"

"Having feelings?" Michael asks and Meric hesitantly nods. "For a student?"

"Yes."

"Ah, well, hmmmm." And he drifts off a minute into some other time, some other place, perhaps light years away. There is this, there is that, faces fading in and out of focus, a brief glimpse of what could only be a thigh, a breast, lips, though whose or when or where, he could not, even when cold stone sober, say. Then he returns to say, "I suppose all teachers at one time or another get to feel something special for a student or two that touches them in a way the others don't, or can't. I guess that's where the term teacher's pet comes from, though I don't think it was ever supposed to imply actual petting."

"So you've had these feelings, too, for a student?"

"There were a few when I was teaching acting back in LA that I had definite feelings for."

"And what did you do about it?"

"Probably the wrong thing each time, though I did different things with each of them."

"Like what?"

214

"Like every variation of the theme," Michael says. "But they were all older students. Or at least I was younger, so they were closer to my age then."

"But I'm young," Meric says.

"Yes," Michael says, looking at him carefully for the first time. "You are."

"So it's okay then? If I do something?"

And here Michael wishes he were someone else, somewhere else, sometime else. But, of course, he isn't, so he makes due the best he can. "I don't know if it's okay or not," Michael says. "But I think if the feelings are genuine on both your sides, well then it doesn't matter what I think, or what anyone thinks. It'll happen anyway." Then he finishes his whiskey and signals for another. "Just be sure it's real," he says. "Then let your heart decide."

İrem finds herself listening to Pelin's troubled heart. "I just don't know what to do," Pelin says and then looks imploringly at İrem. "I give him all the hints but I don't know if he understands them or not."

"If he's like most men," İrem says, "he understands them."

"And do you think it's all right for a student to be involved with a teacher?"

"There are no right or wrong answers there," İrem says. "But if it's real love, then no one can stop you from becoming involved."

Pelin hesitates for a moment, wondering if she should ask the next question on her mind but then decides to ask it anyway. "Did you ever become attracted to a teacher when you were a student?"

İrem looks away for a second, to another time, another place, and smiles a little sadly, Pelin thinks, before she answers. "Once," she says, "in graduate school. There was a teacher there I thought I was in love with,"

"And did you let him know it?"

"He knew it without my telling him."

"And was he in love with you?"

"I don't think you could call it love," İrem says, remembering all too clearly that time, that place, that man. "But he was definitely attracted to me."

"Then what happened?"

"What usually happens when two people are attracted to each other," she says, laughing slightly but without any joy in the laugh. Instead there is a hollow feeling inside her that laughter cannot fill.

Pelin does not know how to ask the next question or whether she should, even if she knows how, but her curiosity is too much for her to bear. "Were you happy?"

"For a while I was," İrem says. "But soon I realized that I wasn't really in love with him, but in love with the idea of him."

"The idea of him?"

"Yes," İrem says, the smile growing sadder as the memory grows more vivid. "He was older, smarter, cultured. I was in awe of him. And I thought I could learn so much from him. He was American, too, and I was in America and that was also part of the attraction."

"Did you?"

"Yes," she says, "though not always what I wanted. And I found out that as I began to learn more, he became more critical of me and less supportive. He had what a friend calls a Henry Higgins complex and didn't want his student to grow independent of him in any way."

"Henry Higgins?"

"He's a character in a play who recreates a woman in his own image but grows unhappy when she starts to become her own person."

"Oh, I see," Pelin says. "That's not good at all."

"No, it isn't."

"But do you still like that type of man?" she asks. "I mean older, more cultured, and experienced."

"Yes," İrem says and suddenly feels a little exposed. "But not in the same way anymore. It could never be in that same way again."

"Why not?"

"Because I'm not that same person, nor am I in those same circumstances. This is my country, my culture. What could someone teach me that I don't already know?"

"But you're planning on going back to the US," Pelin says. "Couldn't it happen again?"

"I'm ten years older than I was then." İrem says. "You change a lot in ten years."

"I hope I never change," Pelin says.

İrem looks at her and smiles tenderly. She thinks she is not so old yet that she has the legitimate right to feel like the wise older person with her, but she also thinks life has taught her a few lessons that have given her a perspective she probably wouldn't have had if she hadn't gone abroad to live and study. And it is from that perspective that she reaches out and pats Pelin's hand affectionately. "I hope so, too," she says.

And they both find their minds wandering off to wonder about men. Pelin to Meric and İrem, without fully understanding why, to Michael.

Katja finds herself choreographing dances with Hasan in mind. It is as if every lovers' ballet is a vision of his courtship of her, or at least in the way she would like to remember it

217

in an idealized fashion. And this pulls her further and further from her every day existence into the play as a fantasy of her aborted romance with Hasan.

And as she watches her two principal dancers, Berat and Elena, become erotically connected in both the dance and their lives outside, it gives her a vicarious feeling of satisfaction and though she thinks perhaps she needs more, she also feels it is enough.

Dave stares out at the sea of faces in his classroom as they work in small groups on creating a role play based on the unit's theme for the week. Their voices fill the air and he tries to concentrate on helping them but since they are all speaking Turkish instead of English, he is at a loss as to what to say. So his mind begins to wander and he finds himself surveying all the women he's been involved with over the last few decades, and all their faces begin to blur as his ex-wife looms over them all, making it impossible for him to see anyone else.

Murat is torn in half. He is pulled by some force he is too weak to resist to Brenda, a love that burns the flesh from his bones, it is that intense. And though he cannot think clearly at night when he is away from her, he still does not have the strength to sever the ties that bind him to Sönmez, the children, his house filled with the mementos of his forty-four years, his life, and ultimately from his family, their friends, who will condemn him for breaking free.

This life, this shared history of twenty-three years has weight, has value, and how does he, in all fairness, walk away from all that? And can he turn his back on all he has built for himself and give it up for a passion he cannot control? A passion that could burn itself out in a week, a month, a year? He trembles with fear and anticipation as he stands on a cliff that every cell in what's left in what should

218

be his rational brain begs him not to step off of, but every fiber of his body longs to give in to the fall.

Jennifer curls up into the pocket that is Deniz and sleeps without dreaming. She is so safe here, so much at home that dreams are no longer necessary. She is living her dreams when awake as long as Deniz is there with her. She is where she has always wanted to be even though she did not know that until she finally arrived.

Dave sits in class listening to speeches about cities from his students and wondering where they get their information. For according to them, Istanbul is the second largest city in the world, the Statue of Liberty in New York Harbor was originally offered to Turkey whose sultan turned it down, and Honolulu is one of the two islands that comprise Hawaii. He shudders as he starts to zone out and wishes, rather wistfully, that he could close his eyes and when opening them again be back in New York, in his house, trimming his hedges, growing tomatoes, feeling the sun on his back, his shoulders, his feet firmly planted on soil he calls his own.

Philip watches people walk by while imagining their lives, what they do for a living, who they live with, what they enjoy eating, drinking, their thoughts on the ruling party, the books they read, the conversations they would likely have with him if they ever stopped to chat. It isn't a game he plays but a novel, or really a series of novels, he is writing in his head that changes from day to day depending on the people he sees, where he is sitting, the weather, the time of day. It is a series of novels he hopes will one day make itself apparent to him with characters he chooses, the situations they find themselves in, the conflicts, if any, they must endure.

And he, at that time, will sit at his desk in the early morning light and write it. Like he is now writing the play

219

for Michael, only it will be his own, not borrowed from Shakespeare, but evolved from his life here in Istanbul, his own fertile ground.

Meric stands his ground outside the club where he knows Pelin is singing, wavering over whether to enter or to keep on walking by. It is so morally confusing in his mind. A student, a teacher, a line crossed, and all the possibilities of that combination whether it goes right or goes wrong. But the attraction he feels, the thrill of potential bliss, songs in the night, and the memory of that slit in her dress, that hitherto undiscovered shapely leg, it all drives him to distraction. And though he cannot think of any reason other than his role as teacher in her life to prevent him from entering the club, he moves off rather slowly, deliberately, down the block, and finds another club to lose himself in and partially satisfy his thirst.

Michael sits alone on his living room floor hunched over in front of his DVD player with stacks of CDs spread out in front of him, his Bose headphones on to block out all sound except the music in his ears. He is playing disc jockey, fueled by a bottle of Irish whiskey within reach on the coffee table, and memories of his past life, the cat sprawled out on the cushion of his couch somewhere behind him fast asleep. He, though, is intent on not dropping off until he has played all the cuts from all the CDs he has laid out before him that conjure up all the scenes of his past in his head, swell in his heart, or has finished the bottle of whiskey which should reduce him to a comatose state, whichever comes first. For he must give in to the memories, put out the campfire and let the wolves that are usually at bay come in, and face every mistake, all the bits of pleasure, each and every painful episode in his gloriously checkered past. And these songs, these songs that bring forth the memories so vividly since they are so connected to his life, will do that.

And he feels a need to cleanse himself somehow of his past so he can move forward once again without hesitation into however long his future is. And it is the future he must cross over to, and let the present slip into the past to be discarded, free himself from his longing for a life he cannot have, and accept the one he has chosen by the very acts he has committed, by the choices he has made.

İrem sits listening to music faintly coming through the walls from her neighbor's apartment, a Turkish song of lament she recognizes from her student days, though she cannot quite place the singer. It is as if all the Western music she has immersed herself with has drowned out the songs of her past. And she cannot help but smile at the irony of it all. For as music from her distant undergraduate days strains to reach her through the walls surrounding her, she holds a letter in her hands of an early acceptance into the PhD program at Stanford University that is fully funded for the next six years she will be enrolled.

A new life awaits her far across the sea. And though she wants to call Michael to tell him of this, she hesitates. Her life is changing, she thinks, and she must tell him, her mentor, her best friend, but something holds her back. Not just yet, she says to herself. Not just now.

And she lays the letter aside, closes her eyes, and falls asleep with the music still faint in her ears.

Scene 7
March

Casting notices are tacked up all over school and students from all the departments with any illusions about an acting career write down the dates, google the play on the internet, and begin to rehearse monologues for the upcoming auditions. And Michael sits with İrem breaking up the scenes they have begrudgingly wrestled from Philip to select audition pieces. And it is then, during that scheduling process, that İrem decides to discuss her future plans with Michael.

"I heard from Stanford," she says.

"Stanford University?" he asks. "In Palo Alto?" And he feels like a fool asking that when he knows, of course, which Stanford she is referring to.

"Yes," she says. "They've accepted me."

"Ah, well, that's great." And he finds his world tilting again ever so slightly, but tilting just the same.

And then she begins telling him about the program, the faculty, the fact that it's fully funded, her excitement barely contained, spilling over the conference table they are working on, pushing aside the play as her life now being envisioned takes over. And Michael, Michael is supportive as he always is, though his heart begins to crack along its well-grooved fault lines. And the only words that keep echoing in his brain are "six years".

Dave has become obsessed with the wall calendar hanging in his kitchen. The page reads March and beyond it are three more pages ending with June. An academic year closes rapidly now, though he must admit to himself, not rapidly enough. And as he crosses out yet another day completed, he thinks of where he is going, what he is leaving, a life of changes where nothing really changes. He'll go from one place to another one year to the next, and still be alone.

Meric wanders the streets at night, unsure of where he is going, what he is doing, but instinctively knowing movement is essential if he wants to survive this state of being he finds himself trapped in.

Murat stares at his wife as she does not ask the questions that have begun to haunt her because she does not want to hear the answers. When does any woman or man want to know that their husband, their wife, their lover, their trusted partner is no longer to be trusted? And when does any husband, wife, lover, trusted partner want to confess to infidelity if they can postpone or avoid it even one second longer? So the two of them stare at each other with unasked and unanswered questions filling up the space between them.

Jennifer feels insecure, really insecure, for the first time in her life and doesn't know if she should say anything or not but all she can think about is what the future holds. This is all so new to her, this being nothing like the relationships she's had before, not just because it is with another woman, though that is, of course, markedly different, but because she has never given so much of herself, so freely, and made to feel so much in return, so complete it is almost frightening to think it could end. And yet she is afraid to broach this subject with Deniz who is so much more at ease, more in control, and Jennifer does not want to expose her vulnerability just yet. That is what frightens her the most.

Deniz, for her part, has no fear at all. She loves like she paints: with fearless abandon. And only expects the same in return.

"I don't know," Brenda says to Philip over draughts of Efes at a club in Kadiköy, "where this is going, or even if it is going anywhere at all but where it is now."

"Which is?" Philip asks.

"An affair," she says. "As simple as that. Nothing more, nothing less."

"And Murat?" he asks. "What does he want?"

"I'm not sure," she says. "After all, it is much more complicated for him. And if he wants more, he also has a helluva lot more to lose to get it."

"But what is your sense of what he wants?"

"The sex, obviously," and she almost laughs but not without a touch of helplessness in it. "He is as starved for it as I am so it is rather intense. And I must admit I love that. Especially after what I lived through in my marriage. But..." and she drifts off here to Murat's sad eyes. "I just don't know how far he is willing to take this."

"And isn't that the age old question?" Philip says.

"Yes," she sighs. "It couldn't be anything else, I suppose, now could it?"

Katja finds herself silently thanking Michael for dreaming up this play because it has given her something to lose herself in so completely that she almost forgets her grief. These lovers become real for her and as she drills Berat and Elena through dance after dance she has created for them alone, she finds she begins to feel hope again. They are an extension of her love for Hasan and through them she lives and loves again. It is so invigorating she almost kisses Michael when she sees him for giving her this gift. But she knows a kiss would not repay him. Only the creation of these dances could. And she devotes herself to that task. For it is her salvation. It has become her life.

Michael meanwhile watches İrem as she begins blocking the scenes as he has imagined them. She can so quickly, so easily read his mind that he often thinks she is more than his assistant but his partner, a part of himself. And this, of course, depresses him to no end as the words Stanford University and six years reverberate in his head.

İrem, however, catches him looking at her in what is for him a rather strange look and she stops her work to ask, "What?"

"What what?" he replies.

"What is that look about?"

"What look?"

"That look on your face a minute ago."

"I had a look on my face?"

"You certainly did."

"And what did it look like exactly?"

"Well if I knew that, I wouldn't be asking you what it was about?"

"Oh," he says. "Right."

And there is a long pause during which they both look somewhat expectantly at each other. Finally İrem, who has less patience for this sort of thing than he does, says, "So?"

"So?" he echoes.

"So what was that look about?"

"That look?"

"Yes," she sighs. "That look."

"Ah well," and he shrugs, "beats me."

"You don't know?"

"I really can't remember," he says. "It was such a long time ago."

And she looks at him for a long moment before she says, "Somehow I knew it was going to end this way."

"What way?" he asks, the picture of innocence.

227

"This way," and she sighs again. Then she returns to the task of blocking while trying her hardest to ignore him.

And Michael, Michael looks at his map of the LA Freeway and tries to imagine California all over again.

Meric finds himself sitting in the club Pelin is singing in and though he sits in the back to be more or less out of sight, she spots him anyway and manages to sing several songs in her set directly to him. Then, to make matters even more complicated, she joins him at his table between her sets.

"I'm glad you came," she says. "How did it sound to you?"

"Great," he says and is in no way being insincere in his critique for she does indeed sound quite wonderful. "You have a great voice," he adds.

"Thanks," she says. "But how do you like my interpretation?" and she almost leans across the table as she says it. "I tried to remember all the things you told me about looking for the story in the songs. Am I successful?"

"Yes," he says. "I believe every word you sing."

"You should," she says and looks meaningfully into his eyes. "I mean you to."

And Meric, of course, doesn't quite know how to take that, or maybe he does but he doesn't want to think he does because thinking he does could get him into a lot of trouble. So he nods, smiles, feels like a fool and says, "I'm looking forward to your next set."

"I hope you stay around afterwards so you can critique me." And she touches his hand as she says, "I value your opinion of me."

And Meric feels his body quiver slightly, heat rising to his face, a stirring in regions below his belt, and thinks he is headed for trouble if he stays, but knows without a doubt that he will stay anyway. That trouble is exactly where he knew

228

he would be going as soon as he crossed the threshold of this club.

Berat studies Elena as she glides across the floor of her room in the apartment she shares with two other girls to go get some wine from their kitchen. He had felt uncomfortable at first staying here but since the girls all seem to disappear into their own rooms once darkness falls, or else never come home but stay at a boyfriend's house somewhere else in the city, it is almost like being alone with her on these weekend nights. He still cannot believe how lucky he is. She moves so effortlessly, her body has feline grace, and he is blessed to be witness to it here and everywhere.

And as she comes toward him carrying two glasses of wine and smiling that enigmatic smile that promises everything but guarantees nothing, he feels his body grow hot with expectation and it isn't wine he thirsts for anymore.

Fersat sits with Meltem in her parents' living room watching a DVD of **Romeo and Juliet**. Her mother brings them cold drinks and is very friendly with Fersat. Her father, too, when he is home treats Fersat as if he were one of the family already and Fersat knows that is because Meltem has told them both that he is special to her. And, of course, they cannot fail to notice how solicitous he is to her, bringing her small gifts, like this movie that he spent hours looking for in numerous DVD shops throughout the city until finding a copy of it in a shop in Eminönö. And they watch the movie while Meltem studies the actress playing Juliet, the part she plans to audition for herself since she thinks no one could be better in that role than her.

"Will you audition, too?" her mother asks Fersat.

"No," he says. "I am not an actor."

"He wants to be a director," Meltem says to her mother. "Like Stanley Kubrick. And Fellini."

229

And they watch the film for a second time, then Meltem strikes a dramatic pose in the middle of the living room and begins reciting the lovers' lines, playing all the parts, changing her vocal tones to indicate each character, jumping around the room, gesticulating wildly. Her mother, who has entered the room carrying a tray filled with snacks, begins laughing.

And Fersat grabs his camera and records it all.

Brenda joins Michael and İrem in their office to discuss photographing the rehearsals and then filming the opening night performance. "Bekir wants us to have a record of this production," she says. "And I was thinking maybe we could even film the process, create a documentary of the making of the play." She looks at Michael and asks, "Is that okay with you?"

"Sure," Michael says. "As long as it's unobtrusive."

"It will be," Brenda says. "I'll make sure the crews are good at keeping things hidden."

And after she leaves, İrem looks over at Michael and says, "Well this gets more interesting with each passing day."

And Michael wants to feel excited by all this but somehow his heart isn't quite in it just yet. His heart seems to be someplace else and he lacks the will to go searching for it.

Dave sits in the cafeteria at the end of the day feeling a great relief to not be hearing his name attached to the word hoca. He just doesn't feel like a teacher at present or at least doesn't want to feel like a teacher but instead would very much like to be just a man sitting in a cafeteria waiting for something or, to be more accurate, someone to come by and call him by a different, more familiar term of endearment.

And as he stares rather wistfully at the door to the canteen, Jennifer appears.

Jennifer smiles when she sees Dave sitting by himself in the corner and walks over carrying her glass of cay. "Do you mind if I join you, boss?" she asks.

"No," he says, stirring slightly in his chair. "Please do."

Jennifer sits and while stirring in her sugar cube says, "You look a little sad today. Is anything wrong?"

"Oh," and he sighs, "maybe just a little homesick." He smiles weakly. "You ever get that?"

"Not anymore," she says. "I did a little in the first year but the city won me over pretty quickly. And the people, too. I'm crazy about the people here."

"Well apart from the students, I haven't really gotten to know the people very well."

"You should mingle more," she says. "The Turkish people are very warm and friendly."

"Well I volunteered to help with the play," he says, thinking he has tried to mingle, or at least to socialize, but he just doesn't seem to be as successful at it as he has been in America.

"That's a start," she says, "even if it's a bit late."

"Well better late than never, right?"

"Yes," she says, and then despite the early warning system flashing in her head, she says, "You never know what you will find if you open yourself up to it." And her mind begins to drift to thoughts of Deniz as she adds, "Sometimes life just goes in directions you don't expect."

Dave nods, says, "Yeah, about half the time." And he tries not to look too far back at his own life which, if he did, would probably be even more full of surprising twists and turns than that.

231

"I certainly didn't expect to fall in love here myself. At least not the way I fell."

"Love has a habit of usually not doing what we expect with whomever we expect it to do things with."

"That's certainly true in my case," Jennifer says, and wonders why she's talking to him like this but then thinks it's probably easier to confess things to people one won't see again, like in an airplane or while folding clothes in a laundromat, or at least, in his case, won't see for very much longer. "I've fallen in love with the wrong sex," she says. "But it seems like the right sex now." Then she looks out the window to the patio beyond where a few smokers, including Philip, stand huddled against the wind. "That certainly wouldn't qualify as normal where I come from."

Dave looks at her carefully for a long second before saying, "Who's to say what is normal or what isn't. That kind of thinking really doesn't apply when love comes knocking on your door."

"You think?" she asks, looking him in the eyes.

"I don't think," he says. "I know."

"And so I shouldn't be concerned about where it's going or what people will think?"

"I never have," he says.

"I should just go with it?"

"You have more to lose if you don't, don't you think?" and he smiles, though there's a tinge of sadness tugging at the corners as he adds, "And there'll be all those sleepless nights wondering what if if you don't."

"And that wouldn't be a good thing, would it?"

"No," he says. "We need all the sleep we can get. And it certainly helps if there's someone sleeping with us who makes us feel good."

Jennifer leans across the table and kisses him softly on the cheek. "Thanks," she says.

Dave is so flustered he almost blushes, but manages to blurt out, "For what?"

"For listening," she says. "And for saying more than you know." Then she gets up to leave. "See you, boss," she says.

And as Dave watches her walk away, he can't help but sigh.

It's been one of those days for Michael where he doesn't know how he makes it through nor does he remember what he has done just a few minutes before. It is as if he is sleepwalking except he knows he is awake but doesn't know anything else. He does know, though, that İrem is sitting opposite him drinking coffee and trying very hard not to look into his eyes.

"Well," İrem says, "you do have some ideas about the casting, don't you?"

"Yes and no," he says. "There are some very talented people in the acting classes but you never know with auditions. There are always surprises."

"So let's be open to surprise?" she says.

"Yes," he goes. "In theatre as well as in life."

She looks at him for a second and then says, "Are you always open for surprises in life?"

"I try to be," he answers but it is a guarded response, as if he is unsure of the fine print. "Why?" he asks. "You don't think I am?"

"No," she says. "I always thought you were very brave. To move to another country, to leave everything behind and start all over again in a place where the language is not your own, I think that is very brave."

"Especially at my age, too," he smiles, though quite a bit sadly at the edges.

233

"Age has nothing to do with it." And she looks at him closely again. "Why do you always bring up your age?"

"It's something I can't seem to ignore. I mean I try," he says, trying to make a joke of it but not feeling very humorous. "But there it is every time I look into the mirror. And I would avoid doing that, too, but I can't very well shave blind."

"You could just grow a beard," İrem says. "That would solve your problem and then you wouldn't be thinking so much about your age."

"You know," he says, "I've thought about that. Even attempted it once. But it was so grey, it depressed me so I shaved it off."

"You're hopeless," she says. "But I know I'm not telling you anything new by saying that."

"Yes, but you still love me anyway," he says, and though it's meant as a joke, the look she gives him takes his breath away for one very long second.

And though she looks away and does not answer him, she is confused by her inability to answer. And Michael is confused by her lack of response. And even though they both continue to work on blocking the script, they are lost to each other in a way they have never been lost before.

Brenda surrenders completely to Murat and is left dazed and exhausted after an hour or two's worth of lovemaking which is as much an assault as it is tender for he twists and turns her body every which way, has her standing in doorways, bent over chairs and her couch, sprawled across her dining room table, kneeling on the bed, and on her back with her ankles wrapped around his neck. He cannot seem to penetrate her enough and is, at times, lost in the act, no longer aware of where he is or who he is with, but just a humping, pumping body in constant motion looking for release. And she is a vessel tossed about on the sea.

"I don't know what I'm doing," Murat later says to Onur in a tavern in Bebek. "I cannot stop myself from going there and yet I know that if I keep seeing her, I will be forced to make a choice between her and Sönmez and the children."

"That is not a choice you want to make," Onur says. "You will lose everything if you leave your wife. And you will be supporting them all while trying to live yourself."

"I know," Murat says, "but I am lost. I cannot help myself."

"Brother, you had better get control," and Onur looks deeply into his old friend's eyes. "And be sure if you really have love for this woman or just lust because it is a heavy price to pay if it's just the sex."

"No," Murat says shaking his head, "it is more than that. I have so much in common with her in terms of work but there is such a vast difference in age, in culture, in history. And with Sönmez, I don't have to explain myself. I just don't feel any passion anymore."

"Are you a kid?" Onur says. "Must you feel passion every time you look at your wife? Passion dies, my friend, but love remains. What will be left when the passion dies with this Brit?"

And Murat stares at his friend unable to answer. There is just that question echoing in his head.

Deniz lies in bed holding Jennifer in her arms and listening to her breathing as she sleeps. She has never really done this before, held someone like this, so possessively, so protectively, as if she is the one responsible for her well-being. She has, instead, always been the first one up after lovemaking and usually out the door before the other awoke. Here, though, she cradles Jennifer's head in her arms, her body up against hers, one leg draped over hers, her arms circling Deniz's waist. Jennifer has not gone to her apartment to sleep since that New Year's Eve night but only to pick up some more clothes and has essentially moved in here with Deniz who has, for the first time in her life, not objected but actually encouraged it. They are a couple now, Deniz realizes, and though they haven't talked about her officially moving in, it is a conversation Deniz knows that must occur. And she will want this, she knows, wholeheartedly. For Deniz there is no doubt. She knows she is in love. Now she just patiently waits for Jennifer to broach the subject with her. And the only fear she has is that Jennifer may not. Then what would she do? How will she cope?

And as she holds Jennifer's warm body against hers this night, Deniz feels her grip tighten just a fraction. And her heart beats a little faster all through the night.

The auditions take place over a week and all through the process, each night, Michael and İrem sit next to each other taking notes. Occasionally one will look at the other and with no words spoken, they both understand the other's interest or dismissal of the talent delivering their monologue. And it is two nights of monologues before they post the list of students who they are calling back for two evenings of reading scenes. And here our full cast is assembled taking note of the proceedings.

Philip sits slumped over in his chair staring at the scenes he has reworked as each student attempts to master simplified Shakespearean dialogue. He occasionally cringes, more often is a bit puzzled not recognizing the words coming out of their mouths, and every so often looks up to see who is speaking so he can write their name down in the margins. He knows, of course, that Michael will make the final determination but also knows from their long association

236

that Michael is also open to suggestions. And though he would like to suggest they do another play, he has surrendered to the inevitable. And he thinks that with two months of rehearsals, they just might manage to pull it off.

Katja, meanwhile, runs the perspective dancers through the paces hoping to see flashes of talent she might have overlooked in her classes. So in a separate rehearsal room, she runs the auditioning dancers through routine after routine, eliminating some, holding onto others, evaluating, reevaluating, creating new movements as she goes along. She doesn't know exactly what she is looking for but knows instinctively that she will recognize it when she sees it. And she uses Berat and Elena to illustrate what she wants from the others and slowly, deliberately begins to weed out those who do not excite her until she is left with a group of twenty dancers who will act as members from both families and also the chorus who will not only move the plot along but will comment upon and complement the action of the play.

Berat and Elena, of course, know what their roles are and the auditions for them are just more opportunities to dance. And dance they do both during the auditions and afterwards on the street, in Elena's apartment, their bodies so adjusted to each other that even their lovemaking is a dance under sheets to music of their own invention.

Deniz meanwhile watches the auditions to get inspiration for the costumes she must design. She is listening for clues as to character which in turn will feed her imagination for color, for fabric, for style, for each group must be individual, distinct, so the audience will recognize them even before they speak. And as she sits there toward the back of the room, with Jennifer by her side absorbed in the audition process, she sketches in her pad almost absentmindedly, but figures appear bearing striking resemblance to the actors being selected for each role.

Meltem acts her heart out and Fersat, working on the film crew for Brenda, has the pleasure of recording it all. She emotes, rhapsodizes, weeps, flirts, runs the scale of human emotions that only a teenage girl in love for the first time would feel so convincingly that Michael can't help but turn to İrem saying, "She certainly has heart."

İrem nods in agreement and says, "I knew you'd like her."

"Yes," he says. "She doesn't treat the text as holy scripture but plays with it, energizes it. That's just what we need."

And Meltem doesn't know it yet but she has captured the lead part she wanted with her fearlessness.

It is a foregone conclusion that Pelin will be the featured singer in the play but even so she auditions under Murat's guidance with the rest since they are trying to find a male singer to represent the male roles and so she is paired with numerous other would be actor/singers from the Music Department with the trio of musicians she sings with acting as accompaniment. Meric finds himself paying as much attention to the couplings as Murat, Michael and İrem but for, he is beginning to realize, much different reasons. And though he doesn't want to admit it, he is finding himself becoming slightly jealous.

And throughout the entire audition process, Brenda supervises her crew to photograph and film everything. Everyone works as a well-orchestrated team with a shorthand of their own. Brenda's crew of six students, two camera crews and two photographers including Fersat, move in and out of view taking still photographs, filming auditions pieces, recording the singing and dancing auditions. And throughout it all, they begin the record of this play.

Dave sits off to the side watching Michael and İrem taking notes, looking at each other without speaking, then taking more notes. He is fascinated by their ability to communicate without words and realizes for the first time that they are a couple even if they don't realize it themselves. He then begins to look at the other couples in the room: Deniz and Jennifer, Murat and Brenda, Berat and Elena, other pairs of students scattered about the room, and begins to feel lonelier than ever. Then as he observes the other two loners in the room—Katja and Philip—and notes their involvement in shaping the play, he also begins for the first time to see the play as an extension of reality and not as theatre at all. And somehow this gives him hope, though he doesn't quite understand how.

And it finally comes down to Michael and İrem at his apartment on Saturday comparing notes while sitting down with the cast of characters to begin filling in names. It really isn't such a hard task after all since they both have come to think so much alike during the last four years that the actual process takes less than an hour. Once they have the final cast on paper, they retire to the kitchen where Michael stands leaning against the doorjamb drinking wine while watching İrem begin preparations for dinner. She looks up at him midway through and stops to say, "Maybe I should start teaching you some of these recipes."

"Why?" he asks.

"So you can cook them when I'm in America."

"Oh," and he sighs, "there's no need. I'll just stop eating after you're gone."

She begins to laugh then, thinking it is a joke, but the rather forlorn look on his face stops her. Her head tilts, her eyes take on that appraising look he has always had a hard time lying to, and she says, "Am I going to have to start worrying about you?"

"You shouldn't worry," he says. "I'll just go back to my old habits. This was just an interlude from them, that's all. And interludes always come to an end."

And here she finds herself for some reason almost offended. "Is that what this was to you?" she asks. "I was just an interlude?"

Somehow, he thinks, he didn't quite express himself correctly and now he is left with the always somewhat difficult task of worming his way out of whatever mess his careless tongue has gotten him into. So he hems a bit, haws, does all the things a person does when they are at a loss for words until something comes to mind to say. And he finally blurts out, "It wasn't like a Eugene O'Neill interlude. It was a good interlude."

"Eugene O'Neill?" she says and struggles to find the connection there. "You mean his play?"

"It was just one of those random associations with the word," he says. "I don't mean anything concrete by it."

"You're just babbling then," she says. "Is that it?"

"More or less," he nods.

She studies him for a long moment which, of course, would make him feel ill at ease if it wasn't for the wine and then she sighs. "Sometimes," she says, "I just don't understand you."

"Really?" he asks. "I always thought you did."

"Most of the time," she says. "But then there are the other times, like now, when I'm at a complete loss."

"Oh," he says, at a loss himself. "I kind of always thought you understood me."

"Usually I do," she says. "Except when I don't."

240

"I'm that difficult, I guess."

"Well you're not easy."

"I've heard that assessment of my character before," he says.

"I'm sure you have." Then she hesitates a moment before finally saying, "Don't you think, though, that it's about time you changed?"

"I'm too old to change."

"You always use age as an excuse."

"Well, there's no denying it's a factor," he says. Then his eyes coat over and a fog descends. He shakes his head as if to clear it, his eyes widening to see better, but neither action seems to help. It's still pretty foggy on the other side of his eyes. "I don't know how I got to be this old really. One day I woke up and looked in the mirror and there was this old guy looking back at me and I didn't recognize him. I said, who are you, old guy? And I saw his mouth move, heard my voice coming out of it, and then I had an epiphany. Christ, I thought. Either this is some sort of optical illusion or that old guy is me."

"I never think of you as old," she says. "Even when you talk like this. I just think you're exaggerating."

"That's kind," he says, "but my body every morning when I wake up tells me differently."

She is still looking at him with that tilted head of hers, those eyes that seem to judge the value of things, the mouth poised to ask a question he will not be able to answer or make a comment that will keep him awake for several nights to come. And finally she says, "You're going to make me worry about you the whole time I'm gone, aren't you?"

"That's not my intention," he sighs. "But six years is a long time. I'm sure you'll get over it eventually."

"You make it sound like the flu."

"Well at least there's no runny nose."

"That's a relief."

And the two of them stare at each other for a minute before İrem turns back to the stove and Michael drinks more wine watching her. A familiar tableau that ends the month but leaves both wondering just what awaits them from now on.

Scene 8
April

Michael knows he's in trouble when he finds himself listening to Frank Sinatra singing *The September of My Years* at two o'clock in the morning. Of course it could be worse, he thinks. He could be playing Mahler's *Ninth Symphony*. So he shifts gears and finds himself listening to Southside Johnny and The Asbury Jukes, dancing in his living room, singing along to those tortured blues, the cat sitting there on the edge of the rug watching him, thinking who knows what in his cat's mind. And Michael, Michael is oblivious to it all. He just slides across the floor, his slippered feet moving as if on ice, and a glass of Irish whiskey in his hand instead of a microphone, his heart, his mind in some other decade, sometime, a long, long time ago.

Dave sits at his computer surfing through amazon's music selections and making additions to his Wish List. He cannot believe he has lived this long without having the Siegel-Schwall Band on CD, or not replaced his old worn albums of the Earl Scruggs Revue and The New Riders of the Purple Sage or Little Feat and Tracy Nelson. He wonders what's wrong with him, this need to hear the music he grew up listening to, and fill the holes in his collection back home in New York. And as he adds one CD after another to his Wish List, he knows he will order them just before he boards the plane back home in June so that they arrive as he is unpacking and fill his house with the sounds of his youth.

Brenda's dream: she is standing watching boats on the horizon of the sea. There is a breeze blowing gently through her hair, she can taste salt on her lips, hear a flute playing somewhere behind her, sea gulls drifting by. She feels such peace, it is as if she has finally come home, and her gaze out to sea is not one of waiting or anticipation, but of an overseer. This is her view, the land behind her where she belongs, and all is right with the world.

Philip sits looking at the play on his desk. It is, he thinks, finished, or at least as finished as possible at this stage. Once rehearsals begin tomorrow night, things will begin to change. He knows this because he has worked with Michael for four years now and though Michael thinks the word is sacred, he also thinks words are living, breathing things and can be changed, adapted, moved around, and even substituted as long as the integrity of the play is not sacrificed. And Shakespeare, like his American Constitution, is open to interpretation.

So Philip sighs, pets the script one last time before stuffing it into an envelope to store away as an historical document in his file cabinet, and gazes out his window hoping to see something as unrelated to the theme of this play as possible to distract him. Unfortunately, all he sees is a couple walking hand in hand down the street. So much for distraction, he thinks, and closes his eyes.

Murat reviews the footage from the auditions and begins composing music for it in his mind. He sees this project now as something that can stand alone apart from the play, whether it is successful or not. For this will be a documentary about the creative process with his score and could play at festivals, in art houses, even be required viewing for anyone interested in or involved in theatre and the arts. And he becomes excited again about something he is doing. And his excitement must show because Sönmez says to him one morning before he leaves, "You seem happy these days."

He is startled at first, not expecting her to take notice of his moods, and looks at her at if for the first time. "Why do you say that?"

"It's obvious," she says.

"Is it?"

"Yes," she nods. "To someone who knows you anyway." Then she looks at him closely before saying, "And I do know you, don't I? Or have you forgotten that?"

"No," he says, almost apologetically. "I haven't forgotten."

"Good," she says and smiles. "That's something anyway."

He is at a loss as to what he should say in response and so he says nothing, just finds himself staring at her.

"Is it something you can tell me?" she asks.

"What?" he asks, momentarily confused.

"Whatever it is that is making you so happy."

And he is relieved then to know what to say next and he begins talking about the music he is composing for both the play itself and the filming of the play, his optimism of it as two separate compact discs, his hopes, his dreams, his desires, and suddenly she is the girl he always spoke to, the one who always listened, all through college, all the years afterwards, for almost two decades before the children came and changed the topic of their conversations. And it surprises him how easy it is to talk, and later, on his way to school to meet Brenda, he begins to feel more than guilt. He begins to feel remorse.

Meric doesn't know what he feels exactly but he does know what he doesn't feel and that is guilty about what he does feel. Instead he finds himself looking forward to the rehearsals, working for Michael as a coach with the actors, giving moral support to Pelin, watching the play begin to take shape, but most importantly, listening to Pelin sing. It is as if every song she sings, every lyric, is directed toward him.

İrem works beside Michael but feels for the first time that there is some gap between them, a barrier of sorts she has never noticed before because it was never there. She does not know how this has happened but for the first time in almost four years they can't seem to talk to each other. It puzzles her because from their very first meeting when Bekir suggested she be his assistant, they seemed to be a perfect match. But, of course, they still work as one person, each understanding intuitively what the other is thinking, but the distance is what happens when the work stops. For suddenly it is as if they have nothing to talk about but the play or any reason to be together except for it. And this depresses her immensely. And she can't seem to find a way to discuss this with him and that depresses her even more.

And the most unsettling thing about it all, the rehearsals take up every weekday night and all day Saturdays and Sundays, so that their routine of dinners at his place are now interrupted until the play is finished. So even though she spends every day and evening with him in the same rooms, they are no longer together like they used to be.

Deniz and Jennifer now paint together: Deniz in her shorts, a t-shirt, barefoot, her hair flowing freely down her back, on her shoulders, a brush held like a baton in her hand attacking the canvas, and Jennifer also in shorts, a halter top, sneakers, her blond hair tied back and swinging like a metronome as the brush in her hand glides across her canvas bringing forth images she doesn't quite understand. And so they now share a process that is integral to the core of Deniz's character. She has deliberately opened up a part of herself that has remained closed to everyone else and invited Jennifer in, not only to witness it, but to share it. And even though Jennifer has little skills or even aptitude for it, she has plunged in with the same intensity her lover possesses to not only understand her better, but to be at one with her, too.

Katja works with her dancers in a separate rehearsal room often visited by Michael who watches, makes a comment or two, then leaves her to immerse herself in the process of bringing to life, through movement, the theme of the play. And this she does with a vengeance, the play now becoming an extension of her own longing for Hasan, and her body grows taut, the muscles stretch, strain, ache for that which is elusive, just out of reach, in another dancer's arms. And the tension she creates on the rehearsal floor mirrors the tension in her own heart.

Brenda's crew is recording first the dancers, then the singers, each in separate rehearsal rooms, while another crew concentrates on the actors in the main room. The photographers float like ghosts through all the rooms, capturing moments, expressions, Fersat finding himself spending most of his time with the actors, trying hard not to take too many pictures of Meltem for fear his love would become obvious, while the other photographer, Kadir, finds himself fascinated by the dancers, and Brenda herself is drawn to the singers, getting lost in the music, the lyrics to the songs, a tendency she was always susceptible to, and drifting off to memories she would rather forget.

Dave is in the main rehearsal room every night coaching some of the actors with their English, especially working on accents that Michael has requested, and finding himself missing America more than he cares to at this point in the time remaining to him here. But one advantage to helping out is he gets to spend some time during the breaks with İrem who he finds out has been accepted to grad school in the US and plans to attend.

"So it's Stanford for you then?" he says over coffee in the cafeteria which Bekir has directed to stay open during rehearsals. "Not New York."

"Yes," she says. "I'll be going there in August to get settled before classes begin."

"You'll like Palo Alto," he says. "And San Francisco is very close so there'll be plenty of opportunity to take advantage of the arts scene there. Of course, it's not New York, but it is my second favorite US city."

"I'm looking forward to being there," she says, but somehow the sight of Michael staring vacantly at the counter while waiting for a cup of coffee disturbs her enough to distract her.

"Yes," Dave continues, "there's a lot there. Great restaurants, a really good opera house, and you can always take a drive up to the wine country. It's very different than here."

"Yes," she says, still only half in the conversation. "I imagine it is."

And Dave begins to wax poetic as he describes his favorite things about the San Francisco area and California in general but İrem isn't really paying very close attention. She is too busy watching Michael as he gingerly handles the rather hot liquid in the paper cup and starts back toward the rehearsal rooms without even glancing her way.

Later, as İrem takes her place beside Michael in the rehearsal room, she casually mentions her conversation with Dave. "He was giving me advice as to things I could do in Northern California."

Michael twitches a bit and says, "But he's living in New York. On Long Island, actually. And he's originally from the Midwest so what could he possibly be advising you about California?"

249

"Well he really seems to know it well," she says.

"From guide books and the movies probably and from his once or twice vacation there," and he can't help it if his tone is a bit derisive. "If you want to know about California and get advice about what to do there, you should talk to someone who's actually lived there for longer than a ten day vacation."

"Someone like you?" she asks, smiling slightly.

"Well, yes," he says. "Yes, I'd be the right one to ask. After all, not only did I live and work there in the theatre, mind you, but I also know you well enough to know what you'd be interested in doing."

"So you think you'd be the better person to be advising me then?" she asks.

"Of course."

"But," she says, slowly giving stress to her response, "you haven't, have you?"

"I haven't?" he says, knowing full well he hasn't but, as usual, being evasive in his reply.

"No," she says. "You haven't."

"Ah well, you know…" and he sort of trails off there, looking toward the actors who are coming back from their break. "We have time, don't we?" he says.

"I suppose."

"I mean you're not leaving yet, are you? We do have the rest of the semester and this play to get through, right?"

"Right," she nods.

"It's not like I don't know I should be telling you things," he says.

"You do?" she asks.

"Sure," he says.

"And you will?" she asks.

"Tell you things?"

"Yes," she says, then adds, "Talk to me."

He looks momentarily confused, then perhaps slightly guilty, though she can't be quite sure, before he answers. "I talk to you, don't I?"

"Yes," she says. "But lately we haven't really talked about anything but the play."

"Ah, well…" and he trails off again, looks around the room as more actors come in and then says, "We will. After this is over." And he smiles at her but it's a bit weak at the edges. "Promise."

And though she wants more, she settles for less as the rehearsals begin again.

And later, during the last break before they call it a night, Philip comes across İrem looking almost lost in the hall. "Are you okay?" he asks.

She looks at him, smiles weakly, and says, "Yes." Then she touches his arm. "Thanks for asking, though."

He nods, says, "I guess you're as tired as the rest of us from these late night rehearsals." Then he adds, "How's Michael holding up?"

"Fine, I guess," she says. Then she shrugs. "It's hard to tell, really. He doesn't talk anymore."

Philip looks at her carefully, not quite sure what to say, or even if anything is necessary. And his hesitancy makes the moment even more awkward than it should be.

"Well I'd better get back," she says. "We're working with the rival gangs and Michael isn't very happy with how it's going. That much is clear anyway."

And Philip watches her go, her shoulders slumped forward from a heaviness in her heart.

After rehearsals are over, Meric finds himself deliberately being slow leaving the building with the hopes that Pelin boards the same bus he does going back to

Karaköy where they can get the ferry across to Kadiköy. And, as luck will have it, he usually succeeds.

"Hi, teach," Pelin says as she slides into a seat next to him on the bus.

"Hi," he says, and can't stop the smile that spreads across his face.

And they converse, lost to the others who sit around them, going to the upper deck of the ferry to be farther away, laughing softly at what passes for witticisms, but neither is really paying much attention to words, just the sound of their voices, looks, half smiles, what passes between their eyes. This is the way they communicate, and they find themselves moving closer to what they actually mean.

Murat cannot say what he is thinking because he hasn't fully worked it out yet, but he knows he can't help being with her, inside her, holding her against his chest, looking into her eyes as they make love. But he also knows it is different somehow, in ways he cannot fully grasp, but now when he is with her he thinks of Sönmez, and when he is with Sönmez, he thinks of her. How can he reconcile the two, not be in inner turmoil as he stares at one, then the other, his eyes are a lie to himself, his life false, and he is less the man he set out to be and more someone else.

Brenda cannot fool herself any longer and says so to Philip at what has become his favorite meeting place in Kadiköy, a bar in what Philip refers to as the seedier part of town. He looks at her a bit sympathetically and says, "What will you do?"

"Get him to talk about it," she says. "We can't go on pretending things haven't changed. It will only make it harder to decide what to do."

"You could lose him if you push too far and too soon."

"Yes, but those are the chances one takes when one is 'the other women.'" And she laughs as she says it, imagining herself a character in some soap opera on TV.

"You're such a practical woman," Philip says, "for someone involved in an illicit love affair."

"Yes," she says and sighs. "It's the English in me. There's just no escaping it."

"Right," he says and takes a long sip of his beer. "Isn't that the truth, though?"

And they both are silent then, drinking their beer, watching what passes for barmaids here rub against the mostly male customers, and listening to the laughter all around them.

Michael is up and out of bed by five this morning, drinking coffee spiked with Bailey's Irish Cream, listening to Brian Ferry singing Dylan, and wondering where the time went. He slept poorly, as usual, and so is now beginning his day in the usual manner of being tired and weary to the bone. He wishes he wasn't so worn out but it seems to be a natural state of being for him and so he accepts it as his fate. Then he looks at the cat who just yawns, closes its eyes, and goes back to sleep.

"Go ahead," Michael says. "Rub it in."

He has his third cup of coffee of the morning and wonders if anyone will notice if he doesn't shave. Then he shaves anyway.

Later, in the cafeteria, Michael has what is his sixth cup of coffee and tries reading the specials menu but can't seem to get pass yumerta. He gives up and stares at the empty chair opposite him until Philip sits down in it.

"Good morning, Michael," Philip says. "You look like you could use some more sleep."

"Don't let looks deceive you," Michael says. "I am beyond sleep. I'm into Zen."

"Really?" Philip raises an eyebrow. "That's rather sixties of you."

"As in my age or the decade?" Michael asks.

"I was thinking the decade but your age could work, too."

"Thanks," Michael says. "I needed to be reminded of both."

"And I guess there's something else you need reminding of," Philip says.

"What's that?"

"Your feelings for İrem."

"Ahhhh," and he rubs his eyes and gives his head a little shake.

"You do remember you have feelings for her, don't you?"

Michael looks at his hands as if expecting some answer there but, of course, there is no answer, just the usual number of fingers in two otherwise empty hands. "There a point here to this question?" he finally says.

"I'm just trying to determine if you know what you're doing," Philip says. "Or rather if you know what you're not doing."

"I'm not sure I follow."

"Talk to her, Michael. You need to talk to her."

"I talk to her."

"Yes," and Philip sighs, "but not about the one thing you should be talking to her about."

Michael looks away, scans the rather empty cafeteria and rubs his eyes again. "I don't know what you mean."

"You love her, Michael. And she needs to know that. This unrequited love business is very much overrated."

"I don't know about that," Michael says. "Let me tell you a little story."

"Is this about you?"

"No, about my mother," he says.

"A family story?" Philip asks.

"More or less. It takes place many years ago, back when my parents were young and newly married. And it also concerns my father's best friend at the time, a guy named Red Felton, who, it seems, was in love with my mother, too, only my father didn't know that. Only my mother suspected it by the way he acted around her. He, though, never acknowledged it, probably out of respect for my father. Anyway the war broke out and Red Felton became a pilot. Before he left for overseas to fly from your country over Germany, he gave my mother his wings to hold for him until he returned."

"His pilot's wings?"

"Yes."

"And why do I have the feeling something bad happened?"

"That's either the writer or the cynic in you," Michael says, "but in either case, you're right. He never returned."

"And your mother kept the wings?"

"Until she gave them to me after telling me that story," Michael says.

"And the point being…"

"That love that is impossible to act on is best left unspoken. Especially," Michael says smiling slightly, "if you plan to go get yourself killed in some war."

"And is that what you're planning?"

"No, but going to America for six years to probably not return, or at least not return here, or, for that matter, to return but find me not here, is close enough to the same thing."

255

"Well it's an interesting story, sad even, but I don't think relevant here. Neither one of you is married and you are both obviously in love, at least obvious to everyone but you two, so I still think you should talk to her about it."

"What would be the point?" Michael says. "I mean, what would really be the point?"

"Well she's planning on going to America for her PhD," Philip says. "That would mean she'll be gone for those six years. If you don't tell her now, it'll be too late after she's gone."

"It's already too late," Michael says. "I'm about thirty years too late."

"Don't you think she should be the judge of that?"

"Judge of what exactly?"

"Whether your age is a matter of concern or not," Philip says. "And if you want my opinion, it is not."

"I didn't ask for your opinion," Michael says. "Did I?"

Philip is silent for a moment, looking at Michael as he stares back. "No," he says finally. "You didn't."

"Well then," Michael says waving a hand through the air, "there you go."

"But I have one," Philip insists.

"Opinions are like noses," Michael says. "We all have one."

"She loves you, you know."

"No, I don't know," Michael says. "I don't know any such thing." He sits back and feels ever so weary, of the conversation, of the coffee that has grown cold in his cup, of the chairs in the cafeteria, of life in general. "We are very good friends. We have been that for these four years and we'll be that until she leaves. Very good friends to the end."

"But don't you owe it to her to tell her how you really feel about her?"

"What I owe her," Michael says, slowly, carefully, so there will be no mistake in Philip's hearing, "is to encourage her in the chance of a lifetime: to get her PhD from a top university in the US so that her career here, there, wherever, will be assured. She is still young enough to have her whole life laid out before her, and that degree, from that university, will give her more options for roads to follow. And I am old enough, have lived long enough, have made enough bad choices in my life to know the value of what she has. And I won't confuse the issue with sentiment."

Philip is silent again for a long second while he watches Michael drink what's left in his cup and signal one of the cafeteria staff for a refill. He takes a deep breath and says, "I think you're making a mistake."

Michael laughs softly, shrugs, says, "It won't be the first, nor the last." Then he looks deeply into Philip's eyes as he adds, "But it is my right to make it, isn't it?"

And there it lies on the table between them and Philip, sensing it is useless to say any more, lets it lie. And as Michael's eyes slowly close, we turn our attention elsewhere.

To Meltem frustrated that her scenes are somehow not playing right and that her partner doesn't seem to be in the same play she is in. She looks helplessly at Michael and İrem who seem, she thinks, to be looking back sympathetically at her. Then Michael whispers something to İrem who nods and calls a break. "I think," he says to the two lovers, "you both need to watch a couple of movies so you get the idea of what I want from you."

Then they adjourn to an empty classroom where İrem plays **Roman Holiday** and **Tootsie**. And between the laughs, İrem asks if they are beginning to understand how Michael wants the lovers to act, and Meltem, of course, has understood from the beginning and the actor playing Romeo starts to nod and afterwards, on their way home, they both begin to rethink their scenes while İrem looks for Michael who is nowhere to be found. Instead she finds herself sharing a taxi with Brenda to the ferry at Karaköy.

"The play looks like it's coming along very nicely," Brenda says.

"Really?" İrem says. "Sometimes, when you're as close to it as I am, you're just not sure."

"No," Brenda says. "I think it's shaping up very nicely." Then she smiles. "I understand you showed the lovers **Roman Holiday** tonight."

"Yes," İrem says. "And **Tootsie**, too. It was Michael's idea. To get them to see the kind of tone he wants for the lovers' scenes. He wants them to understand about people in love trying to bridge what appears to be impossible barriers and sometimes getting it and other times being unable to surmount the obstacles."

"Romantic comedy," and Brenda laughs. "What a great idea."

"He wanted to also show **Bringing Up Baby** but we didn't have enough time."

"Did the students get it?"

"I think so. One, Meltem, already was playing it right."

"You two, Michael and you, I mean, seem very close."

"We are," İrem says, "were, still are, I guess." And she sighs. Then, for reasons she fully doesn't understand, she says, "It's all a bit confusing now."

"I don't mean to pry," Brenda says, "but I always thought that you two were…" and she hesitates slightly before she says, "…involved."

"No," İrem says, shaking her head perhaps a little bit too much. "We're just friends." Then she adds, "At least I think we're friends, but sometimes I just don't know."

And Brenda, sensing a comrade-in-arms, says, "Would you like to stop for a drink somewhere before going home?" And when İrem looks at her unsure exactly what is being offered, Brenda adds, "I could use another woman to talk to myself."

And once the ferry docks, they settle on a club Brenda knows from outings with Philip.

Meanwhile, up the hill on Bar Street, Meric and Pelin are sharing a table, drinking beer and trying rather unsuccessfully not to look too deeply into each other's eyes. They also are unsuccessful at keeping their hands apart, and soon, with fingers intertwined, and eyes locked, the inevitable question arises with the expected answer to follow and with beer still in their glasses, Meric pays the tab and leads her home to hear her sing love songs exclusively to him all night long in his bed.

And Deniz is emptying drawers to accommodate Jennifer's accumulated pile of clothes. And as she empties one more drawer, she turns to Jennifer and asks, "How much more do you have at your place?"

"Maybe a little more than is here already."

"Hmmm," Deniz goes, then looks at the already full bureau and says, "Perhaps we should get another closet." And she looks at Jennifer. "What do you think?"

"You want me to bring the rest of my clothes here?" Jennifer asks, almost afraid as she asks the question of the possible answer.

"Well it makes sense, doesn't it? I mean, you're practically living here so you might as well just move in."

"You really want me to?"

"I do if you do," Deniz says and her eyes stay fixed on Jennifer as she adds, "Do you?"

"Oh yes," Jennifer says, then flies into Deniz's arms. "Yes, yes, yes."

And they tumble onto the bed, the clothes left half in, half out of the opened drawers, to be dealt with in the morning.

And Elena and Berat are dancing under the stars on the roof of her building oblivious to the world below.

Dave sits with the door to his balcony open and gazes down at the now empty, dark school buildings. Now that his time here is drawing to a close with just two months to go, he has regrets that he had not become more involved in the life of the city, had not explored more, had not really become friends with anyone here.

Katja choreographs dances in her head, tries out steps in her living room, dreams sequences in her sleep. Her partner is always Hasan, light as air, nimble on his feet, his arms lift her through space.

Philip begins to lose himself in the outline of his book. The characters in his mind are beginning to take shape, bits of dialogue are scribbled in his notebook, and what once was going to be a screenplay is now most definitely a novel. He cannot help feeling a certain joy to be working again on his own project and though he knows he'll be called on by Michael to make certain changes in the play, he also knows he is free to begin losing himself in his own make believe world. And he can't help but feel immense relief at that prospect.

Brenda doesn't know why but she feels a certain lifting of a burden as she talks with İrem. She finds she can tell her things that she could not share with anyone else, especially a man. For only a woman, she thinks, can truly understand

260

her dilemma. "I just hate thinking of myself as a home wrecker. It is just not the person I set out to be. I am really much too morally traditional for this."

"It's funny how we often end up being or doing things we would not have thought possible," İrem says. "I still don't understand my relationship with Michael. Sometimes I think it is one thing and then at other times it seems to be something else."

"What does he think it is?"

"That's another problem I have," she sighs. "It's impossible to know just what he thinks. The better I know him, the less I understand him."

"I think that's the problem with men in general," Brenda says. "They seem simple enough but they're never as simple as they seem. I think we women are much easier to understand because we basically only want two things from men: for them to respect us and for them to be honest in their love." She also sighs. "But men usually fall short on those, especially that second one."

"Is Murat dishonest with you?"

"Well just the fact that he's cheating on his wife puts his honesty in question, don't you think?"

"I see what you mean."

"And he's putting me in that position, too. If only he'd make up his mind one way or the other. Or is he just trying to have it both ways, which would cause me to lose all respect for him."

"Do you regret getting involved with him?"

"Yes," Brenda says and sighs once more. "At first I was just carried away with the thrill of it all. I mean, it was so different from my marriage that I was literally swept away with the passion. But now I feel cheap in a way and I don't want to have this feeling, if you know what I mean. I want to either be legitimately his or else I want it to end. I need some sort of resolution here." She looks at İrem with what could be tears in her eyes, though her voice is firm, almost violent in tone. "Do you understand?"

"Yes," İrem says. "I more or less feel the same way. I would like to know what Michael feels so I can decide whether to go to America or not."

"You would give it up for him?"

"He is my best friend," İrem says. "And I just don't think I'll feel what I feel for him for anyone else. I mean, I'm 32 years old. I'm not some kid who's never been in love before. But these last four years I haven't even looked at another man. So that must mean something, right?""

"I think," Brenda says, reaching over and putting her hand on İrem's forearm, "that we both need to have a serious talk with our respective men." And she smiles as best she can as she adds, "And that's a scary thought, isn't it?"

And both end the evening wondering why they didn't become friends before this night. But they are both grateful that they finally have, for the comfort they both feel in their shared hope and fear.

Michael sits in the dark when he comes home. In the dark waiting for daylight, which he knows will come, with new thoughts, new revelations, new insights into the past, the present, the future, and old truths, too. For surely those await him also, in the daylight that is sure to come. So he sits, a glass of whiskey in his hand, the cat curled up on the couch near him, and waits. He is in no hurry. He has done this before and will do it again, all the nights still left to him, waiting for all the days he has yet to endure.

Scene 9
May

İrem wakes with her heart pounding in her chest, a dream so vivid in her mind that she cannot help but believe in the truth of it. In it, she sees Michael standing on a pier with a crowd of people looking out to sea, resting on a shaft, his body leaning into that wind that blows in from the sea, and in his eyes there is such a mournful expression that it breaks her heart to see him. And in the dream she does see them as she stands on the deck of that ship, her arm upraised, her palm open, she is waving goodbye. The ship is pulling out, passengers all around her on the deck, there are people shouting, a horn is blowing, and she knows she is leaving forever, a heaviness in her soul. And as the ship pulls farther away, the crowd on the shore shrinking in the distance, his face looms over her, her hand reaches out, she can almost touch his face, there are tears in his eyes, in hers, and she opens her mouth to speak but nothing comes out, just the ship's horn, and his face, his face there in front of her, his face.

She wakes with that face still in her mind. His face.

Meric wakes up half expecting to find an empty bed, last night being some dream he had that he is sorry to wake from, but there she is, asleep, her hair spread out on his pillow, her mouth slightly open, her breathing regular and peaceful, her leg half exposed as it sticks out from under the sheet. Pelin, he thinks. Here. In my bed.

He stares at her in wonder. She is so beautiful, he thinks. And last night was a revelation, the sex so intense, and yet so tender at times to be almost heartbreaking, the way her eyes locked on his, how she responded to every move, every flex of every muscle, her body twitching with pleasure, her organisms frequent and prolonged, her moans still reverberating in his ears.

He grows hard remembering and cannot stop himself from lifting the sheet and easing himself inside her, she who is already wet waiting. And the night might be over, but the morning lies ahead as those moans begin to fill his ears once more.

Katja has begun to speak to Hasan in the kitchen as she prepares her breakfast. She knows, of course, he is not there but she speaks anyway for it comforts her to speak to him in Bosnian, a language she was teaching him much as he taught her Turkish, by the sound mixed with actions, by words mingled with her hands, as if she is weaving a picture on a loom in the air. And it is the language she speaks only to him in this country. And she knows he can hear her. She knows this with all her heart and that knowledge gives her peace.

Murat finds himself eating breakfast with Sönmez, the kids packed off to school or her mother's, the house finally quiet, like in the early days of their marriage. Sönmez is pouring him a second cup of coffee which he is sipping pensively as he stares at the remnants of the food on his plate. He looks up at her, her eyes watching him intently, and smiles. He almost says something but realizes there is really nothing to say, this moment is perfect without words, the look in her eyes warm and understanding, that he feels, for the first time in a long time, at peace in his own home.

Dave has begun to pack. He knows it is still too early but he can't help it if he starts to put things away in one of the suitcases he brought. It is winter clothing, after all, and he knows there is no sense in leaving it out, he'll never wear any of these clothes in this country again. Sweaters mostly, and some wool pants, a down vest he bought from L.L. Bean, and his silk long johns. The weather now is so warm, not hot yet, but definitely just jacket weather in the evenings, and since he lives so close to campus, he really doesn't even have a need for that. It is only just a short walk back after rehearsals and since he's there every night, including the weekends, he could even pack them. And the packing actually relaxes him. He has these clear visions of being home again, seeing old friends, plucking weeds in his garden, eating Chinese take-out, drinking Chilean wine. And it's that thought that makes him wistfully think of a missed opportunity with İrem, but there's no point trying to pick up whatever strand there might be from that. No, he reasons. It is time to look forward to going home. And the play, with all the romantic tensions, makes him long for familiar territory once again.

Brenda deletes yet another email from Mark. She has read it, of course, this time because she has not read any of the previous ones and her mother had called a few days ago to ask why she was being so rude to him so she read this last one to perhaps contemplate answering it but words just would not come and in the end she hit the delete button. What could she say? she thinks. She cannot even clearly remember what he looks like, his face sometimes just a faded photograph from some distant place in her past. It seems so strange to her that that is so but then again he rarely enters her mind anymore. Murat helped erase him from her consciousness, helped to put him into the past tense of all her sentences and that has given her a great deal of relief. But lately Murat, too, is receding from her present, or at least minimizing his role in her life, he having not come to her place for over three weeks now, for as long as the play has been in rehearsal, and she knows it is difficult with this schedule that leaves little time for anything outside teaching and the play, but still, she knows something has shifted in him and perhaps in her, too. Life is so strange, she thinks, and sighs as she begins getting ready for school.

Jennifer spends her breaks in the costume shop watching Deniz work. The sketches are all approved and now she is creating the various costumes out of different fabrics for each group of characters. And the actors come in to try them on, modeling them for Deniz as she makes adjustments, changes colors, takes in or lets out hems. And Meltem is there, twirling around the shop in her white cotton dress with Fersat taking pictures. The dancers are the easiest since they will wear nothing but flesh colored body stockings and the cabaret act that will also act as transitions are dressed as if they are performing at a Manhattan supper club: Pelin in an evening gown, the trio in dinner jackets.

And later, after the shop is closed and everyone is at rehearsals, Jennifer models some of the costumes for Deniz and Deniz, to both their delight, gets to help her dress which leads to helping her undress which leads to some very heavy panting on top of fabric on the floor.

Philip roams throughout the neighborhood between his classes and the play rehearsals. Though he is actively involved in rewriting some scenes for Michael, his mind is really on something else: his own vision of lovers, mix-ups, confusion reigning, but not in the characters on stage but in the ones spread throughout the seats in the rehearsal rooms, on the production staff, the film crews, his colleagues stumbling through their own lives, in Istanbul, and the people living in it with them. And he draws his inspiration from his walks, his solitary research gathering jaunts throughout the neighborhoods, his eyes absorbing everything, his mind always active, remembering conversations, recording looks, sighs, the missed opportunities, the book taking shape in his head.

Michael rests his head in his hands, closes his eyes, and thinks he really needs to get some sleep. He is not, after all, young anymore and as one ages, one needs more rest. At least that's what they say in those magazine articles that he tends not to read. But not reading them does not mean he does not know what they say because he has enough people around him who seem to memorize them and repeat them verbatim whenever they get the chance. And, of course, they're right, for he feels it in his bones and finally can't resist the temptation to lay his head down on his arms on the desk and let his mind empty.

"You really need to get more sleep," İrem says, confirming what he already knows, that she is one of those people who reads those articles.

He looks up at her and smiles weakly. "That was what I was trying to do."

"Not here," she says. "You should get more sleep at home. Like in a bed. You know," she adds "like normal people do."

"Are you insinuating I'm not normal?" and he tries for some indignation but it doesn't come out right. He thinks perhaps he can't really be indignant with her and she, of course, probably knows that.

"No," she sighs. "I'm just saying that you need to get more sleep."

"Well you know," he says, flourishing a hand rather weakly through the air, "the play, classes, the semester drawing to a close." He sighs dramatically. "It's all a bit much, isn't it?"

"Yes," she says, tentatively, watching him carefully.

"So who has time for sleep?"

"We all need to make time for sleep," she says. "Otherwise we won't have the energy we need to accomplish all the things we need to do."

"Ah," he goes. "Logic."

"Yes," she says. "I know it's not something you like hearing."

"No," he says. "I have nothing against logic. It's just I'm not necessarily good at it."

"That," she concurs, "is an understatement."

"It's why I have you around," he says, then remembers that he won't have her around much longer and begins to feel sadness settling in. How, he wonders, will he ever be able to get his mouth to speak after his brain has begun working.

"Well," she says, "what will you do when I'm in California?"

"Become even more illogical, I guess."

"That is not what I was hoping to hear."

"And it's not what I would like to say, but as usual I say it anyway."

She sighs then. Says, "You're not giving me peace of mind about leaving."

"Don't worry," he says in what should be his most reassuring voice but somehow doesn't sound very reassuring to her or to him. "I've been this way so long that it's the only way I function."

And though he feels even more exhausted than he felt before, he knows he has lost any desire to sleep.

Even though they work together every night and on the weekends during rehearsals, Brenda does not really have much opportunity to speak with Murat. They are involved in different aspects of the production, working with different groups, which is part of the problem, but also she notices a frosting, almost, in his attitude, as if they are colleagues who

269

barely know each other. This is somewhat upsetting to her but she does not speak of it with him, partly out of pride or vanity, maybe, but also out of fear. For she is not certain she would like to hear his answers to her questions and finds herself hoping this will pass.

Murat, meanwhile, is finding himself confused about everything. Whenever he sees Brenda he undresses her in his mind, bends her over, and fucks her till it hurts. But whenever he doesn't see her, his mind drifts to Sönmez, sees pictures of their life float by in that camera in his mind, and can't help but be mystified as well as grateful for the fact that they spend each morning having breakfast together while talking about the day that is unfolding before them, the one that passed, the tomorrows that lie ahead. And it seems to him that just as he was finally beginning to make a choice, he finds he cannot. For how does one choose the future when the future is uncertain no matter how he decides to live it? So Murat buries his head in his score and concentrates on orchestrating lovers as confused as he is.

And the play takes shape, the nights, the weekends, all pass, the actors are off book, costumes are fitted, the set rises around them, technical issues like projecting subtitles are tackled and solved, the orchestra of musicians and the singers along with the dancers help carry the action forward, and everyone connected with the play begins to glow as they sense something special happening in these rehearsal rooms, on the stage once they enter the tech and then dress rehearsals. And Michael and İrem would be happier if it wasn't for the fact that this is their last production together. And though the play is essentially a romance with a happy ending now, after all the confusion a sadness descends where the director and his assistant sit trying to shape the play in their own image but their own image is far removed from the play.

Fiction reflects life but life, they both realize, does not always reflect fiction.

And finally, the play. We now go to opening night and sit in attendance with the rest of the audience. There is Michael, his grey suit reflecting a face made for poker, his eyes half closed, a curtain drawn on his rapidly beating heart, and İrem sitting next to him there in the front, a black silk dress hugging her slim body, her legs crossed right over left, her arms resting on the armrests of her seat, her eyes focused steadily on the curtain that has not risen yet though it takes all her self-control not to look Michael's way. Katja sits on Michael's other side, dressed in a tight red dress that allows those shapely dancer legs to bask in the admiring glances of anyone lucky enough to view them, though she is not aware of any interest in her since she is too preoccupied running the dances she choreographed through her head and hoping her dancers are doing the same thing.

Philip is in the next row with Brenda next to him, his head buried in the program as if looking for typos with his one pair of black dress shoes shined on his way here by a bootblack in Eminönü, an appropriate colored tie borrowed from Michael for the occasion, and a new haircut just for opening night. Brenda, meanwhile, is preoccupied with wondering what Murat must be doing since he is in charge of the orchestra for this night's performance. She is, though, looking almost radiant in a blue satin evening dress with a plunging neckline and bare back, her blond hair shimmering in the light. She has never felt so much like a woman as she does this night.

And in the rows behind and to the side sit the other members of our cast mixed in with other university personnel as well as members of the Board of Directors with Bekir and Özge in front looking elegant in formal attire, Jennifer and Deniz both dressed in black silk dresses that reveal legs that are crossed in toward each other, and Dave a few rows back surrounded by Prep teachers. And finally Meric is there, also, shifting nervously in his seat, dressed in his black suit and feeling somewhat stifled by his red striped tie.

The house lights dim and the members of the trio take their positions for the opening song, their instruments play the introduction to the Cole Porter tune *Let's Do It* and Pelin appears in a shimmering green evening dress, a cordless microphone in her hand, and she begins to hum along before breaking into a jazzy, sexy rendition of the song. Midway through, the curtain rises on the bare stage and the orchestra then begins as Elena and Berat stand motionless in the center, then twist out of their embrace and begin a coy dance of seduction, moving toward, then pulling away from each other as the music ends, the dancers run off into the wings stage left and from the wings on stage right the members of the rival families appear and the action of the play begins.

The first scene is on the street with all the actors of the two families dressed in contrasting colors as members of two rival street gangs. And the orchestra plays, the dancers begin to fill the stage with movement, with swirling color, and an energy passes from the stage to the audience as the dancers part onstage to reveal Berat and Elena, who do the first of a series of variations on the lovers' dance, and as it ends, the heads of the two families meet and the story commences. There are the age old arguments, spoken in two languages, Turkish by one family, English by the other, with subtitles superimposed on monitor screens above and to both sides of the stage. The misunderstandings, the fighting, the feud explained, and as both families part, our Romeo and Meltem as our Juliet are left staring at one another from opposite sides of the stage.

And here the play becomes a romantic comedy of mutual attraction but without a common language so there is miscommunication, misunderstandings, as two potential lovers try to navigate the chasm of language separating them from bliss. And their young friends act like two rival rap groups trying to outdo each other in song, in dance, in verbal insult, while keeping the lovers apart. And people bump, people grind, they rock, they roll, the stage is alive with music and dance, and the audience claps along, stomps their feet, sways in their seats, a Turkish audience in love with music, it being in their souls, and the two languages at first clash, but soon mesh, and by the end of the first act, there is wild applause as the curtain drops.

And it is here, Michael knows, that the audience has accepted the concept for the play since they are eager to laugh, and do so in all the right places, and it is then that Michael turns to İrem smiling for they both know they have passed the first hurtle and can now sit back and relax for both know they have a hit on their hands. İrem squeezes Michael's hand as the first act ends with thunderous applause and says, "Well it looks like you're the man of the hour."

"Not just me," he says, "but everyone involved, including you." And before he can continue, Bekir is standing before him with his wife beaming broadly.

"Well Michael Bay, we have a success here."

And Katja is backstage with her dancers, Meric is coaching Pelin, Deniz is backstage also making some adjustments on the lovers' costumes, and Philip who was prepared to slink further down into his seat is now outside enjoying his cigarette while Murat keeps him company and

Brenda supervises the film crew circulating through the audience filming reactions to the play.

The lights flicker during Philip's third cigarette calling them all back to their seats to the second half of this lovers' comedy to watch the lovers' dance, the brushing of hair in couples, in threesomes, hands passing through hair as if stroking the very skin of their beloved. And this dance starts the act as couples twist and turn, led by Berat and Elena, to fall in and out of love and then back in, as things change only to go back to where they should have been, and hearts that are broken are mended whole. And in the end, a wedding and all is well within all the worlds, the languages mesh, the tableaus are arranged, and joy lights up the stage before the lights fade to give everyone their peace in a night of endless love.

The audience rises to its feet, clapping their hands, stomping their feet, shouting bravo to the cast, the crew, the musicians, the singers, the dancers, a beaming choreographer, a director and his assistant holding hands, a triumph for the end of the school year. And though this will run for two more weeks, this is the night they will all remember in years to come. And Michael and İrem, still clutching hands, lead them all in one final curtain call, their eyes misting over as the world they once envisioned together steps one foot closer to reality.

Later, after the dust has settled, the audience departed, make-up washed off, costumes changed for street clothes, they all gather in the gallery for a cast party hosted by Bekir and the school. There is food, there is drink, music to dance to, a kind of gaiety reserved for those who have climbed to heaven and seen the light. The dancers, of course, dominate the dance floor, twirling and twisting like modern day Dervishes, with Berat and Elena in the center until Katja is coaxed out onto the floor by Dave who seems to have left his inhibitions at the door, though his free style rock and roll cannot compete with her fiery temperament as she shows them all what a pair of legs and hips can do. And soon almost everyone is out on the floor, in couples, in threesomes, even solo, they glide across the gallery floor as the band shifts from song to song, with many singing along to a familiar tune, and as İrem takes the floor with an empowered Dave, her dress floating in the air, her slender legs causing Michael to turn away lest he fall in love all over again. And as the floor vibrates with all this festive spirit, Michael drifts off to the garden outside where Philip sits on a bench enjoying the night air and a cigarette.

"Well if it isn't the man of the hour," Philip says. "Why aren't you in there dancing away?"

"Somehow," he says, sighing as he sits on the bench next to him, "I think sitting is more desirable at this point. Enjoying the night air, and talking with a friend."

Philip looks at him closely and then says, "Do I detect a note of melancholy here?"

"Perhaps," Michael says. "It never seems to be far away these days."

"But you should be basking in your success."

"Well I am," Michael says. "More or less, anyway."

"And which is that exactly?" Philip asks. "More or less?"

Michael looks at him and makes what could pass for a disgusted face if they were anything but friends. "If you're going to be a pain in the you-know-where," he says, "I'll sit at another bench."

"Sorry," Philip says. "It's just this writer's mind of mine, looking for answers to questions I probably shouldn't ask in the first place."

"I think they call that curiosity," Michael says. "And it's not listed with the seven virtues." He then looks at Philip and asks, "There are seven, right?"

"Beats me," Philip says. "I always came up short when it came to virtues."

"Hmmmm," Michael goes. They sit in silence then, each lost in some private world of their own before Michael stirs and says, "What's up with you anyway? You've been awfully quiet of late."

"It's this book in my head," Philip says. "I am having visions."

"That's dangerous stuff," Michael says. "Though, of course, the only actual visions I had were related to substance abuse, which, I'm glad to report, are all behind me now."

"Well the play was a vision."

"Of a different, more benign sort," Michael agrees.

"And that's the kind my book is."

"Well you're safe then from sainthood or the nuthouse."

"That's a relief."

And they both drift back into silence while the party rages on without them. And as we turn our attention back inside, we see Deniz and Jennifer in the middle of the floor dancing with Meltem as Fersat frantically clicks away. And Pelin is swept along in Meric's arms. Elena meanwhile dazzles Berat with her own seductive dance and takes the tie he wore just for her into her hands and leads him away from the dance floor, out to the garden, off to the street beyond. She flags down a taxi to take them back to her apartment where she will dance naked in candlelight for his eyes alone, a dance he will remember in candle glow in his mind's eye, long after she has left for Kiev to begin her life as a professional dancer and he has returned to Adana to open a dance studio for children, their lives forever from this night forward to be lived apart.

Meltem, though, will not abandon Fersat but will continue to be his muse, posing for what should be candid shots, though there will be nothing candid about her, for many years to come. And the other couples—Meric and Pelin, Deniz and Jennifer—will continue their dancing at home. Katja will also dance at home but with her invisible partner, his arms encircling her waist, his breath on her neck, his eyes boring holes into her dreams. Dave, too, will have dreams of whirling women with quivering thighs dancing on tables for his eyes alone.

It is only İrem who will not continue dancing but will work her way through the crowded floor seeking Michael, only to find him out in the garden sharing that bench with Philip. "Why aren't you dancing?" she asks as she stands before him.

"Ah, well I'm sitting here chatting with my old friend Philip. Keeping him company, I guess you could say, since he's such a miserable dancer and feels so left out."

"I'm not that miserable," Philip says. "Just in the wrong decade for the kind of dancing I do best."

"That's one way to look at it," Michael says. "But what decade you belong in is open for some heated debate."

"And you," İrem says. "Are you going to sit there and pass up the chance to dance with me at what is our last cast party for our last production together?"

Michael looks almost stunned by that remark and for once can think of nothing to say. He just stares at her with his mouth slightly open.

"Well?" she says.

"He's speechless," Philip says and laughs. "Will wonders never cease?"

Michael looks over at him and his lip curls slightly. "I don't need any comments from the Peanut Gallery."

"A reference to what?" Philip asks. "Something obviously American."

"I keep forgetting," Michael says, "that I am surrounded by foreigners."

"Take heart, old boy," and Philip pats him on the back. "We both are."

"As amusing as this might possibly be," İrem says, "I'm still waiting for my dance."

And Michael looks at her again with admiration in his eye, even if his heart sits heavily in his chest. "I'm all yours," he says and stands.

And though somehow they both don't know quite how to take that, Irem puts out her hand, which he takes, and leads him inside to dance their hearts out. And the night ends with her in his arms on the dance floor and Philip filing one more memory away for safe keeping.

Jennifer feels at a loss since she does not know how to make her life with Deniz work. Neither one of them is part of a gay community, there are no other gay couples they know, no clubs that they frequent, no gay vacation packages they have booked, and so how do they continue in this very straight world as a couple when they don't exactly think of themselves as gay, just as two people who happen to be the same sex that are in love. Deniz is no help since she does not care how the world views her, has always been unconventional in her lifestyle, and so does not even think in these terms. But Jennifer's Midwestern upbringing forces her to look at things, even things that are not traditional, in a traditional way, and so she finds herself trying to define what they are in conventional terms. But Deniz only laughs.

"Why must you label things, us, the way we will live? Just forget all that and enjoy what we have. Who cares about what we are called?"

"But other people will define us," Jennifer says. "So we might as well define ourselves first."

"You are my other half," Deniz says and looks deeply into her eyes. "Is that not definition enough?"

"And we will tell our parents that?" Jennifer asks. "Our friends?"

"We don't have to tell them anything," Deniz says. "We will just be and they will either accept it or not. But as long as we accept it ourselves, that is all that really matters."

"Is it really as simple as that?"

"For me, it is," Deniz says. "What about for you?"

And here Jennifer can think of no reply except to reach out and pull Deniz to her. "I can't breathe without you," she says and holds her tightly against her chest.

"Then breathe," Deniz says, her mouth in her ear, her hand rubbing her head, tangling itself in her hair. "Breathe." And their mouths become one and suddenly Jennifer finds labels superfluous. The only thing important is what she feels in her heart.

Meric finds bits and pieces of Pelin's clothing everywhere, a pair of shoes he almost trips over, a pair of panties and bra in his underwear drawer, a dress hanging in his closet, a pair of jeans draped over a chair. It would have made him uneasy in the past but now he finds it rather appealing. She is, after all, young, vibrant, sexy, and he finds himself tingling with anticipation just thinking about her. And seeing these bits of clothing only excites him more. He refrains from fondling them, though, because he doesn't want to think of himself as developing a fetish, but his hands itch to touch her. And knowing he will see her tonight, first at the club where she sings, then in his own bed for a private encore, makes him giddy with desire.

Murat sits in his living room drinking raki with Onur while their wives discuss a Turkish soap opera. The men look at each other over their raised glasses and Murat can tell that Onur is saying silently that he made the right choice. Murat, though, thinks he made a choice by not making a choice which isn't quite the same thing but good enough. He has opted for the path of least resistance and though he should be at least satisfied with that, he feels instead a lingering regret for what might have been if he was the man he had always thought he was. But nothing is as simple as he once thought and though he isn't unhappy seeing Sönmez smiling before him as she chatters on with the wife of his best friend, he is though strangely numb. But this will pass, he thinks, and life will continue the way it was meant to go. It really can't go any other way. And he will be happy one day, he tells himself. One day he will forget even that he could have made a choice. One day.

Brenda stares at the toothbrush Murat used that sits rather forlornly in a glass by the bathroom sink. She can't help but think she went through this same situation after Mark left and it saddens her to think she may have to go through it yet again. This is the nature of relationships in the 21st Century, she thinks, and though she wishes it weren't so, she is resigned to the inevitable change of lovers, a sort of seasonal affair, and one not without its source of mystery and adventure, but one which, she is sure, will eventually lose its novelty as she grows older. But she surprises herself by not feeling any remorse at the end of her affair with Murat. Instead she is almost grateful, for he helped her overcome the inertia she felt after her marriage failed and gave her a new sense of herself as a sexual animal. And an abandoned toothbrush is a very small price to pay for her own liberation.

Katja feels suddenly adrift. It is as if once the play is finished, she has lost her purpose, her function in life. She finds she has no energy, is listless around the house, sleeps late, does not dream, but lies there as if dead to the world. It is as if she has lost her will to live and, though it should frighten her, it does not. She thinks she wants death, will find all that she lost, all those who are gone forever will be waiting for her somewhere. And it is in this state that Hasan comes back to her, lies next to her in bed, whispers in her ear. She had lost him momentarily but now that he has returned, she feels the blood flowing in her veins, heat in her body, dances coming as visions in her head. She can feel his weight on the bed, his hand stroking her thigh, his tongue in her ear. And she begins to dance in her nightgown on her living room floor, barefoot, her arms floating in the air, her hair wild and free. She is alive and going nowhere. She is at home.

Dave prepares his final report on the exam results and finds he is both satisfied with the passing rate of 80 % and also with the fact that this is the last report he will have to write here. His bags are mostly packed, his e-ticket printed out for his flight home in three days, and though he plans to do a little last minute shopping for gifts for his brother and some friends, he is anxious to be going home. The adventure is over for him now and he longs to sleep in his own bed again, to hear the birds chirping in his own backyard, to cook breakfast in his own kitchen, to settle back comfortably in his office back in his own school. For now he knows beyond any doubt that he truly belongs back in New York. And he never wants to leave it again except for maybe a two week vacation.

And İrem prepares dinner for Michael on the Saturday after graduation. It is fish, of course, since she knows he loves that, with rice, a salad, and homemade hummus and eggplant dip. He opens the bottle of wine, a Zinfandel from Francis Ford Coppola's vineyard which he bought earlier at Rind in Moda, and they eat in almost total silence, neither knowing how to talk since summer is finally here and her departure only a month away. This will be their last dinner together that she cooks since she will be leaving for Izmir on Monday and won't return to Istanbul until the night before she departs for America.

He looks at her thinking he could never get tired of looking at her face, then realizes, of course, that soon he will only have pictures to gaze at, and his heart cracks. She, meanwhile, wonders what he is thinking and why he doesn't say anything. Then she wonders why she isn't talking either and that makes her feel, for the first time, self-conscious in his presence.

So they eat, clear the table when they're done, he washes the dishes while she brews some Turkish coffee, and they settle down in the living room to watch one last movie together. He plays *Shane* for her, not remembering that he showed her this film on one of their first evenings together almost four years ago, and she, of course, remembers but doesn't say anything, knowing it is one of his all-time favorite films and just watches it again, drinking more wine after the coffee, nibbling on crackers and her hummus, some grapes, pineapple slices, and nuts. And when it's over, they both feel immensely sad, though neither vocalizes that, or the possible reason for it, the emotions that the film has touched in both their hearts.

They listen to music, talk about the play, never mention her upcoming departure, and finally, before she is ready to call a taxi to take her home at three in the morning, he brings out a box that holds his gift for her.

"It's just something to symbolize your new adventure," he says, finally articulating what lies ahead.

"A gift for me?" she asks, touched and surprised at the same time.

"Yes," he says. "But it's not a big gift, just something personal I would like you to have."

"Personal?" and now she is intrigued.

He gives her the box and she opens it with fingers that tremble slightly. And there it is, lying face up, a pair of silver wings. She looks at him quizzically and asks, "This is...?"

"They're a pilot's wings," he says. "They belonged to my mother's favorite cousin who gave them to her to hold for him until he returned from the war," Michael says. "He never did and so she kept them all the years after until I graduated college and decided to move to LA. Then she gave them to me saying they would bring me luck on my new adventure spreading my wings and flying off toward my future."

"What a lovely story," İrem says. "But sad, too, since he never returned."

"But not sad for you," he says. And though he is partially lying by not telling her the real story, he justifies it in his mind by bending the story to fit the circumstances, her circumstances anyway, at least the way he sees them. "These wings are for you what they were for me: the start of a new phase of your life. And for both of us it is in California."

"You'll visit me there, won't you?" she asks, suddenly fearful of a future without him in it in some capacity.

"Sure," he lies. "We're best friends, aren't we?"

"Yes," she says. "We are." Her eyes seem to lose focus for a second but she blinks and he comes in clearly once again. "And you'll come with me to the airport when I leave next month?"

"Wild horses couldn't keep me away."

And they face each other, the wings held in between, a gulf beginning to open that those wings will not be able to traverse.

And we finally end the month with Philip who is getting ready to stay with his friends in Sinop where he will have the peace and quiet he will need to begin his book in earnest. For it is coming together in his head, the characters all loosely based on the people in his life, his own modern retelling of **Romeo and Juliet** with Turks and Brits and Americans circling, bumping into each other while trying to grab a little bit of happiness in a world where happiness is suspect. And he knows he is not Shakespeare but then again what he will write is not a comedy or a tragedy, just a glimpse of life in the city that straddles two continents that he has learned to love. It will be about love as a transitional stage toward self-enlightenment. And in that sense, all the stories will have happy endings even when they end in tears of despair. He thinks of a quote from the American writer Ben Hecht that went something like love is a hole in the heart. A hole that cannot be filled, a hole one learns to live with for the rest of one's life.

And Philip sighs as he thinks of the weight of this book but knows it will not be difficult writing it for as long as he keeps the people he knows in his mind, it will write itself.

Coda

Meric listens to Pelin singing in the kitchen as she slices tomatoes for their breakfast of menemen which she will cook and which he has found he cannot live without. Her voice fills his apartment, the eggs and tomatoes simmering in the skillet changing the atmosphere in his rooms, and his heart, his heart almost bursts as she turns to him and smiles, wearing just his t-shirt from the night before, and holding all his love in her eyes.

Murat watches his wife breast feed their baby daughter and though he himself would rather be sucking on her breast, he knows he will have his turn later as she cradles his head in her arms and lets him sleep, while thoughts of Brenda and what almost was drift away.

Brenda sits at an outdoor café along the Bosporus with the wind in her hair and a tan on her bare legs and arms. Her legs are crossed and a sandal dangles from one foot as she sips a cold glass of white wine while reading a Nick Hornby novel. She finds herself laughing out loud and though she doesn't notice, she gets some admiring looks from a couple of men sitting a few tables away. They whisper to each other, debating on whether or not to approach her, but she is so intently focused on the novel, they hesitate. Brenda, of course, would not be interested since they are younger than her, are actually only out of university for a few years now, but she looks so young with her hair tied back into a ponytail, that deep tan, sunglasses shading her eyes, that the thought never occurs to them that she is almost a decade older.

But she does not feel older. Instead she feels young again, as if she is just entering the world from school herself, ready for whatever adventures lie ahead. And as she reads on, laughing at the foibles of those so inadequately prepared for love, she feels wise, in control, a woman who may not have everything she wants, but at least knows what she lacks and is no longer afraid to seek it wherever it may be.

Philip is in Sinop listening to the lone man walking the streets at 2:15am beating the drums calling those who have fasted during the day and are sleeping now to eat, dogs howling, and Philip rising to write. It is so peaceful here, the Black Sea, Karadeniz, outside his window, a breeze blowing in, cooling his body and his mind. He will write now until morning, then leisurely walk down to the cafés at the harbor, settling in the one with the most people, and watching them as he has his glass of cay, a simit, and picks up more vocabulary for his notebook. His summer life unfolding around him.

Berat is walking the streets of Adana, imaging Kiev with Elena revisiting, in his mind, the cafés she adores, remembering the pulse of what must be her life there, and though he is unsure of just how long this longing will last, he surrenders to the moment and cherishes it all the more because it is, like his love, fragile but holy as well.

Fersat is sitting with Meltem in her parents' living room eating popcorn and watching yet another DVD which she will enact for him after it's done, and he will record it all, his favorite actress performing all the parts just for him.

Deniz wakes with the thought in her head that the furniture needs rearranging and Jennifer is only too glad to help. And as they move the couch to another wall, adjust the rug, drink a mug of coffee when surveying what they have done, she looks at Jennifer who looks back, her hand extending to nestle in hers, and they lean against each other, drinking their coffee, in their living room, and both sigh with

287

satisfaction, pleased with what they see, where they are, together at home, and knowing this is like it is supposed to be.

Katja turns in her bed, naked under the sheets, her skin tingling as Hasan's fingers run their course over it, his tongue in her ear, her breath constricted, her heart beating loudly, pushing against her chest, wanting so desperately to break through, to a new day, an old day, a day she has been denied but refuses so stubbornly to give up. And though she knows deep in that part of her brain she ignores that this is not real, she clings to it anyway. For her love is deep and long and will never quit. And no one, no power on earth, can withhold this love from her.

Dave stands, as he often does these summer days, contemplating his deck. It really needs to be repainted, the old paint is peeling in spots and must be scraped off, the wood sanded, and perhaps this time he will just varnish it instead. Put a coat of polyurethane over it to protect it from the weather. There are other jobs, too, to be done: pulling up the weeds, resodding the front lawn, repairing the fence along the back. He really should have started earlier, but he had so little energy when he returned from Turkey that he slept two weeks away before finally rousing himself. And now he must prepare to entertain some friends who are coming over later to barbecue, a bottle of Pinot Noir is opened, breathing just for him, with others in reserve, as well as beer in the ice chest, and life is, after all, continuing, and today, on this typical summer day, he will continue along with it, here, at home, once again.

And in another city far away, Michael helps her with her bags, passing them to the cab driver who does his best to arrange them in the trunk, the one odd large brown suitcase left sitting on the passenger seat up front. And Michael sits in the back with İrem, their hands almost touching for the long ride through Istanbul traffic to Ataturk Airport. Once there, there is the check-in counter at Turkish Airlines, the answers to the questions about who packed her bags, and İrem glancing back over her shoulder more often than she would have thought possible to make sure he is still waiting back there. Then that long, almost silent, awkward vigil at Gloria Jean's Coffee as they both have tost and coffee postponing the inevitable long good-bye.

Finally, she takes her place on the long queue waiting to get past the security check and Michael stands helplessly watching her go, a last wave good-bye and then she is lost to his sight as she turns left toward her gate.

İrem will board the plane in Group A and take her seat in the rear and try to read the book Michael gave her for the flight, *Little Novels of Sicily* by Giovanni Verga, but her mind will still see him, that last sorrowful look before she waved, and she will, for many years to come, wonder what if she had stayed.

And finally to Michael, standing barefoot on his balcony in the early morning hours, remembering his father's words of wisdom: "You win, you win. You lose, you don't win."

And Michael, with his hands in his pockets, nodding in the sun.